BRUKEN

MORAG EDWARDS

Published by Goldcrest Books International Ltd
www.goldcrestbooks.com
publish@goldcrestbooks.com

ISBN: 978-1-913719-46-3
eISBN: 978-1-913719-47-0

*'... to live again among men and women,
to return to that place where one's ties
with the human broke ...'*

When One Has Lived a Long Time Alone
Galway Kinnell
1990

CHAPTER 1

The slow night pulsed with the breathing of four women and the newborn sounds from their babies. A blue light fell from the corridor through high screens surrounding their beds. Ros pulled herself up to sit against the pillows, feeling the tug of her stitches. She looked over at Anna. Was she awake? Anna's bed was closest to the corridor and the strange light draped her bed in blue gauze. Her open mouth looked purple and her blonde hair, spread across the pillow, seemed grey. In the day, Ros liked to watch Anna, fussing around her bed, chatting to everyone, or reading books with an irritating intensity, twisting a strand of hair and chewing on her lip.

Ros leaned over to look into Jake's plastic bassinet. She'd intended to bottle-feed but the nurses had grabbed her tits and shown Jake what to do. He'd got it straight away, even though he was a thin, ratty-looking little thing. It was good that one of them knew what it was all about because soon they'd be going home together; Ros and Jake, friends for life. At least for the rest of my life, Ros thought. He'll get a short break from me at the end.

Ros often thought about life and death. Had even written a poem about it at sixth form college, which won a prize. She'd been clever for as long as she could remember but not the sort of clever anyone knew what to do with. *Too clever by half.* If she'd only been half as clever, she might have been okay. Her half-as-clever classmates, those sensible enough to avoid three years at university, now had jobs in call centres or supermarkets, money in their pockets, boyfriends. Ros had four A levels, all starred As, and now Jake. Her teachers had expected her to go to university, told her she must fill in a UCAS form because everyone else was. All through the course they had banged on about 'outcomes' but when she'd asked what the exact outcome for her would be if she went to university, they'd come up with vague stuff about choices and friendships and improved earnings in some unspecified future. Maybe if she'd had a plan, other than having Jake, she might have applied. Some of her class were there now and their postings on Instagram didn't tell her much except they were 'having a laugh'.

A nurse's shadow crept across the floor, framed in a trapezium of light, as she pushed aside one of the screens. She was checking on the woman who hadn't stopped crying since she'd arrived on the ward, except for tonight when she was silent, which was even more worrying. She instructed another nurse, too loudly for the middle of the night, to check the blood pressure of Mrs Adams in Bay 4 who Anna had whispered was being kept in because she was ill. Anna seemed to know everything about everyone, except for her. Ros hunched down, pretending to be asleep but felt the weight of a nurse leaning over her, breathing hard into her face.

'Feed your baby.' The nurse spoke in a flat tone, empty of either interest or hostility. Ros picked up Jake and helped him to find her nipple. His gulping and swallowing sounded too loud in the quiet ward. While he fed, Ros looked at her phone. If she didn't go home soon, she'd run out of battery and she'd forgotten her charger.

This ward was the place where mothers who weren't allowed to go home were detained. Anna had already told her that she was staying in because it was her fourth baby and only eleven months since her last. Ros guessed why she was being held, but she didn't say.

The phone screen said half past four. Soon, the day would start. The cleaner came at five and breakfast was at seven. Yesterday, because she'd just had Jake, she slept through breakfast and woke to sodden Weetabix and cold tea left on her tray. Then there was the day, which lasted for fifteen hours, before lights out at ten. A complicated device hung over her bed where she could pay for television or radio on a credit card but since she didn't have one, she had pushed it away to face the wall. Ros liked to watch the visitors before and after the mothers' 'rest' in the afternoon.

Anna's husband came yesterday, bringing their two daughters and the baby boy. Ros thought the husband looked angry and in a rush. His hair stood up as if he'd forgotten to brush it because he kept sweeping it back with his fingers. He didn't pay much attention to the new baby and when he kissed Anna he looked over at Ros. Anna said later that he was a doctor, and he wasn't too pleased about another baby. His colleagues had made comments about further training on contraception. Anna giggled at this, as if she'd told Ros something funny. One of Anna's friends came in the evening, and they'd whispered about something and looked at her baby, who seemed full and pink, with hair that was so white his head could have been smeared in Vaseline.

Ros remembered to change Jake's nappy and put him back in the bassinet, where he stared at her until she felt uncomfortable. She swung her legs over the edge of the high bed and padded on bare feet to the toilet. The nurses at the station stopped talking as she passed.

Back on the ward, Anna was sitting up too.

'You alright?' Anna mouthed.

'Fine,' Ros whispered back. She didn't want a night-time chat with Anna. Night was her special time, for thinking. She stood at the window and looked down five floors to the car park and beyond to the prison and the rows of terraced houses that fanned out from the walls. It was dark outside and would stay that way for hours, but already there were lights on in upstairs windows, a man walked a dog on the green, cars were still leaving the hospital. She turned back to look at Anna, now a mound of bedclothes. She didn't think that Anna remembered her from when they met once at antenatal class. Her midwife had told her classes would help with the birth, but Ros went only once. In the end, Jake had ripped out of her body in one long yell. Antenatal classes wouldn't have helped with that. Anna had her baby the same night and they'd been wheeled onto the ward together. At the class, Ros thought Anna was somebody's grandmother, which is why she'd remembered her so well the night Jake was born. She hadn't realised that Anna had been pregnant too.

At six, Ros changed Jake from his hospital gown into a sleepsuit she'd bought at Primark. It was way too big, and he looked like a clown with his dark hair sticking up from the top of his head. Anna had said she should try to talk to him, that he would know her voice. He preferred to stare at her, so she stuck her tongue out at him and he stuck his out at her. She lifted Jake from the cot and propped him up against her knees, watching Anna get up. She had a funny way of getting out of bed backwards, her feet searching in turn across the floor for her slippers before she stood up. From this angle her bum looked very wide. Anna pushed stray clumps of hair behind her ears and turned to Ros.

'Can you watch him while I go and shower?'

Ros nodded and carried Jake, pressed against her shoulder, to sit on the edge of Anna's bed. Watching Anna stomp out of the ward, her towel over her shoulder, Ros thought she must walk like that because her thighs were too close together. 'Chafing' her mum had said one hot summer. 'My thighs are chafing. You're lucky, you're a stick insect.' Anna's baby (he had no name) started to fuss, and Ros hoped she wouldn't have to pick him up. He looked sticky, like a half-sucked bit of seaside rock.

Anna had dressed him in a washed-out pink sleepsuit left over from her girls.

'He doesn't know the difference, why waste them?' she'd said.

Anna seemed in a bad mood when she got back. 'Bloody water was cold. I hope I can go home today.' Ros didn't bother to have one; maybe she would go home today too.

The ward round was at ten, after the elevenses had been cleared away. When it was Ros's turn, the doctor scanned the notes and muttered something to the nurse standing at her elbow. Ros was used to this. Because she was a care leaver and Jake had a social worker, people assumed things about her and treated her differently. They suspected she had problems and avoided her eyes. The doctor leaned on the end of her bed, with both hands, as if she wanted to push it closer to the wall.

'I should discharge you, Ros. You're ready to go home but there's an outstanding issue with Social Care. As soon as it's sorted, you can go. I won't need to see you again.'

Ros noticed that Anna had to wait most of the day for her husband to collect her, sitting fully dressed beside the bed, her case packed. Sometimes she wandered over to talk to Ros, but she kept looking over her shoulder towards the corridor. He arrived about five, just as the patients were being served dinner, and hopped around his wife's sluggish movements, made even slower by her stitches. As he passed the end of Ros's bed he grimaced, baring all his teeth in a way that most people would think was an attempt at a smile, but from her A level psychology notes Ros knew it was actually a threat. He drummed his fingers on the nurses' station, while Anna spent too long saying goodbye, passing the small suitcase from hand to hand and jiggling his car keys in his pocket. Anna turned to wave to Ros, miming a phone call and Ros waved her fingers back at Anna, like seaweed under water.

Because of the problem (unspecified), she had been moved into a side room with Jake. She sat on the bed with her arms folded, watching pigeons land on the flat roof opposite. They avoided vents of steam from four polished chimneys at each corner, searching optimistically for insects amongst the gravel spread on the felt. Occasionally, forgetting it was November, they made half-hearted attempts to mount each other, which resulted in quarrelling and feathers left in disarray. This meant spending some time adjusting their appearance, but mostly they waddled back and forth like clockwork, heads and necks in perpetual motion until a bird-brain decision was made to fly off and repeat the exercise elsewhere. Ros fed Jake and watched him sleep. She spoke a few words to the woman who pushed a broom halfway under her bed and flicked a cloth around her windowsill and had a longer conversation with the woman who took her order for tomorrow's lunch and dinner. They agreed that the fish would be nice for lunch and then maybe sandwiches and yoghurt would do for tea, whoever had to eat it.

Since there was no food in the flat, Ros decided to eat her hospital tea, but had made up her mind to go home. She dressed herself and the baby, checked her pockets for bus money and tried to walk off the ward with the evening visitors. At the nurses' station, her way was barred.

'Back to bed young lady!'

'I'm going home, you can't stop me.'

'When your social worker and mother visited yesterday, we were told you couldn't go home until your flat had been checked. Your social worker is sick, so it can't happen today. They're sending someone else out tomorrow. You'll have to wait.'

'Okay,' Ros replied, in the patient, low voice she had copied from the adults who had once cared for her. 'That woman was not my mother, she was my personal adviser. The social worker is Jake's. It's not my fault that the flat hasn't been checked. I'm going home.'

The nurse folded her arms but smiled. 'Back to bed!'

'You don't get it,' Ros argued, remembering too late that it wasn't helpful to point out to an adult that they were wrong. 'I'm not a risk to my baby. I'm an adult trying to leave this hospital. It's up to me whether my flat is suitable for Jake.'

'I do get it,' the nurse leaned forward, staring at Ros with eyes that threatened to pop out of her head, 'and you listen to me. You are a care leaver, and I am the responsible adult here. What I say goes. Now get back to bed.'

A grey light filtered through the unlined curtains. Anna chewed on her lip, a lifelong habit when worries tiptoed along the edge of anxiety. She'd meant to line those curtains and even had the lining in a drawer, still in the bag with a receipt. Anna shifted the baby, but it was useless. He'd fallen asleep in the middle of the feed, limp like a rag doll in the fold of her elbow. She lifted her bottom to pull her sticky pyjamas away from her skin and the movement caused the baby to stir but not wake. She studied Nick, his face pushed fiercely into the pillow, crumpled with resentment as if he suspected someone might snatch his sleep away. Anna noticed that his hair was receding.

She slipped out of the bed, careful not to wake him, and placed the baby in his Moses basket. It was obvious that he needed to be changed but that would have to wait. The door to the next room was slightly ajar. This was a perfect room, decorated by Anna and Nick for their last baby, Christopher. Pastel stencils of a retro train with a cheerful but deranged expression romped under the cornice of the Edwardian house, chased by clouds of steam and repeating sunbeams. The folds of the matching curtains foreshortened the train's progress in a way that Anna had always found unsatisfactory.

The planned child slept on his back with his face turned towards the wall. Anna gazed at the curve of his cheek, the night light shining through the translucent tip of his ear. Anna bent over the cot, forgetting to lower the side, and heaved him out, feeling the strain on her weakened belly. She held him close, scenting his familiar night odour of sour milk and urine as she buried her face in his neck. She carried him to a cane chair in the bay of the window, covered by a throw she had made herself at quilting classes, from squares cut from the girls' outgrown summer dresses. Christopher found her breast with the familiarity of a long-term lover. Anna closed her eyes and dozed, her quilt around her shoulders.

Once Christopher was asleep, Anna logged onto TheBump.net and skimmed through recent posts. She clicked the link to her blog, and since there were several comments asking whether she'd had the baby, she began to type.

Well, I'm back after the birth and it all went better than expected. Another little boy, so that makes two of each, a perfect family. I was in labour for about twenty-five hours but the second stage only lasted twenty minutes. And for those doubters out there, I didn't need any pain relief except for gas and air, so ha ha to those who say older mums have a more difficult time. The baby's fine, not feeding too well but it's early days. I met this little girl on the ward, just eighteen, having her first baby. It was so sweet, she didn't have a clue, so I showed her how to breastfeed (round of applause!). She didn't have any visitors, so I'm going to make her into a bit of a project, sort of mentor her I suppose. Before I'm deluged with critical comments, I do know that most teenage girls make lovely mums. I'll keep you posted. Goodnight all you long-suffering night owls. If you're reading this—get some sleep!

Anna skimmed through the comments from her last post, blocking one writer that called her a 'smug cow'.

She slipped back into bed, pressing her cold feet against the back of Nick's thighs. Too late, Anna remembered that she hadn't changed the other baby. Sleep pushed her body deep into the mattress and the duvet settled around her neck. She would do it when she woke, she bargained, it would only be a couple of hours.

Through his jersey jogging bottoms, which he wore only in winter, Nick felt the chill of Anna's feet and grunted, shifting further away. Now awake, he patted the bedside table to find his phone. It was almost five, that unsatisfactory time of night when there wasn't enough sleep left to enjoy but it was too early to get up. He raised himself onto his elbows and leaned over Anna to check how soundly she was sleeping before he clicked onto an app, hidden within a folder, to see if there were any messages from women he had contacted. He tried to shade the phone's light, so bright that she was bound to stir, but Anna slept on, snoring softly.

Aha! There were six messages ... interesting. Nick leaned over Anna again, listening to her breathing but decided that not even he would risk checking his messages right next to his wife, even if she did seem out for the count. The site he'd found was aimed at married women who were tired of their old man and looking for a bit of no-questions-asked. He'd managed a few meetings already but had grown tired of the coffees, then lunch, then another coffee and wondered how it was ever going to be possible to get to the business. One of them had even accused him of taking years from his age on his profile, which was true, but looking at her, she was every bit as guilty.

Nick flicked again through the new crop of messages. The names they thought to call themselves! Here was one,

'SimmeringSue', and another, 'JuicyJaquie', ridiculous and a bit sad to be honest, when you met them.

His curiosity won, and edging around the bed in the half-light, Nick almost stumbled into the Moses basket. He peered into the cot, trying to see whether he had woken the child but there was no sound from the tiny baby, spreadeagled on his back. He crept along the landing to the top of the stairs but made it no further.

'Daddy, where are you going?' Jess stood in the doorway to her bedroom, rubbing one eye and frowning at him with the other.

'I'm getting a drink of water. Would you like one?' Nick slid his phone into the pocket of his jogging bottoms. Jess nodded and disappeared into her room.

Nick filled two glasses and crept into the girls' bedroom. Cara's back looked firmly asleep, but Jess waited for him in her bed, the book in her hand only too visible in the night light. It was Nick's worst story, the one about going on a bear hunt. Somehow, he couldn't read it in any way that made it interesting, unlike Anna who had taught for years in primary schools.

Jess sipped at her water and patted a space amongst her garish, bright-eyed menagerie, whose names he was expected to remember but never could.

'Dad, read me a story.'

'Can't we read a different one?'

Jess's bottom lip started to tremble. 'But I want this one, Daddy,' she whined, sounding as if this was the only thing that could be expected from any reasonable person in the middle of the night.

Fearing a full-blown crying episode Nick gave in, and after the fourth reading Jess slept, and finally so did he, with Bumble, Mumble and Jumble, or whatever their names were, pressed into his back.

CHAPTER 2

Unable to tolerate her penetrating glare, Ros swung back from the nurse's face, forcing down the rage in her chest. In her room she lifted Jake from the sling and placed him on the bed, her hand gently cradling his head in case he startled. She wanted to trash the room, to throw the chair through the window, kick the bedside chest aside and hear the delicious crash of the water jug on the tiles, but all she could permit herself was to press her brow against the cool glass of the windowpane and clench and unclench her hands until her fingernails left deep trenches in her palms.

Jake started to breathe faster, making sounds that grumbled and whimpered, building to a full-pitched cry that wailed like a police siren on a dark night. In the days since she had known him Jake had been a polite baby who had cried only when absolutely necessary, and Ros turned, incredulous at his red face and tight fists, witnessing a rage that matched, even surpassed, her own.

'Respect, Jake!' As she spoke, her voice immediately stopped the cry. She lifted him and folded his trembling body against her own. Jake's mouth rooted across her neck, searching for her breast, and she kissed the top of his head. Ros lifted her tee shirt and they lay curled on the crumpled sheet, fully clothed, tension draining from them both.

Ros woke at three, jolted by the sound of a trolley as it passed her room. She changed Jake, remembering Anna's warning, 'You must change him after a feed; nappy rash is easy to get but hard to shift.' He yawned but didn't wake. Ros looked out at the quiet streets, the tarmac shining in the phosphorescent light. She wanted to walk out there and smell the night. The shadow of her packed rucksack was cast back by the light from the glass pane in her door, turning a corner of the window into a mirror. This might be her moment to try again, when one of the nurses was busy on the ward. But then she remembered that the buses wouldn't be running, not for another two hours at least, and she didn't have enough money for a taxi. Ros undressed Jake and he began to whimper, so she fed him again until he slept. Sitting alone with her hands in her lap, Ros watched the world on the streets unfold.

'Still with us then?' The nurse from last night burst into her dream. In a house with many doors, the people behind each one had asked her what she wanted but she couldn't say the words. Waking sounds came from the corridor. Her breakfast tray lay untouched. Ros lifted her head and saw the congealed cereal and the oil slick on the mug of tea and tried to make sense of where she was.

The nurse made a 'tsk' sound as she carried the tray outside.

'You go and shower while I watch the baby. What's he called?' She peered at the label on the plastic crib. 'Jake … that's a nice easy name for him to spell.' The nurse laughed, more than her comment deserved, then flapped hands at Ros, as if shooing away a fly. 'Go on, go on. I'll make you some tea and toast when you're back. Your care pathway says you're to be shown how to give the baby a bath before you leave hospital. Now, some toast is worth staying for, isn't it?'

Ros privately agreed, as she bit into thick slices of hot toast dripping with catering margarine and gulped down a mug of tea that was almost, but not quite, too hot. The nurse wheeled in a bath of warm water and laid out the things they would need. Next to these, she placed a clean towel for the baby. Ros watched her, licking the oil from the tips of her fingers, enjoying the comfort of order and routine.

She said this aloud and the nurse seemed pleased, taking it as a compliment. Ros hadn't meant to praise her, she had only spoken her thoughts, but she could see that this parenting thing, these soothing routines, might suit her. Jake's eyes widened as he felt the water on his skin and startled, flinging his arms wide. For a moment it looked as if he might repeat last night's ill temper, but he must have changed his mind as her warm hands soaped his skin.

'They don't mind this bit,' the nurse warned her, 'after all, it's only a few days since he spent all his time in a warm bath. It's the next bit he'll hate.'

Ros lifted Jake onto the towel, and on cue he began to shake and tremble as if he had been left out in the rain, his face reddened and crumpled with rage.

'He can't regulate his body temperature,' the nurse explained, 'that's why you have to be quick. He'll need a feed afterwards to settle him. You don't need to bath him every day. Do you have everything you need at home?'

Fumbling with tapes that wouldn't stick, Ros nodded. The nurse tutted again and shook her head. 'You see, you're all fingers and thumbs and now you've got cream on the tape. We'll just throw this one away.' She laughed, deep in her chest. 'But at home you won't want to waste them so keep a roll of surgical tape in your bath kit. I'll give you some before you go.'

Ros wished she had got it right but had heard the magical words about going home. The nurse was enjoying being the expert, it was putting her in a good mood and Ros knew how to turn this to her advantage. 'Let yourself be taught,' her counsellor had said, 'there's no shame in not knowing something and it makes the person teaching you feel better.' Ros squeezed her nails into her palms. That's what they thought. The truth was, you humoured them until you could get your own way.

The nurse folded her arms and sat in the visitor's chair at the side of the bed.

'He's feeding well,' she said, nodding approvingly. 'You've done a good job to get it going so quickly.' Ros felt a movement in her chest, something she recognised as pride.

'You know why I've done all this with you this morning? The baby's social worker is still sick, and your flat hasn't been checked but I'm allowed to say you can go, if I'm happy with your progress. I can see you're a sensible girl and a quick learner. We don't want you hanging around here any longer, do we? By my reckoning, if they need to check your flat, they can do it after you're home. I'd feel a bit happier if you had a mum, or auntie, you could call on but that can't be helped.'

'There's Anna, the woman who was on the ward. She said I could ring her anytime.'

'Ah, Mrs McNeill.' The nurse slapped her thigh. 'She'll keep you right.'

Ros didn't like the idea of Anna 'keeping her right' but she knew it was important to stay in the game.

'So, I'm discharged?'

The nurse beamed a wide smile. 'You're discharged!'

Ros found gratitude hard, most often because it was undeserved. People expected thanks for doing things that were quite ordinary.

'Thank you.' She smiled, making sure she looked straight into the nurse's eyes, as she had been taught. 'You've been such a help.'

Ros walked the long corridor away from the ward. At first, only patients scuffed alongside her in ill-fitting slippers pushing their drips ahead of them like flags into battle. Down an escalator she reached the public areas of the hospital; there were too many people crowding forward to join the rows already waiting in outpatients, too many bodies swaying towards her, three abreast, in padded coats. Even the outside was crowded, as patients gathered to draw a last drag from their cigarettes.

She shivered at the bus stop, Jake zipped inside her coat, feeling a confused nostalgia for the closed ward she had left behind. The traffic whished past, tyres spinning on wet tarmac and the brakes of the bus made a long, mournful cry as it stopped to pick her up. Putting one hand against her chest to protect Jake, Ros had to use her other hand to carry the rucksack and find her balance when the bus churned away from the stop.

Before Jake was born, she would have been indifferent to the man sitting next to her, nodding his head in time to the fractious whine from his earphones and thumping a closed fist against his knee with rhythmic aggression. She wouldn't have seen the young mother pick up her baby's dummy from the floor of the bus and push it back into the child's mouth. The world seemed full of danger. Couldn't everyone see the threat?

She turned her back towards her neighbour, as far as the cramped seat would allow. Jake moved against her chest and the warm scent of her newborn child drifted up from the gap in her coat. She pretended to look out of a window streaming with vapour from other people's breath and counted the lurching stops until she could escape. The streets near her flat were empty of human life, but dogs and at least one rat were already out, scavenging last night's takeaway wrappers. Sparrows picked at vomit spattered across the pavement.

Inside her flat, Ros leaned her back against the closed front door and inhaled the brown silence. She travelled the narrow, dark corridor to her sitting room and threw her rucksack onto the floor. At the window that looked down onto the street, there was a table, against which the landlord had optimistically set two chairs. Ros sat on the leatherette cover of one of these, feeling her bottom sink into the pit made by all the bums that had sat there before. The varnish on the table had peeled, leaving marooned patches of shining islands.

She didn't know what to do with Jake. There was a cot in her bedroom, but that room was dark and smelt of mildew, and he would be too far away. She removed her coat, eased Jake from the sling and carried him over to her single armchair. She left him there, curled on his side, and walked back to her seat at the table, tracking the coastline of the varnish with the tip of one finger. She wasn't thirsty but making a cup of tea would create some sounds; the fizz as the water began to boil, the chink of the spoon in the cup, the satisfying suck as she pulled the fridge door open.

Ros unscrewed the lid and recoiled from the smell of the milk. She hadn't expected to be in hospital so long and it had soured. The kettle boiled and she poured steaming water over a teabag. By the time she got back from the shop downstairs, it would have brewed. In the hall, she pulled on her jacket and searched her purse. She had enough cash for some cigarette papers and tobacco, as well as milk. Her first fag in ten months would be amazing. The door was open in her hand when she remembered Jake. She pushed it closed with both palms.

Standing over the sleeping baby, she weighed up the odds. If she left him alone for the few minutes it would take to run down to the shop, he would surely be fine but after that she'd do it again. And again. If she made a rule now, never ever to leave him alone, it would stop her taking risks. It might save her worry. She sat down again at her seat by the window, picking at the varnish with her nail. Making her decision, she went back into the kitchen alcove and tipped the blackened tea into the sink. The bag lay plump and moist against the white enamel, trails of caramel fluid circling towards the drain.

Jake stirred, beginning the snuffling sound that would quickly become a wail. She bent over him, watching him wriggle and twist with growing agitation and stroked his back. Her touch settled the baby for a few minutes, until she found matches and lit the gas fire, turning the setting to low. Ros lifted Jake from the chair, kissed both his cheeks and wrapped him in her coat, before carrying him downstairs with her to the shop.

Steam from Jake's bath dripped down the windows and Ros drew the curtains, since the light was already fading. She emptied the basin of tepid water into the kitchen sink and left it propped against the taps. The living room floor was littered with baby detritus and the cold, bare flat had become warm and untidy. She picked up a soiled nappy and rolled it for the bin. Pushing to one side the changing mat and the bale of tiny nappies, Ros went into her bathroom and sat on the toilet seat to roll cigarettes no wider than the cotton buds she had been warned not to use on Jake's ears. She worked quickly, her fingers becoming stiff and clumsy with cold. Standing up, she saw her own reflection in the bamboo-framed mirror over the sink; her short black hair, her small, pointed chin and the prominent ears, exaggerated by the row of studs that descended in order of size from the tip to the lobe. Ros lit one of her home-made cigarettes and watched herself take the first draw. It tasted so good, burning at the back of her throat. Like a child hiding from a parent, she stood on the toilet seat and opened the bathroom window. Resting her elbow on the frame, she tried to exhale through the narrow gap, wafting at the smoke with her hand as the warm air hit the resistance of the icy inward draft. Sounds from outside travelled in with the smoke. The evening hum of the city provided a chorus for the closer voice of someone calling to a child and the noise from the television next door.

Ros had no television, but she still had her laptop and internet access, paid for by Derbyshire Council. Her teachers had made the case at her first PEP meeting in sixth form that it was essential for her exams, but someone in the local authority had forgotten that she'd left school and Ros wasn't planning to remind them. Back at her table, she logged onto Snapchat and scrolled through recent photos, but there was little of interest in the strange details of university life, or the latest party held on a Thai beach. Some friends from school had posted photos of a student event called Carnage and she flicked through the pictures of shining faces, their mouths open and features floppy, leaning against each other outside some bar or another. When they were at school, she thought, none of this lot would have known what carnage meant. Ros took a photo of Jake, asleep in the corner of what was now 'his' armchair and wrote, 'I've had the baby. It was easy. I'm calling him Jake.' She hesitated, her finger poised over the key, and then deleted the message.

CHAPTER 3

Nick's car was still in the driveway when Anna arrived home from taking the girls to school. She could see his shadow through the mosaic of stained glass in the front door, yet he made no effort to open the door for her, although he must have heard her key. Not looking at her, but continuing to pack his medical case, Nick said: 'Jane Clark is waiting for you. Had you forgotten?'

'No.' Anna sighed and put Christopher down onto the polished wood floor. He crawled across to his father and pulled himself up against his legs. Nick lifted the baby and Christopher leaned far back against his father's arm, confident and fearless. Nick began to tickle him, and Christopher's laughter rang out like a bell in the silence between them. 'It's okay,' Anna added, 'I hadn't forgotten.' What she meant was, she hadn't forgotten that the health visitor was coming but had forgotten the exact day. She would have preferred it if Nick and Jane hadn't met. He would have hated being questioned about the new baby.

The practice where they were patients was a neighbour to the one where Nick worked, and there must have been gossip between the health visitors. Nick McNeill's wife pregnant so soon!

Nick placed Christopher on the floor and stood up to collect his bag. He bent down again to kiss the child and pushed past Anna. He turned back, as if he had forgotten something.

'By the way, you've left our youngest child in the car and the door's standing open.'

Anna hurried to lift the baby from his car seat, his hands, and cheeks cold to her lips, but at least he had escaped the worst of the rain. I wish he would cry sometimes, she thought, then I would have to notice him. Anna used her legs to guide Christopher through the open front door, just as he was turning to crawl backwards down the step. Frustrated, he began to protest until his attention was caught by a dead fly under the hall table. Anna closed the door behind her, leant back against it and heard the latch click.

'Coffee, Jane?' she called, hoping to warm the baby's hands and cheeks in the kitchen. She looked around the sitting room door where the health visitor was writing notes. After three children, now four, under her care, Jane was almost a friend but not quite.

'Not just yet.' Jane looked up and smiled at Anna. 'Let's weigh the baby first. Got a name for him yet?'

We haven't even discussed it, Anna thought but said, 'No, we can't decide.'

'You know the midwife was concerned about his weight, that's why I've called today. When was his last feed?' Jane stripped the baby exposing his pathetic limbs and yellow stained nappy. Anna saw her frown, her large hands registering his cold limbs as she supported his head and back and placed him onto her portable scales.

'It's a long, cold drive to the school.' Anna felt she had to explain. 'I don't feel I can ask Nick for help. It might well be a few hours since his last feed,' she confessed.

'I think I'll have that coffee now. We need to talk.'

Anna listened to the water in the kettle bubble and roar and watched the instant coffee froth under the boiling water. She pulled her cardigan more tightly around her waist and held it in place with her elbows, pressing her fingertips against her temples. She knew what was coming.

'Are you still feeding Christopher?' Jane asked, sipping her coffee. Christopher, emptying her handbag, turned around at the sound of his name. Not waiting for a response from Anna, she continued. 'You have a weak, underweight baby. He's lost too much weight since he came out of hospital.'

Anna defended herself: 'He doesn't have much appetite. He doesn't swallow well.'

'If you really cannot give up feeding—' Jane glanced at the offending child, as did Anna, and together they noticed that he was chewing on a tampon from Jane's bag. Jane snatched it from him and continued as best she could as Christopher screamed and tried to stand, dragging on her tights for support.

'If you can't give up feeding Christopher,' Jane shouted, the string of the tampon dangling from her fingers as she held it out of reach, 'why not bottle-feed the baby? He needs to be fed every two hours. Bring him back to the clinic in three days for weighing. I'm sorry, Anna, I've known you for years, but I must speak frankly. You can't hide from me that this child is dirty and cold, so I'll wait for ten minutes and play with Christopher while you clean him up.' Her voice softened. 'I know it must be hard with two babies under a year. Have you thought about getting any help in the house?'

'I don't have help as such,' Anna searched for anything that might make her seem more in control, as if this ghastly situation was unique to this day, 'but I met a girl— a woman—in hospital and she's been coming here almost every day. She has a baby the same age, but he sleeps a lot, so she's able to help out.'

From the landing Anna could hear Jane reading Christopher a story. She ran a warm bath for the baby and lowered his tiny, scarecrow body into the water. He arched his back, his arms spread wide in alarm as the water touched his translucent skin, but there was no cry. His old man's face rippled with ill-defined emotion. Anna briskly soaped his smeared skin and wrapped him in a soft towel. She rested him on the bed and stroked his cheek. He turned towards her touch, his gaze unfocused, his mouth working. Who are you? Where did you come from? she thought.

After the health visitor left, Anna sat with her head back and her eyes closed, trying to feed the baby. Christopher pulled himself up against the sofa and cruised its length. He considered the gap between the end of the sofa and his mother's knee and whimpered but his mother ignored him. He stood for a few moments more, his hands resting on the cushion. One thumb went into his mouth and his other hand reached up to stroke his ear. His eyes slowly closed, his head fell forward onto the sofa, and he slept, still upright.

Anna felt sick. She hadn't followed professional advice; she'd forgotten to bath her baby and he'd been left outside in the cold. How could she have let this happen? The doorbell rang, causing Christopher to lose his balance and he hit his head on a toy car parked under the sofa. She scooped him up and hurried to the door, kissing his head and wiping his wet cheeks with her thumb, the new baby slumped into the crook of her other arm.

'Put your boobs away, it's not a pretty sight,' said Ros, waiting on the doorstep, her hair sparkling from a light fleck of snow. Anna put Christopher down and passed the baby over to Ros, while she buttoned up her shirt. Once inside, Ros unzipped her parka, revealing Jake. The extra bulk of the child only added some normality to her tiny frame, and it seemed to Anna like a new surprise each time he appeared from inside Ros's coat.

'I saw that old bitch leave,' said Ros, handing her jacket to Anna. 'I was hiding behind the wall. What did she want?'

Anna winced. Jane was younger than she was.

'Just checking on the baby, routine ... you know how it is. She had to talk to me about Christopher as well. He's due some vaccinations.' The detail revealed the lie. Anna saw that Ros had noticed, saw her eyes dart around, trying to avoid looking down at the baby.

'I'm glad she doesn't visit me anymore. She used to really piss me off with her questions. Last week she said I could just bring him down to the clinic if I'm worried, which I won't be.'

'She's only doing her job, after all you—'

'What? Looked as though I'd be a bad mother? Well, I've passed the fucking test, whatever it was.'

'I'd prefer it if you didn't swear in front of Christopher. It's not a test, my circumstances are quite different from yours. My age, two babies so close together …'

'Whatever. Do you want to finish feeding the baby?'

'No, I think he's had as much as he can take. I'll tuck him into in his Moses basket … you could put Jake in beside him. Can you play with Christopher, and I'll make some coffee?' Anna hoped that Ros hadn't heard the catch in her voice.

Nick parked in a side street near his own house, waiting. If that girl was there, she'd leave before three because Anna had to pick up the children from school. He lowered both windows and smelt dusk and wood smoke on the frosted air, hoping the draught would lift the smell of sex from his body. He hadn't showered afterwards. Lifting his elbow, he sniffed his armpit. Yes, he needed one. Nick pushed down into his seat and closed his eyes. God, he could still taste her! If Anna kissed him, she'd know.

Once there had been drug reps, women away from home ready to kick off their high heels in a Travelodge, but now the reps stared at him with youthful intensity, shining under the haloes of their first-class degrees in pharmacy.

The men were the worst, with their pointed brown shoes and tight-legged navy suits, trying to persuade him to prescribe the latest overpriced wonder drug.

And there was Jenny, his Jennifer. Once you were being unfaithful, Nick had worked out, then what was the point of sticking with just one? If Anna found out about Jenny, he would give her up of course, but there would still be the women on the site. It made perfect sense.

But I think I might love Jenny, Nick thought. 'I'm in love,' he said aloud, his eyes still closed. He sat up and straightened his tie in the rear-view mirror. 'I think I love you,' he sang, pushing back his hair and frowning at the widow's peak curved into his receding hairline like a sandbank. There was a tap at the window and Nick spun around to see the scrawny girl, his wife's latest acolyte, smiling at him. He grinned back and pretended to search in his case, as if he'd just arrived.

She crossed the road and waited for a bus, staring across at him. If she didn't go soon, he'd have to get out of the car and face Anna before he was ready. Thank goodness, a bus rattled towards the stop, and he watched the girl find a seat. In the twilight, the few passengers were like shadow puppets, their shapes defined by the light from the windows. He didn't return her wave.

Nick waited until Anna had reversed her car out of the driveway before he went in. He loved the house when it was empty, even if it did reek of soiled nappies, but there wasn't time to sit and absorb the silence. He had to shower. When he heard her tyres on the gravel, he was already back in the hall. Anna came in first, carrying the babies.

'Hello!' she said, 'I saw your car.'

Nick crouched down. 'Here come the girls!' he shouted as Cara and Jess tumbled over the doorstep, pushing at each other to be the first into his arms. They brought school with them, in their hair and their uniforms, that curious mix of cooked food and cloakrooms. They quickly tired of his embrace and dropped their bags for Nick to pick up, running off together to watch television. Christopher crawled after them, whining.

'Stay and have some tea with me?' Anna asked, passing him the baby. She touched the strands of wet hair on his neck. 'Why have you showered? Haven't you got surgery at five?'

'Yeah, but I can stay for a few minutes. Tea would be lovely. I've been on a visit, an elderly patient, no family. I felt I needed to shower afterwards.'

Anna frowned and wrinkled her nose. 'I remember that smell from visiting families when I was teaching. In staff meetings, we used to call it the smell of poverty. Some children carried it into school on their clothes.'

They sipped their tea across the kitchen table, the sound of cartoons drifting from the sitting room.

Nick looked down at the child in his arms. 'We'll have to call him something. There's only a week left before we have to register the birth.'

'What about Hugh?'

'After my father? You must be joking!'

'I think he looks like him, and anyway, he might be pleased.'

Nick held the baby up and studied his profile. 'Okay,

let's call him Hugh, it suits him. Does that girl have to be here every day?'

'You mean Ros? She's not here every day.'

'Anna, you know nothing about her. Can't you see your other friends?'

'My friends are at work, or out playing tennis, or having lunch. I'm at a different life stage to most of them. I can help Ros, she has no one else.'

Nick stood up and drained his mug, passing Hugh over to Anna.

'I'm not happy about it but it's your choice. I would have thought you had enough to do.'

'Yes, I have more than enough to do and that's why it's sometimes useful to have Ros here. I help her and she helps me.'

Nick judged that a change of subject was needed. 'What did Jane Clark want?'

'It was nothing, more of a social call really.'

Nick knew this couldn't possibly be true, given health visitor caseloads, but Anna's hard stare, one he knew well, reminded him to take no further risks with this conversation.

On his way out, Nick paused at the open sitting room door to watch his daughters and Christopher, transfixed by the burbling screen. These three were enough, he thought. They should have been enough.

CHAPTER 4

Ros loved Anna's house with its high ceilings and huge fireplaces. One day she would have rooms like this, ones that smelt of polish and with furniture she had chosen herself. She undid the straps of her sling and bent forward, kissing both of Jake's cheeks and laughing as his head turned sharply each way, in an instinctive search for food. Ros clapped his hands together and a ghost of a smile drifted across his mouth and eyes.

Anna's baby lay curled in his basket. He stirred and Ros lifted Jake from his harness and placed him down next to the other child. He already looked quite different despite being born on the same day. He was much larger, of course, but Anna's baby still seemed new. Ros lifted Christopher onto her knee and showed him her phone, his favourite activity.

Anna frowned at Christopher as she carried in their tray, but Ros ignored her, lifting the small boy onto the sofa next to her, without trying to retrieve her phone. She settled back into the soft cushions and felt content; fresh coffee, chocolate biscuits, her unexpectedly beautiful baby and this perfect home. Anna knelt to stoke the fire and leaned back as flames caught on a log, wiping soot onto her jeans, telling Ros about the health visitor's handbag and the tampon. Ros liked to hear Anna tell stories—the way she paused at the right moment and added bits that they both knew were a bit exaggerated. Both women laughed, wiping tears from their cheeks with the backs of their hands, until she noticed that Anna was crying proper tears. This wasn't how it was supposed to be. She wanted it back to how it was, where Anna was in charge, and she was the one being looked after.

'Um ... do you want to talk to me about anything?'

Anna shook her head. 'I'm tired, or hormonal, or both. It's the birth and feeding. Everything goes haywire don't you find?'

'Too right,' Ros agreed, but she hadn't noticed much difference.

'Tell me about you,' Anna asked, 'do you have some family?'

Answers that contained some of the truth were always best, Ros thought. Lies were too difficult to remember.

'They're here in Leicester but we don't meet up.'

'So, you don't ever see your mother? I'm sorry, do you mind me asking?'

Ros smiled. She recognised the moment. It was payback time, time to settle the account for the things Anna had lent her, the hours she spent here keeping warm and being fed. She reached for another chocolate biscuit.

'We fell out. I don't get on with her boyfriend.' All true so far, although she had never met her mother's new man.

'And your father?' Anna bit into her own biscuit, her eyes narrowed with interest.

Ros shrugged and took the last biscuit. She saw Anna glance at the plate.

'I've never met my father, and the last I heard of him, my stepfather is in prison.' Still the truth.

'And Jake's father?'

This is the bit she really wants. 'A boy in my class at school. He's doing a degree at Durham.' Ros wiped chocolate from the corner of her mouth with her little finger. 'I haven't told him; he needs to focus on his work.'

'Oh, you poor little thing.' Anna leaned back, satisfied.

Ros scuffed late-fallen leaves with her boots as she trudged home, head down. It started to rain. She pulled her jacket more tightly around Jake and kicked a Pepsi can into the gutter, the jarring clatter causing two pensioners outside the post office to frown at her. Ros glowered back, challenging them with a stare. She heard one of them 'tut', but she pretended she hadn't heard. The street changed as she walked its length, the trees becoming fewer, the houses smaller and closer together, until she reached the parade of shops that serviced the grey ranks of houses where she lived. There were six shops, three were boarded up and covered in graffiti, but there remained the fish and chip shop where Ros had her flat, a newsagent and general store (only two school children allowed in at any time) and a tool hire shop. Nothing was displayed in the shop windows, which were protected by steel shutters covered with flyers. It was difficult to find the door to the newsagent, except that it was marked by a finer pattern of steel mesh and responded to her push.

Inside the store was dark, lit only by electric light, and smelt of cardboard boxes and rotten bananas. Mrs Lapinsky was on a step ladder, replacing cans of lager. She turned at the sound of the door and smiled at Ros.

'Ah, Rosemary, I'll be with you in a moment.'

Ros winced. In fact, her name was meant to be Rosalind, but Mrs Lapinsky had never checked.

'How is your beautiful baby? You need to get some money, get a job. You could work here a few hours a week. I'll ask Josef.'

'I'll think about it.' Ros tilted her head as if seriously considering Mrs Lapinsky's offer. She couldn't just stand there, filling in time, using up someone else's light and heat. She would have to buy something. Ros walked over to the brightly lit counter that displayed multicoloured packets of sweets and looked at the cigarette packets behind, visible only because the screen had been left open.

'Just a lighter and a Mars bar.'

'You mustn't smoke around the baby.' Mrs Lapinsky held out an open palm for her money.

Ros smiled and nodded. 'I'm trying to give it up.' She knew how to keep people happy, to give them just enough to keep them interested.

Outside, Ros leaned against the wall and lit a roll-up. In fact, she had promised Jane Clark that she would stop smoking and mostly she had. She drew deeply as the wind whipped around her face, lifting crisp bags and small plumes of dust from the pavement. Ros didn't want to spend any more time in her flat than she had to, and she needed some food. The one place where there was plenty of food, apart from Anna's, was her mother's house and she could break in easily if her mother hadn't changed the locks. It wouldn't be stealing, just taking what she was owed, since her mother must have saved a shedload of cash by handing her care over to the state. Ros turned to see the time on the clock hanging from the white-tiled wall of Kyprianou's fish and chip shop. It was almost three. Her mother and brother would be at work and wouldn't be home until later, but her sister would soon be home from school. It was a brilliant idea, Ros thought, but perhaps not today.

Jake wriggled in his sling and began the small choking sounds that meant he would have to be fed. It was time to go home. Ros put out her cigarette and walked up the metal staircase that led to the walkway along the back of the flats. In her narrow hallway, Ros studied herself in the mirror, hung in an attempt to catch some light from the pane of glass in the door. She didn't look eighteen. Her cheeks were pinched and white and the dark circles underneath her eyes were magnified by the low light. Inevitably, the flat smelt, being above a fish and chip shop, but there was something else, a rank, musty odour that she didn't know how to get rid of.

Ros had no idea how to clean a house. They hadn't shown her, where she'd lived after she left the other place, and she wasn't going to start by asking Mrs Lapinsky which products to buy; it was obvious where that would lead. The funny thing was, she didn't notice the smell after a while, only after she'd been out. Jake's social worker thought the flat was okay for a baby, and since she was on her own, it didn't matter. She hoped other people couldn't smell it on her clothes, but they probably could. Next time she saw Anna she'd ask, but that might be risky too.

Ros sat in a chair to feed Jake. She would have liked to put the fire on, but she couldn't afford it in the afternoon, and anyway the health visitor had said that Jake was better off being a little too cold than too hot. Anna had lent her an old radio, so she sang along with the music and listened to the news about everyone struggling to get home from work. Jake seemed to like the sound of her voice, his dark eyes never leaving her face. He looked so like her, it was hard to see how anyone else had a part in his making. Once Jake was changed, she eased him into his sling and slipped downstairs to the chip shop. Mr Kyprianou allowed her to buy a child's portion, which was half the adult price.

'After all, you are little more than child,' he said, and smiled as he passed over the fragrant package.

Ros had eaten half her chips before the kettle boiled. She used the last of her milk, pouring it on top of the teabag in the mug, watching the brown and white fluids mingle. She lifted the teabag and placed it on a saucer to use later. Ros drank her tea looking down into the street. There was no one there, not like in the evenings when a crowd of kids her age stood below and swore and spat.

She wondered what it would be like to go down and stand about with them, to smoke together and pass something around, laughing too loudly.

Later, when Jake was asleep and wouldn't wake again until his midnight feed, Ros watched from behind her part-drawn curtain. The young people had gathered, mostly boys but she could just spot two girls, their long hair swinging forward across their faces as they bent to light a fag. The kids moved in and out of the light from the chip shop, their shapes forming and disappearing in the shadows, so it was hard to see how many there were. Of course, they were several years younger than her, she could see that now.

Mr Kyprianou came out of his empty shop and shared a cigarette with the gang and Ros wondered if one of them was family. But then he tried to move them on, kindly at first, then more insistent and they mocked him, moving only a few metres to stand under a streetlight. Ros heard the girls giggle when two boys sneaked back and jumped up from below the shop window, shouting abuse at Mr Kyprianou. What happened next was inevitable. One of the kids under the streetlight picked up a stone and lobbed it towards the lit-up target of the chip shop. Whether he simply meant to scare Mr Kyprianou or his friends, his aim was too clean, and the window cracked then shattered. The kids scattered, the girls screaming, all except one of the youths crouching below the broken window, his back showered with glass. Ros must have moved, her shape lit from behind by a low table lamp she had forgotten to switch off. The youth stayed, in no hurry to run from the devastation of Mr Kyprianou's shop and glanced up at her window. She stepped back behind the curtain, creating a chink between the fabric and the wall to see what happened next. The boy pushed up on his knee and stared, right at her, as if he could see her face. He raised two fingers, pointed at his own eyes and then at arm's length, pointed his fingers at her. His message was clear, 'I can see you. I know where you are.'

CHAPTER 5

Anna logged on to The Bump.net and linked to her blog, pleased that it was attracting a large number of hits. People seemed interested in her work with Ros, which showed how worthwhile it was, but there was the usual crop of unhelpful comments. She thought about blocking them but decided to leave them to be roasted by her loyal followers.

Anna replied to a few questions, *No, she hadn't introduced Ros to cloth nappies and a laundry service.* She felt a brief needle of guilt, since she'd meant to use terry nappies herself but was still using disposables with both boys. Well, she wasn't going to admit to that! *Yes, she would show Ros how to make her own baby food and thanks for the recipes.* Anna clicked onto New Post and chewed her lip.

Ros brings Jake around nearly every day now. Her fingers stabbed at the keys. *To be honest, I don't know what she does on the days we're not together and I feel I should know. Jake is growing well, smiling and is always clean and warm. Hugh is catching up a bit weight-wise now that Christopher has decided to wean himself. Just shows how right I was to persist. It all worked out in the end. What do these health visitors know?*

I think Ros might be smoking because I can smell it on her breath. I'll choose my moment carefully because she can be a bit prickly. I worry about her lack of family and with Christmas coming up I'm wondering what to do. I don't even know if she has any friends. The ones she had at school all seem to be at university. At least they'll be home soon, so maybe she'll be able to get out a bit more with people her own age. I don't think she can afford babysitters, so I hope she's sensible if she asks friends round to her flat. My husband isn't keen on having Ros with us for Christmas. I said it would be an extra pair of hands, but he reminded me that my mother-in-law is coming. More of that later! Thanks for all the advice about dads not bonding with their babies. I understand it's not an automatic thing for some men and I will be patient.

Anna's idea for today was that they should walk. She had enjoyed the infant weeks in front of the fire with Ros and Jake for company, and Ros had been surprisingly good at playing with Christopher while she ran around the house hauling laundry from the washing machine and pulling duvets up over tousled sheets, but Christopher was walking now and needed to go out. It would be good for

Ros, Anna thought, to get into the habit of a daily walk, whatever the weather. The outside was free after all.

Ros felt disappointed when Anna met her at the door, already dressed in a thick cardigan that was almost a coat, with matching hat and gloves. She'd been up every couple of hours with Jake through the night, and on the long walk over had enjoyed fantasies about closing her eyes briefly in Anna's warm sitting room.

'The park, we're going to the park,' Anna chivvied, turning Ros around to face the street. Pushing her new double buggy along the uneven streets and up and down kerbs tested Anna's flaccid muscles and she developed a stitch. She stopped and rested her hands on her generous hips, then stretched up and down again, to touch her toes. Her breath drifted, powdery in the quiet air as the tugging pain from her side eased. Ros, who had been walking slightly ahead, paused, and waited but didn't turn around. She's sulking, Anna thought.

Anna caught up with her. 'Shows how unfit I am. This is such a good idea. Let's head for the café and then Christopher can try the swings. I brought the girls here all the time when they were little.'

'Do you want me to push your buggy for a bit?' Ros offered, frowning at the slope ahead.

'Goodness me no, I need the exercise. Onwards and upwards!' Anna leaned into the buggy as if she was mowing a lawn.

The park was deserted apart from an elderly woman and her dog that puffed its obese way behind his owner's already slow pace, stopping to sniff the air as the buggy passed in front of its opaque eyes. The woman said, 'Good morning,' as people did in parks.

The trees were black against a sky the colour of pearls; any leaves that persisted glowed like toffee apples whenever the sun broke through the thin cloud. Anna rested at the summit and gazed around, pleased with her day.

'Come on, cheer up. This is okay, isn't it?'

Ros was cold, frozen in fact. She could no longer feel her toes. She had already been cold when she reached Anna's and had no need of exercise, since she walked everywhere. If Anna needed to get fit, Ros thought, she ought to go to the gym.

'I'm fine, Anna. It's good.' She shrugged. 'Let's go on. I'm cold and Hugh looks cold too.'

Anna peered at Ros's parka and felt its weight between her fingers.

'Maybe we should get you a thicker coat. I'm sure I've several I could spare. Remind me when we get home.'

Yeah, right, Ros thought but said, 'Is that the cafe over there?' lifting her voice as if some enthusiasm had at last crept into her mood.

The windows of the cafe were haphazardly sprayed with artificial snow in each corner, as if Leicester had been caught in an unexpected blizzard. They dripped with steam from an urn that boiled behind the counter, the shiny coffee machine redundant and used to dry tea towels. Frayed tinsel looped across the ceiling and a solitary star hung above the chalkboard on the wall, where someone had scrawled 'Season's Greetings'. The menu, folded on the table, had a smudged robin in one corner, as if someone had used a child's printing set.

Anna put the card down and gave Ros enough money for their coffee and a bacon and egg roll for herself. The cafe felt damp, and a haze of hot fat stung her eyes. She pulled off her cardigan and hung it on the back of her chair, hoping that her clothes wouldn't smell of burnt fat at home. Anna leaned forward to take off Christopher's coat and lifted him onto her knee. Hugh was asleep, so she left him where he was.

'I got you a mince pie, since it's Christmas.' Ros tumbled the change onto the table. Anna pushed the mince pie back and said, 'You eat it. I don't need the calories.' Ros found a highchair for Christopher and broke the mince pie into pieces on his tray. Anna knew she should remove it, but Christopher's tantrum would spoil any chance of a proper talk with Ros. It was a dilemma worth exploring on her blog, she thought. Should a mother always ban sweet, fatty foods or were there times when expediency mattered more?

Anna sipped her coffee from the translucent melamine mug and found it weak and thin. She held the cup in both hands and told Ros that Nick's mother would be spending Christmas with them. It seemed a safe way of bringing up Ros's own situation.

'What's she like, your mother-in-law?' Ros's interest was unusual, and Anna felt encouraged by the question.

'I used to be terrified of her when I was first married, but after she left Edinburgh and surfaced in America she seems to have mellowed. She has a Canadian husband we've never met. And she's only seen the girls, never these two.' Anna tipped her head towards Christopher, cramming mince pie into his mouth, and Hugh still asleep in the buggy, his cheeks pink. 'Nick's her only child.'

Ros unzipped her parka to let Jake look around and he blinked, caught sight of Anna, and gave her a perfect, newly minted smile.

'You will come over at Christmas, won't you?' Anna held one of Jake's hands and looked up at Ros. 'Harriet will love to see this little one.'

Ros bit deeply into her roll and a trickle of yolk oozed onto her lips. She wiped her mouth with the back of her hand and Anna tugged at the napkin dispenser, passing her a tissue. Ros took it and wiped her lips, her hazel eyes never leaving Anna's face.

'Last year Christopher was a tiny baby,' Anna continued, 'babies and Christmas ... it's special. How did you spend last Christmas? Were you with your family?'

Ros nodded. 'We are your family now. We'll do our best.' That's what they had said four years ago when she had stood in their kitchen with her rucksack, so she could reply truthfully to Anna's question.

'I was with some of my family but not my mum or brother and sister.'

'Poor Ros,' Anna said and frowned. 'You and your mum must have had such a falling out. What was it about?'

'I didn't like my stepfather. I told my mother what I'd seen on his computer, so she threw me out.'

Anna gasped. 'But that's shocking. He was the adult ... he was responsible!'

'That's why he's in prison. But not for anything to do with me.'

Anna fell silent. This was not what she had expected and guessed that there must be more. From her experience, Anna knew that to remove Ros from her family, social workers must have thought she was at significant risk. She watched Ros finish her roll and wipe the egg-smeared plate with her fingertips, sucking each one.

Ros smiled at her but Anna couldn't judge the smile. The girl seemed satisfied, as if something had been accomplished. Perhaps she had told her story so often, to teachers and social workers, it no longer distressed her. That must be it, Anna reasoned.

They walked around the ponds, allowing Christopher out of the buggy to throw a crust of bread to the ducks. Anna hadn't seen Ros push the leftover bread from the cafe into her pocket and such a small but thoughtful act only made her seem more of an enigma. I must stop probing and accept her as she is, Anna reprimanded herself. Whatever her past, I have to trust her. She's had enough rejection.

Christopher tried to copy Ros throwing the bread, but it fell behind him onto the tarmac. Ros laughed and picked up the crusts, kneeling down to his level. 'Ga' he said to Ros pointing to the ducks, 'Ga.'

'Anna, he said "ducks". Did you hear him?' Ros turned towards Anna, her eyes bright. Anna smiled back. She could be his sister, she thought, my own child. She must come to no more harm.

The ice on the pond was frozen, making soft, cracking sounds as the ducks hurried across to be first at the bread.

Starlings gathered in the branches of the trees above them, swooping and sighing on long, falling notes as they settled. Suddenly, the park felt sterile and empty, and Anna shivered, keen to leave.

Anna's unease evaporated into the domestic routine of home, and she felt foolish to have rushed them back. Ros seemed anxious to please and offered to help empty the dishwasher and tidy the children's bedrooms. Anna found her in the girls' room, kneeling in front of a doll's house, given to Cara by Nick's father when she was born. It was elaborate, not a child's toy at all, but Ros was absorbed, taking out each piece of miniature furniture and rearranging the rooms, with the stiff little family posed in the middle of a silent conversation. Anna sat down on Cara's bed and watched her play, stroking Jake's cheek as he slept.

'Cara never plays with it. You should sit with her one day and try to encourage her interest.'

'I will.' Ros didn't turn around. 'We can play in the holidays when she's home from school.'

'Yes,' said Anna, 'you must come often after they break up. It will be fun for the girls, like having a grown-up sister.'

When Jake woke, Ros decided to take the two buses across the city to her mother's house, gambling that if her sister was already home from school, she would let her in.

Emily was in the kitchen making toast when Ros tapped on the window.

'You're not allowed here. Mum will kill me if she finds out.' Emily said, peering through the door at her half-sister. She looked so different from last year when Ros had seen her at a contact meeting. Then, Emily had still been at primary school. Now, her thin legs balanced above shiny wedges and continued, shapeless, into a short navy skirt, which swung around undeveloped hips. Her school shirt was pulled out over the skirt, practically covering its length, and underneath, just visible through the cheap cotton, she wore a vest covered in pink hearts.

'Got any fags?' Emily asked.

'Yes, but not for you. You're too young to smoke. Make me a cup of tea and some toast and I'll show you the baby.'

Emily pulled the door wide to let her sister pass.

'I'll tell Mum you were here.'

'Okay, I'll give you one but don't smoke now, not around Jake. Anyway, it'll make your breath smell.'

'Yours does anyway.' Emily reached across for the roll-up.

The sisters ate toast and drank tea, watching each other across the table. Ros looked over Emily's dark hair at her mother's small and ordinary kitchen and envied its cleanliness, its order, its abundance.

'I'm going to watch telly now. Can I hold the baby? Can he watch with me?'

Ros unstrapped Jake and sat him on her sister's lap in front of the television in her mother's neat sitting room. He tried his new smile, but Emily wasn't looking. Ros smiled back at him and returned to the kitchen, opening cupboard after cupboard. There was so much of everything. Why did she need so much?

Taking a carrier bag from the drawer, the same drawer where they had always been kept, Ros took a little of whatever she could: a single egg, a few teabags, some cereal. She would do this again. If she took just a little, every so often, nothing would be missed. As she moved around the kitchen, she noticed the washing machine. Next time she'd bring her laundry, there was plenty of time even to dry it, as long as she took care to remember her mother's shifts. Ros glanced at the clock above the cooker; it was already five.

'What's happened to the new boyfriend?' Ros asked her sister.

'Mm?' Emily replied at last.

'What about Mum's boyfriend. Where is he?'

'Dunno, he just went.' Emily shrugged without shifting her eyes from the screen.

Ros made them both a poached egg and tinned spaghetti and sat down next to her sister to eat. Jake lay on the floor, asleep, where Emily had put him down.

'You shouldn't be eating that,' Emily said, her mouth full, turning her large eyes towards Ros. 'It's stealing.'

'So what? She'll never notice. Not if you don't tell. If she asks, just say you were hungry.'

'Give me another fag then.'

'No. If you want me to come and make your tea for you again, you'll shut up about this.'

'Sean will be home in a minute, and he'll tell on you even if I don't.'

Emily was right. Ros could manage her little sister but not her brother.

'Where is he anyway?' She stood to clear their plates.

'He works at Aldi after college. He gives Mum ten pounds a week and she gets a discount there as well.'

'Oh, well done Sean,' Ros said, with sarcasm.

She carried their plates through to the kitchen and dumped them in the sink. 'You'll have to wash those dishes before he gets back, or he'll know you let someone in.'

'You made half the mess!' Emily protested.

'If you want me to come again,' Ros called, 'get those plates washed.' She left by the back door, pausing only to lift a spare key from under a loose brick. Her mother still lacked imagination.

CHAPTER 6

Nick lifted a strand of Jenny's hair from his chest, where it was tickling his armpit. He moved slowly, so she wouldn't waken, placing his hand back onto the nape of her neck. He felt rather than heard her breathe, her whole body stretched the length of his, chest to chest, stomach to stomach, legs tangled. Outside the sky was already darkening and he knew he would soon have to rouse her.

The music matched his mood of mellow gratitude, a female jazz singer from Jenny's collection and not his usual taste, which was frozen in time from his days at medical school. Nick stroked her hair and moved his head backwards onto the pillow to look at her face. Jenny ... new into the practice; her enthusiasm for life, for the work and unexpectedly for him, had elevated him to feel— what was it? Not joy, or happiness, but utter contentment. In this actual moment, he loved her more than any other person in the world.

Jenny raised her head and frowned up at him.

'What time is it?'

Nick glanced over at the bedside clock, the digital numerals bright and trembling.

'Almost four, we have to go soon.'

'I don't.' She yawned. 'I'm not on the five-to-midnight stretch, so I'm staying here to work on a research paper.'

'God knows I fought tooth and nail to reverse our management's twenty-four-hour open-surgery idea, but I have to admit,' Nick said, grinning into the half-light, 'it's made our affair possible. Working these shifts means that at home I hardly ever have to account for my time.'

'It suits me, or I wouldn't have taken the post.' Jenny rolled onto her back. 'It's actually only the pharmacy that's open twenty-four hours, and the shifts aren't bad, except the really early one.'

Nick felt as if his skin had been peeled away as he lost the warmth from Jenny's body. He pushed up onto his elbow and the sight of her breasts, silhouetted in the light from the streetlamp, made him want to reach across and run his fingers down the curves and hollows of her body.

Jenny turned back towards him, also resting on her elbow.

'How is the baby?'

Nick pushed thoughts of more sex with Jenny from his mind.

'He's almost two months now. The early problems with weight loss seem to be over but there are still some concerns about his development, not that Anna will accept it. We've called him Hugh, after my father.'

'I thought you hated your father.'

'It was Anna's idea, and he does look very like him. We decided one afternoon after I'd been with you. I think my mind was elsewhere.'

Jenny frowned. 'You weren't with me. We haven't had any time together for over a month.'

Too late, Nick remembered that afternoon; it was when Simmering Sue had unexpectedly come up trumps. But Jenny had closed her eyes, as if she was considering the discrepancy in his account and Nick had to wait longer than was comfortable for her to speak.

'I don't know how you manage four children and do your job. You must be exhausted all the time.'

'If I'm honest, I don't do much with the children. Anna couldn't face the way education was going, so she gave up work after Cara was born. We made some sort of unspoken pact that children were her department, bringing in income was mine. I'm not one of those fathers who changes nappies or gets up in the night. I don't do the family thing at all well.' Nick was aware that he was rambling—relief had made him garrulous.

'From what you've said, you had no blueprint to build on.'

'Yeah.' Nick grinned. 'Let's blame our parents. It's always safe.'

Jenny leaned forward and kissed him. The tips of her nipples brushed against his arm, and he rested his hand on the curve of her hips, wondering if there was still time.

'I'm puzzled why you had so many kids, if you're not really into them,' Jenny murmured, after the kiss.

'Me too.' Nick withdrew his hand and brushed back his hair. 'I'm amazed every time I see them. After I met Anna, I was determined to work as a GP in the most deprived areas of the city, and she felt the same about teaching. Kids just weren't on the agenda. She was incredibly committed as a teacher, so I should have guessed that she would become a full-on mother.'

'Maybe she's trying to have a whole class.' Jenny laughed.

Nick felt irritated by this jibe at Anna and swung his legs over the side of the bed.

'Not if I have anything to do with it. I'd better get showered or I'll be late for the medical challenges of evening surgery.'

'Go on then.' Jenny pushed at his backside with her foot. 'I'll make you a cup of tea.'

Nick stood by the curtains and sipped tea from one of Jenny's mugs, looking down onto the wet pavement. Lights picked out the silver roofs of cars parked tightly together on both sides of the street. He could see into every room of the student house opposite, each one ablaze with light. A mother and child walked home from school, hand in hand. Some youths ran past them, laughing, their voices echoing down the narrow street. He felt something close to guilt, not about Anna but for Jenny, that she'd almost found out about the other women. Nick turned to look at her, already at the desk, studying the manuscript she had been working on earlier. Nick watched Jenny's careful movements. She had slipped a tee shirt over her naked body, and without taking her eyes from the page, she folded her body onto a chair, her free hand tucking the shirt under her bottom. Still reading, she leaned across the desk, switched on the computer, and began to tap at the keys, totally absorbed. Jenny trusted him, and he had lied to her.

In his car, Nick stabbed his mobile phone back to life and found three missed calls, a voicemail and a text from Anna. He was already going to be late for his first patient and hesitated before listening to her message. Thank goodness, it was about Ros, not one of the children. He wouldn't have to turn up at Children's A&E and face awkward questions about where he'd been. Anna sounded frantic. Ros hadn't turned up today.

'And what the fuck am I supposed to do about it?' Nick said aloud, as he looked up at the flat's first floor window, seeing only Jenny's shadow reflected on the ceiling.

CHAPTER 7

When Ros didn't turn up the next day Anna's mood swung between worry and irritation. She hoped Ros had met up with old friends, and with teenage carelessness, had forgotten to tell her she wouldn't be coming. By the end of the day, she felt sure this was the explanation and her irritation rose. If Ros came tomorrow, she would talk to her about thinking of others. After all, she was a mother now. She wrote about it at length on her blog when both the babies were napping and the girls not yet back from school, developing her theme that teenagers, who were intrinsically selfish, must struggle to put their baby first and that was why it was so crucial their own mothers were involved.

The replies, when they came in, reminded her to make sure she had Ros's address and mobile number. She, or the baby, could be ill and who would know? Anna agreed with them, wondering how on earth she could have overlooked something so basic. But then, Ros had never offered to share such personal information.

Nick, eating a late, microwaved dinner at the kitchen table, was unsympathetic.

'Come on Anna, it's time you gave her up. Maybe this is for the best. We know almost nothing about her.'

'But I gave her my old ski jacket,' she replied, adding that she was perfectly aware she had just made a fatuous remark, before Nick could say anything. Anna hadn't told Nick what Ros had said about her stepfather or that she'd been in care. She felt a needle of worry over keeping this secret, which she rapidly twisted into righteous indignation on Ros's behalf. 'She's had so little support, her own mother has nothing to do with her. I'm not going to turn my back on her now.'

Nick forked in another mouthful of shepherd's pie and Anna had to wait until he'd swallowed before he replied.

'That's my point.' Nick jabbed his fork at her. 'Why does her mother have nothing to do with her? You're letting her hang around my kids. God knows what's happened to her in the past, or what she wants from you. I'm not happy about it.'

'Our kids,' Anna corrected him.

Paradoxically, since starting his affair with Jenny, Nick found that he was more tolerant of Anna. She lived in one box, marked wife and mother, and Jenny was in another, labelled sex and fun. He didn't expect either of them to pretend that he was *everything*, that he actually mattered. So, instead of starting an argument with Anna, which once he would have done, he sat back and wiped his mouth with a paper napkin, screwed it into a ball and attempted an overarm bowl into the wastepaper basket in the corner.

'If you'd given that old coat to me, I'd have tried to avoid you too.'

Seeing Anna's expression, he winked, but she obviously wasn't in the mood for jokes.

'It's got nothing to do with the coat. What if she's ill? I don't have a clue where she lives,' Anna paraphrased TheBump.net's consensus.

Nick stood up and scraped his leftovers into the bin.

'I've got work to do in the study. You decide—she's your friend. Just be careful, that's all I ask.'

In his untidy office, a room that was for some reason excluded from Anna's haphazard cleaning rota, Nick listened to the sounds of the children's bedtime and guessed that he had twenty minutes before the goodnight ritual. He retrieved his mobile from his jacket pocket and flicking through new messages from the site, saw that there was one from SimmeringSue. She didn't want to see him again, he read, he wasn't her 'type'. Nick felt his face flush with resentment and was trying to frame a suitably cutting response when Anna put her head around the door.

'Look after this one can you? He won't settle, and I've got my arms full.' Nick tried to hide his phone, even though there were at least twenty legitimate reasons why he might be scanning his messages, but in the end the deceitful object was left dangling in his hand when he was forced to reach out his arms for baby Hugh, before Anna swept out of the room in a haze of baby oil. Holding Hugh against his shoulder, Nick squinted at the phone and tapped out a reply that he hoped was uncaring and therefore hurtful. The response from the site was immediate; he was already blocked.

CHAPTER 8

It was ten o'clock but barely light when Ros reached the city centre for a meeting with her personal adviser. At the bus station she noticed a young man leaning against the wall where the national, rather than local, buses drew in. Her glance absorbed and then dismissed him, his short hair, scarred face, and prominent ears.

Claire's office was in a building on the edge of the centre that might once have been a shop. Ros was asked to wait in a cramped seating area while the key for the meeting room was found. Through the glass panes that separated her from the workspace behind, she noticed a Costa takeaway cup on Claire's desk, lying next to the back of her computer. The three advisers and the secretaries had made some attempt at decorating the room for Christmas; strings of flickering lights hung over their computer screens and pocket-sized Christmas trees lolled against sandwich wrappers. Claire had pinned several cards to the wall behind her desk and Ros realised that she hadn't thought to bring her one. Perhaps Anna would lend her a card and she could post it tomorrow. There was still time.

The meeting room was cold with an unused feel, and Ros wrapped Anna's jacket more tightly around Jake's sling.

Claire noticed and apologised. 'I'm really sorry there's no radiator in here and our fan heater has vanished. Still, we won't be long. How are things? Jake's growing well, isn't he?'

'He's fine but the flat's cold and damp. I'm sure it's not healthy.' Ros was keen that this meeting wasn't going to be a hurried pre-Christmas round of self-congratulatory platitudes.

'We did advise you to stay in Derby,' Claire reminded Ros, as if she really needed to hear this again. 'Your decision to move to independent accommodation in Leicester was rushed and wasn't one we were happy with. We agreed that you wouldn't make any contact with your family, and I hope you've stuck to this?'

Ros hesitated. Did Claire know?

'Of course, I haven't,' she chose to risk a lie, 'but I'm not guilty of anything, I should be able to contact them if I want to.'

'We can't stop you meeting Emily but not at her home. Please don't try to make contact with anyone else in your family—it's the only way your mother will accept having you in Leicester. Anyway, I'm pleased to tell you that Social Care are planning to drop Jake down from being a child in need, so he won't have a social worker for much longer. We know you're a good mother, Ros.'

'He was always safe,' Ros argued, trying to hide the tremor in her voice that betrayed the months of resentment she had carried since their totally unfair decision that Jake needed a social worker. 'I didn't do anything.'

Claire allowed a short silence between them, one that seemed to convey her agreement, before lifting the lid of her laptop.

'We need to review your plan, Ros. Having a baby has set things back but we should try to get down some next steps. Your bursary will finish as soon as you're nineteen, so after our next meeting you'll need to sign on for Universal Credit. And what about college or university next September?'

'He didn't set me back.' Ros needed to get this clear between them.

'Sorry, that was a clumsy of me.' Claire closed her laptop. 'I was trying to say that I recognise you have to think about Jake as well. I know that an accidental pregnancy isn't a barrier to anything.'

'But he's part of the plan—Jake wasn't an accident. I've had my child and there won't be any more. I have a family of my own and I'm ready to do the degree and career thing. I can see the point of it now that he's here. I want him to live in a warm house that doesn't smell. I want him to know the right words. I want him to open the fridge and have a choice of what to eat.'

'Yes of course.' Claire folded her arms and nodded. 'You're so right. And he'll be proud to say you're his mum.'

The boy was waiting for Ros as she left the office and he whistled two sharp notes to catch her attention. She ignored him and quickly walked on. He followed her, not catching up, just keeping pace, his tuneless piping whistle reminding her of his constant presence. Once, she turned and looked at him and he winked at her.

'Piss off!' she yelled but he just grinned with his yellow, pointed teeth. Ros walked on, but more slowly. If she took the bus to Anna's, as she had intended, he would know where Anna lived and perhaps neither of them would be safe. He seemed familiar. Did she know him from primary school? Why was he following her? Walking away from the city led her into an area of small workshops and industrial units, empty of their workers. Her fear began to turn to anger. Why should she be frightened of a puny little thug no taller than she was? She would challenge him.

Ros turned around, hands on hips, adopting her most aggressive stance, but this left Jake horribly exposed. She held the thick jacket tight against her chest with one fist.

'What do you want?' she snapped as the youth strolled up. Her legs were shaking.

He grinned again, a snide, leering grimace that made her want to slap him.

'Dave wants a word with you,' he said at last, having first brushed some imaginary dust from his trousers.

'He's in prison,' said Ros, her voice sounding less confident than she would have liked. It was a senseless comment, spoken only to buy time.

The youth shook his head and grinned again, feigning disapproval.

'Never been to visit, and him like a father to you.'

Ros stared, her breathing shallow.

'I don't want to see him. Anyway, I can't. It's not allowed.'

'Well, he wants to see you. You're eighteen.' The youth's tone hardened as he pushed his hand against Ros's shoulder in time with each word, forcing her back against the wall. She crossed her arms over Jake.

'He's got nothing to do with me. He's never been my father.'

The youth put a hand on each side of Ros's head and pushed his face into hers. She could smell his breath and feel his spit as he spoke.

'He's coming out soon. Served his time you see. And he wants to see yer.'

Ros cried out as he squeezed her lips together with one hand and forced his tongue into her mouth. She brought up her knee into his groin. His head went back in a roar of pain. Ros whipped her forehead down hard against his and he stumbled back against the door of a supplier of bathroom fittings. The metal frame rang out melodically as he slid down its length. Ros kicked him again and ran back into the city.

Ros knew she must look wild or strange as passers-by first glanced at her, then turned back to stare. She found a cafe she remembered was cheap and bought a mug of tea. The families around her were weary of shopping and each other, the parents slouched in their seats, plastic shopping bags strewn at their feet, their pale pre-school children whining from buggies. Ros ignored their whispers as she unzipped Jake from his sling and fed him, exposing her breasts. This calmed her and as she smoothed the top of his head, her hands stopped shaking. In the single toilet she rinsed her mouth with water, shocked at her appearance in the mirror; deep red marks on either side of her mouth and a bruise swelling on her forehead.

Gradually, as the hours passed, the cafe emptied and the solitary employee, a boy in an outsized apron, swept the floor around her. There were no doors or windows and the endless loop of taped music from the main concourse cycled through a celebration of sleigh rides and little drummer boys. Jake wouldn't settle. He whimpered then raged as his mother sat, immobile, her body fitting into the smallest space possible, as if she did not exist. Eventually, he stopped crying but still called out occasionally across the empty tables to the boy in the apron. Then he slept.

CHAPTER 9

It felt so ordinary, to stand in a queue and wait for coffee, to choose a table by the window and spread out a newspaper and read in the filmy, winter sunlight. The tables around her were busy with conversation and Anna eavesdropped on sounds from an unfamiliar adult world. She watched the women lean close, heads almost touching, their eyes connected, sharing things that mustn't be overheard. Couples faced each other across the table, making lists and plans for the holiday ahead. A single man read a text and smiled. To his phantom correspondent he shrugged as if to say he didn't know, he wasn't sure. Anna wanted to know what the question was.

She'd promised Nick that she would be home by twelve, and finished her coffee, tipping her head back to swallow the chocolate and froth. The texting man smiled at her, and Anna wiped her lip, hoping that she didn't have a chocolate moustache. She was aware that his eyes were tracking her when she left the cafe and returned his smile, as she pulled at the heavy door. At least someone finds me attractive, she thought, pushing troublesome thoughts about Nick from her mind. They would find a way back to each other; it was perfectly normal for a couple's relationship to be tested by young children. And his new shifts didn't help—she never knew when she would see him, let alone find the time to talk.

It was several days since she had last seen Ros, but Anna felt confident that she would see her again. Her present was the last one to buy and Anna stopped at All Saints and bought some vouchers. It was disappointing, she would have preferred to help the girl choose something, but what else could she do? She glanced at her watch and knew she must hurry home.

The shops were crowded, and she had to slow her pace, glancing up at the pink and grey ribbons and baubles suspended from the atrium, spinning in the heat from the bodies below. It must have rained outside the centre, as most shoppers swayed under wet coats and dripping carrier bags, partially folded umbrellas acting as weapons, pointed towards the unwary walking behind. Anna was taller than most and as she dropped her eyes to look ahead, a girl who might have been Ros was in the distance, pushing past a family. Anna stumbled and caught the heel of the woman in front and with the apologies, smiles and complaints about how busy it was, the moment was lost. When Anna reached the point where she thought she had seen Ros, the girl was gone.

Ros used her mother's key, pleased that her theft hadn't been discovered and the locks changed. It was only a matter of time. She couldn't face Anna, not with her face as it was, and phoning was out of the question. Phoning would have meant lies and lies were best avoided. The kitchen smelt of toast and Ros leaned against the back door and imagined the room only an hour before; the bodies darting, voices competing with the tiny television on the counter, the smells of morning.

Jake wriggled in his sling, and she lifted him out, holding him in the crook of her arm as she filled her mother's washing machine with laundry, tipped out from her rucksack. They watched the cycle whirr and click reassuringly to the end, the suds flailing at the window like a winter storm. Ros found a laundry basket and propped Jake up amongst some towels as she dried and folded their clothes, pressing them down while they were hot to smooth out the creases. She helped herself to cheese, bread and a banana and made a mug of tea, remembering to replace the hot water in the kettle with cold.

In the sitting room, her mother had a Christmas tree in the corner next to the television. It was a new one, made of trembling purple foil, the branches hung with opaque white baubles. Ros would have liked to put on the tree lights but couldn't risk attracting attention from her mother's neighbours. She knelt and looked at the presents, clumsily wrapped and tied with ribbon that didn't match. Her mother was obviously still careless about things that mattered. She read the labels, written in pink gel pen in her mother's childlike writing, gifts for Emily and Sean, Nan and Gramps.

Jake was clingy and she lifted him up to read the Christmas cards on the windowsill. She didn't recognise any of the names. She carried him upstairs and showed him the soft toys in her sister's bedroom, smelling the sour mix of cheap deodorant and sweat from the pile of dirty clothes bundled on Emily's floor. On the bed, amongst discarded textbooks, a broken pencil and a crisp bag, there was a letter from the school, reminding parents that the Christmas holidays started on Friday. Ros picked up Emily's English workbook and flicked through the pages. She shook her head at the crossings out, the dreadful spelling. Her sister wasn't getting an education, not compared to hers.

Sean's bedroom door was closed. In her mother's room there was a photograph of a baby on the dressing table. Ros turned it over not wanting to see the child's face, and searched the drawers, sifting through her mother's underwear. She wrinkled her nose at finding a half-finished packet of contraceptive pills and a sticky tube of lubricant. She sat on the bed to feed Jake, examining her bruised profile in the mirror, turning her head from left to right. Her face throbbed and she could still taste his coated tongue in her mouth. At least she was safe here; it was the last place anyone would think to look for her.

In the bathroom, Ros found samples of shower gel and shampoo in the cluttered cabinets and slipped them into her pocket. Retracing her steps, she checked each room, tugging at the tell-tale dip in her mother's duvet and puffing up the dent in the pillow.

Downstairs, the sitting room was darkening. She heard the whoomp of the central heating, set to warm the house for Emily's return. The radiators ticked as hot water travelled through the pipes. It was almost three and time she was gone. The traffic was heavy and car headlights were already bright against the gathering night. Ros walked along the street to the bus stop and as she waited to cross the road, she looked back towards her mother's house. She thought she saw a tall figure swing around the gate and up the path, but to her relief she realised it wasn't a stranger, it was Sean. Her legs felt weak; she had just escaped a confrontation that would have been almost as bad as yesterday's.

Outside Kyprianou's fish and chip shop Ros hesitated, preferring the bright lights of the still-trading shops to the anonymity of the flats behind. She waited for a few minutes before she faced the darkness, hurrying past the skips at the side of the shops, piled with rubbish, until she found the unlit metal staircase, her feet ringing on each step. She imagined that some part of the shadows below was more substantial than the rest and ran to her door, glancing behind her. Breathing heavily, she waited for the thump of footsteps but there was silence. No one was there. She was safe.

Jake had suddenly become a good sleeper, in bed for eight and only needing to be fed again at midnight before waking at six. Anna had said she should be proud, 'An evening to yourself, amazing!', but tonight, the silent, empty space of her flat felt hollow and unwelcoming. Listening to Jake's breathing, Ros flicked through the messages on her phone. They were all home for the holidays, her friends pouting for the camera before a club night in Derby. They might come here, Ros thought, I can't go out with them, but they could come here. Why not? Nights out in Leicester had been common during her sixth form. I won't go on to the clubs, but I can invite them here first. Before she could change her mind, Ros drafted a group message and pressed 'send'. The replies came quickly, pinging reassurance into the heavy silence. They were coming!

CHAPTER 10

It was nearly midday when Anna returned from a rushed visit to the supermarket. She stepped into the hall and closed the door, leaning against it. No one was crying. The burble of cartoons drifted from the sitting room, and she peered around the door. Christopher was there, on Nick's knee, a stethoscope dangling precariously from his ears as he listened to his father's chest. The remains of Nick's lunch, which he had obviously shared with Christopher, were scattered across the cushions. The crusts of a sandwich formed a neat rectangle on Nick's briefcase and an empty pot of yoghurt lay on its side beside his mobile, toppled by the weight of the spoon still inside. Fragments of crisps smattered the carpet. There was no sign of Hugh.

Nick looked up when he heard the jangle of her keys.

'You've got a visitor, in the kitchen.'

Ros was there, Hugh in her arms, walking him around the oak table and talking softly, with her back to Anna. Jake chewed his fingers, his eyes following his mother from Hugh's baby chair on the floor. She turned around and smiled at Anna.

'Hi, I've been helping Nick. I got here about ten minutes ago. Did you get everything you needed?'

Anna sat down and pulled off her gloves.

'I've been so worried about you. Why didn't you call me? I couldn't begin to think what had happened.'

'I'm so sorry, we've been ill. I had a really bad cold and so did Jake. I didn't want you to catch it.'

Anna sighed. 'But that's ridiculous. You know I would have helped. I'm cross and disappointed you didn't let me know.'

Ros hesitated. 'I didn't want you to come around to my flat. I'm ashamed of it. It's filthy.'

'Oh Ros.' Anna smiled with relief. 'Is that all? You are silly. Remind me to help you get it tidied up. With all the fuss over Christmas I might forget.'

That's unlikely, Ros thought.

'Pass Hugh over for his feed,' Anna continued, 'and then I'll make us all some lunch. We can talk about Christmas, and you can come with us this afternoon to see the girls' nativity play. By the way, I thought I saw you in town yesterday?'

Ros shook her head. 'What would I be doing in town? I've no money to spend.'

Anna leaned over and peered at Ros across the table. It looked like she had a bruise under her eye, covered by thick make-up. The inspection made Ros touch her cheek.

'I tripped climbing up the stairs to my flat. There's no light at the back of the shops. Luckily Jake wasn't hurt. I think I must have been feverish.'

Anna frowned. 'It's definitely time I saw your flat. I might be able to help, speak to the council or whatever. I did it all the time for families when I was teaching, so I know the system.'

Nick looked at his watch, edging it out from under the cuff in case he was seen. He had worked out that he had eleven more of these events ahead of him, which in total added up to fifteen years of nativity plays. He tilted his head and scanned the vaulted ceiling and thick, dark beams of the school hall. The windows, set high in the walls, allowed Victorian children no wandering of attention, no dreaming of an alternative future. He would be fifty-seven when this ended.

Metal frames supporting climbing ropes were pushed against the wall, since the hall was still used for PE, and there was an aroma of generations of lunch. Some things never change and that could either feel comforting or like a trap. Right now, Nick was feeling trapped. He stifled a yawn.

Jess was on the stage, one of at least fifty children who had tripped across waving to their parents, in the demanding role of villagers. There was no singing and the children mimed to taped music from 1950s American musicals. Nick pondered the cultural significance of Bing Crosby and wondered if he should reconsider his father's offer to pay for private schooling, not because he had a clue about Cara and Jess's education, but because it would screw his father for thousands of pounds. But Anna wouldn't hear of it: 'If state education is good enough for the children I teach, then it's good enough for ours.' Their argument had lasted some time, he recalled, because he had stupidly reminded Anna that she didn't teach any longer, which had been the wrong thing to say.

The infant school was hustled out of the hall and the junior department arrived. Nick thought that the Year 6 kids, as he had learnt to call them, looked distinctly uncomfortable, shambling into the hall, hands in pockets, squeezing together onto the floor, too large and too cool for such capers. Lucky them, he thought, they've made it to the end. Cara pranced onto the stage in a costume that was too tight and performed the Little Mix number he had already admired at least twenty times at home.

He slipped his mobile phone from his pocket and read a text from Jenny. What were they going to do about 'their' Christmas? That was an interesting thought ... a novel idea. He hadn't realised that he and Jenny would need to 'have a Christmas'. He'd bought a present for her, of course, hidden in a drawer at work but clearly more was expected. He texted back, promising they would talk about it tomorrow.

Nick saw that Ros had noticed him slide his phone into his pocket. She felt too close, their elbows jammed together as they sat, scrunched on miniature chairs. Had she been able to read the text? He smiled at her, and she smiled back, so he thought it was unlikely.

At lunch Anna had tried to force Ros to spend Christmas Day with them, despite his attempts to catch her eye hoping she might notice the tiny shake of his head, but luckily the girl had refused, claiming to have family to visit. He had seen that Anna was about to interrogate Ros about the mystery 'family' and he rescued her, insisting that Anna leave her alone. The girl had looked grateful, just as he had been grateful to her for rescuing him from Hugh this morning. They had reached a compromise; Boxing Day would have to do. Thank goodness. His mother and father would be quite enough on Christmas Day.

Anna was a Christmas enthusiast. She had a fantasy about family Christmases that Nick knew was unshakeable. Her family ran a garden centre, or nursery as his father-in-law insisted, but a changing society had meant the inevitable opening of a gift shop and cafe and a grotto at Christmas. He had heard many times from Anna about Christmas being the nursery's busiest time, of a childhood spent helping other families choose trees and baubles, her mother exhausted and an undecorated house on Christmas Day. His own had been an empty, adult day always spent with his mother, his father if he wasn't on call, which he too often was, and his mother's two sisters. His presents were always book tokens or a magazine subscription and after his parents' divorce, only a cheque from his father.

This year, with three children and a new baby, it was surely the time when they should draw the curtains, light the fire, and eat from Marks and Spencer's. But that wasn't Anna's way. She would try harder, exhaust herself and become red-faced and difficult. It wasn't as if his mother would help. Harriet had tried to have as little as possible to do with him when he was a baby, and he couldn't imagine that she would want to spend time peeling potatoes or playing with her grandchildren.

The junior school marched out of the hall to 'Rudolph the Red Nose Reindeer'. The head teacher, a harassed-looking man who had received notification of an Ofsted visit two days into the new term, invited the parents to stay for tea and a mince pie. Nick had learnt about the inspection from Anna, who was still on the information highway of teacher gossip, and seeing the man's face he remembered this particular nugget with a frisson of pleasure.

Nick stood with Anna and Ros juggling a cup and saucer, trying to control pastry which shattered as he bit into it. The scalding filling burned the roof of his mouth so that he couldn't speak. He found himself nodding in agreement with the cluster of parents around Anna and Ros; the concert had been 'wonderful' and the infant children 'so sweet'. If you overlooked the head, who was clearly on something stronger than tea, he was the only man in the room. Several of the parents were his patients, noting his presence on a Wednesday afternoon, when they hadn't been able to get an appointment with him for weeks.

Soothing his burnt mouth with gulps of tea he overheard Anna tell Ros that she should try to get Jake's name down for the school. She could use their address, Anna said, since it was unlikely Ros could ever afford to live in the area. Nick had a vision of the future; Ros and Jake being shifted into their household, inch by inch, even if was the last thing the girl wanted. He knew how Anna worked.

'It's time we collected Jess and Cara,' he interrupted before Ros could open her mouth. 'Christopher's looking hot. We should make our way home.'

Again, Ros seemed grateful.

'I'm going to catch the bus from outside the school, so I won't walk back with you, if that's okay.'

'Oh,' Anna looked disappointed. 'I've sorted out some cleaning stuff for you. Never mind, you can pick it up tomorrow. Enjoy your party tonight.' Anna leaned forward and kissed her theatrically on both cheeks.

Nick watched Ros push through the parents. At the door to the hall, she turned and waved a small, gloved hand.

Anna turned to him, frowning. 'It's time we got that girl a pushchair. She'll get back trouble if she carries on with that papoose. What happened to our old single buggy? Is it in the garage? When we get home, Nick, you must see if you can find it.'

Ros felt uncomfortable and wondered if she hadn't been hanging around Anna for too long. Instead of the easy come, easy go of last year, here she was, laying out bowls of crisps and checking that the sausage rolls weren't burnt, counting and re-counting bottles of beer and touching the cap of each bottle of vodka. The sausage rolls were Anna's idea. Ros would have been happy with cheese and onion crisps, but Anna pressed on her three bags of Waitrose organic sausage rolls, with one packet suitable for vegans—young people shouldn't drink on an empty stomach.

Ros had regretted saying anything at all about her little gathering, as it had become swept up onto Anna's list of projects, of which there were many. The candles were Anna's, the tablecloth was Anna's, the Christmas lights that stretched above the alcove into the kitchen were Anna's, apparently bought at a knockdown price from Habitat before they closed their shop in Leicester.

Ros sat down to feed Jake, and looking around, felt quite pleased. It would have been easy to just *pretend* to use Anna's stuff, she would never have known but actually, it was okay. The flat was warm and with the curtains drawn the stained walls and chipped skirting boards flickered with interesting shadows thrown by the candles. Even the flat's habitual smell of a hamster cage left-too-long was masked by the scent, since the candles were perfumed with Christmas spices. Now, Ros thought, I must try to relax and get Jake off to sleep.

It was a struggle. Jake sensed she had other plans. These had included washing and straightening her hair and a long soak in her mother's 'age-defying' almond bath oil. In the end, Ros managed a quick shower and a grimace at her face in the mottled mirror on the bedroom wall, before she closed the bedroom door firmly on Jake, who remained stubbornly indecisive about sleeping. Immediately, Ros heard giggling and a shriek from the walkway outside. Her friends had arrived. Jake would have to be ignored.

They seemed different. They were different. Even their bodies seemed to have changed. The boys were taller, the girls thinner. Their faces were changing too;

their cheekbones casting new angles in the light from the candles. Ros couldn't keep up with the talk. She didn't have the words. It was a vocabulary laden with experiences she hadn't shared. She couldn't sustain the drinking either, and as the room filled with smoke from the thin and fragile roll-ups they turned with agile fingers, she began to feel an overpowering need to sleep. Jake's piercing cry silenced their chatter.

'The baby!' Emma squealed, as if she had forgotten the one reason why Ros wasn't at university with them. 'Can we see him? Please Ros ... oh please!'

Ros hesitated, reluctant to subject Jake to the smoke-filled room, but she was proud too, so she lifted him from the cot whispering, 'Come on, Jake, it's time to meet your dad,' into his damp neck.

Ros watched Jake's passage from arm to arm, bestowing each young person with his dazzling smile, as if he had spent his entire short life practising for this moment of deserved adoration. She held her breath, anticipating the moment when Joe would hold him. When it came, she covered her mouth. Surely everyone must see; it was so obvious. She scrambled for her phone and took a photograph, father and son, cheek to cheek. The moment passed, and Ros photographed Jake with the all the others, in case anyone questioned why she had singled out Joe. The conversation moved on, they tired of the baby, so Ros took him into the bedroom, using the smoke as an excuse, but feeling too uncomfortable to expose her breasts to these old, new friends. In the dark, as Jake fed, she listened to the rhythm of their conversation. It was like the sea, the suck and crash of waves breaking on a rocky beach, their laughter the sound of gulls circling. She held on tight to the small victory of seeing the father hold his son. She would never tell Joe and he would never ask, since their one night of drunken passion must already be lost from his well-ordered catalogue of what was important. But she had a photograph to show Jake when he asked her, which one day he would. She settled Jake back into his cot and leaned her head on the crook of her elbow, bending over the rail to stroke his hair. Once Jake slept, she eased her stiff back and thought how restful it would be to lie down on her bed, just for a moment. At once, she was asleep.

When Jake woke at six, Ros struggled to remember why she was lying on her bed dressed in party clothes. She stumbled into the sitting room, where candles had formed pools of melted wax, drips suspended over the sticky carpet. The fairy lights still glimmered and in the rosy light, she read a note that had been left for her.

'Great party,' it said, followed by an exclamation mark and several kisses. Written by a girl, Ros thought. She made tea and slowly chewed through a plate of cold vegan sausage rolls for breakfast. Checking Instagram— she had been tagged in many unflattering photographs— she scrolled through posts describing an 'amazing' party she seemed to have missed. Ros stretched and yawned. She had planned a party and her friends had come. The amazement was that it had happened at all.

CHAPTER 11

Nick opened a bottle of wine in Jenny's kitchen. Like Jenny, the kitchen was tiny but perfect. It reminded him of one of those rooms in a museum, where things had been crammed in because they ought to be there, but it couldn't possibly work as a habitable space. Nick suspected she hardly ever used it and tonight's stirring, tasting and whisking were all for his benefit. But he had enjoyed squeezing past her to reach the corkscrew, her bottom, wrapped in a tight, silk dress, brushing against his groin. He'd adored the stretch of the fabric across her breasts as she reached up behind his head for plates and he'd leaned forward to kiss her neck. Any ideas of having her there against the silent-close drawer unit faded when she firmly handed him two glasses and left him alone, standing by the counter.

Nick carried the glasses into the dining room, which led into the front sitting room, which in turn led directly onto the street. Nick was familiar with the Victorian terraced house as he had lived in one himself when he left medical school. Jenny's was a fine example, with an original fireplace and cornices. Too dark and confined for much of the year, these narrow houses blossomed at Christmas, when glitter and fires lightened the gloom. Pinheads of light glinted amongst the green leaves and pink bows on the mantelpiece and smoke-free coals glowed in the miniature grate. Jenny lit the candles on the table and waited for his reaction. He smiled, passing her a glass of wine.

'It's lovely, Jenny, thank you. This is such a good idea.'

'I wanted us to celebrate Christmas properly, as if we're a couple. Let's pretend for a few hours.'

Nick slipped his arm around her waist and kissed her, but she pulled away from him when the kiss ended.

'Tonight's for food and conversation, nothing else,' she said with a scolding tease in her voice. 'I must check our dinner.'

Nick sighed and drank his wine in deep gulps, the backs of his calves warming against the fire. He listened to Jenny moving in the kitchen. They were certainly like a couple tonight, he thought, and it was all a bit too familiar. He preferred toast in bed, rumpled sheets, the mess and disorder of sex and passion. Why did women need to create scenes where men had to act out a role? Or maybe it was just the women he chose. Oh my God, he thought, is she a younger version of Anna?

Jenny came in with their first course and Nick sat down in his place, at right angles to her, so that they could both admire the fire and the decorations. The mirror above the mantelpiece reflected Jenny's profile, a tilted nose and slightly prominent chin, while Nick had a hunted, shifty look he didn't like. After a few mouthfuls, Nick became aware of Jenny's silence. Some gesture from him was expected. He reached over for her hand.

'You look beautiful tonight. This is fabulous.' He motioned towards his plate. He wasn't exaggerating, it was delicious. 'Where did you learn to cook?'

'My mother ... like most Thai women it was part of her culture. She didn't cook our meals herself but supervised everything that happened in the kitchen. She was a very traditional wife.'

'So she encouraged you to cook?'

'Not at all. She wanted everything to be different for me, the education, the profession, the things she didn't have. But I grew up knowing how good food should taste. Not even a traditional English education or university hall of residence catering could take that from me.'

'It certainly did it for me.' Nick grimaced. 'But then my mother was no cook. So she was the original Thai bride, your mother?'

'No, she wasn't!' Nick saw Jenny's cheeks flush. 'My father met my mother in his first post. She was his secretary. He was a diplomat in Bangkok—I've told you before.'

She stood up and stacked their plates, creating more noise than Nick thought was necessary. He studied his reflection, running a finger down the deep gullies that were forming on either side of his mouth, as his face slid towards the grave. This wasn't going well.

They ate the next course in silence, their mirror images reflecting every awkward touch of face or neck, the sideways glances noticed but ignored. Nick thought how ugly people looked as they chewed and questioned the merit of food as an aphrodisiac. But every mouthful was a glorious fusion of fragrant ingredients, and after another glass of wine, he began to feel better. He sat back in his chair and pushed his fingers through his hair.

'God, I'm hopeless. Of course, you told me. I was trying to make a stupid joke. I'm just so tense. It was really difficult for me to get away because I was on a late shift last night.'

Jenny's expression lost its severity, and her lips formed a half-smile, as if she was thinking 'poor you'. He pushed his advantage.

'I thought about telling Anna there was a surgery outing, which would have contained a grain of truth, but it wouldn't have taken much for her to find out it never happened, so I said I was going to the gym. In case she checked, I've had to join one. This is supposed to be my induction night.'

'That was an expensive lie but surely worth it to be with me. It means we can see each other more often. You can become a gym fanatic.' Jenny laughed, and Nick could see she was pleased. She didn't look at all guilty about the money he'd had to fork out, just to be with her. Jenny wasn't like Anna at all.

Nick felt irritated but tried to be humorous. 'Well at least I'll get plenty of exercise, wherever I am.' He knew this was crass and the words soured in his mouth.

'Let's go through.' Jenny brushed his hand. 'I've got some fabulous chocolates we can have with coffee. I bought them in Paris when I was on that conference.'

Nick tilted his head and looked down at her, trying to mimic a teacher's scowl. 'The practice doesn't send you to conferences so that you can shop for expensive chocolates.' Oh, shut up Nick, he thought.

He waited for Jenny in the front room, crowded by a sofa, a television, and a small Christmas tree. The door to the street was protected by a velvet curtain that folded onto the floor like whipped cream. The only light in the room came from a scattering of white lights on the tree and another set framing the archway into the dining room. The tree was decorated with coordinating silver bows and baubles, quite unlike the chaotic, home-made decorations on the tree at home.

In fact, it hadn't been a problem for him to get out. When he left, the girls were whispering behind their closed bedroom door, Christopher slept on his back like a starfish and Anna sat feeding Hugh at the long kitchen table, studying Christmas recipes, and making lists with her free hand. He watched her from the doorway, chewing her bottom lip. She had barely looked up when he'd said goodbye.

Underneath Jenny's tree was a parcel wrapped in embossed silver paper, tied with a grey ribbon. The single package stirred something inside him, like a reproach. It occurred to him that she might be lonely. He checked his jacket pocket for her present. At least he could do this for her but the rest of it, whatever Jenny's life amounted to when they weren't together, wasn't his responsibility.

'Your mother's coming for Christmas?' Jenny asked Nick, looking at him over the top of her mug.

He felt weary of all this family talk, but still feeling guilty about his stupid mistake over *her* mother, tried to make an effort.

'When I finished university, she went to live in Canada. She married a retired civil engineer from Vancouver. I've never met him. They've got a condo in Florida, whatever that is. She came over when Jess was born and now she's coming to see her grandsons.'

'One visit for every two kids,' Jenny remarked.

'Yeah, family life in neat packages. Sounds like my mother. You've never met her, and you've already got her sussed.'

Nick thought Jenny looked pleased. 'My father's coming as well. He always does. He didn't take the hint that he should give us a miss this year. I don't think my parents have been in the same room for twenty years. It should be interesting.' He glanced at his watch. 'Look, I hate to be boring but it's already ten. I'd better get home. Shall we do presents?'

'At last, I thought you'd never ask!' Jenny reached under the tree and passed Nick the silver package. He slowly unwrapped it, admiring the neatly folded paper and the silky ribbon. It was a set of cufflinks. When could he ever wear these without attracting unhelpful questions from Anna?

As if she heard the thought Jenny leaned over and kissed him.

'Happy Christmas, my love, you can wear them here when we're together.'

Nick put his hand behind Jenny's neck and kissed her properly. He reached into his jacket pocket for his gift, aware of the scrunched ends and heavy use of Sellotape, but her careful unfolding mirrored his and he colluded with the pretence that he had taken care with the wrapping.

'Oh.' It was a single sound, not even a word. Jenny looked down and turned the perfume box over in her hand. The gift wrap fell to the floor.

'Don't you like it?' He felt betrayed. The woman in John Lewis had said it was a top seller, the best.

'It's just …'

Nick sighed. He must leave soon. 'Just what?'

'Perfume's such a personal thing. I'm sure I'll love it. My mother loved it. It was her favourite.'

He remembered, with a thud in his chest, that Jenny's mother was dead. The facts streamed out from a neglected file stored somewhere in his memory, onto the tip of his tongue. It was only last year, when she was still his trainee, not his lover. He remembered her mother's stroke, the rush to Chester … she had arrived too late. Oh shit, he thought.

'Jenny I'm so sorry. I'd forgotten that your mother died last year. It must be close to the anniversary.'

'It was yesterday.' Jenny spoke to him over her shoulder as she fetched his coat from the cupboard under the stairs. She handed him the jacket and Nick, seeing that the collar was shiny with grease from his hair, snatched it from her with needless force. They kissed farewell inside the room, not wanting to risk being seen on the doorstep.

Jenny looked up at Nick, her expression unreadable.

'I'm sorry too, this probably wasn't the best idea. At least, not this week.'

Nick scrabbled with the heavy curtain, in an effort to reach the door handle, reminding himself of a shambling comedy act, as he tried to convince Jenny that the evening had been perfect.

In the car he waited for hot air from the blower to clear the condensation. He checked his texts before turning the engine. There was one from Anna. Would he pick up toilet paper on his way home?

Anna stacked the dishwasher and wondered why Nick had been in such a bad mood this morning. It could have been because the girls were running around in their pyjamas when he tried to leave for work, or more likely because he had to drive to Heathrow after lunch to pick up his mother.

It was a beautiful day. She stood and pushed her palms against her back, easing her muscles. I must get fit after Christmas, she thought, looking out at the garden. Perhaps I'll join the same gym as Nick.

She liked the winter garden. The wall at the end, hidden in summer, provided a rich background for the tangled branches of climbing shrubs and the bare earth looked dark and fertile. There were more birds than usual, scouring the bushes for leftover seeds and berries.

After a visit to Nick's surgery to drop off presents, Anna planned to take all the children and Ros to a farm in the countryside, where she'd read there was a Father

Christmas and some animals they could feed. She would take the chance to visit the farm shop, which she'd heard was good. For a moment she leaned against the sink, chewing her bottom lip, trying to remember the few things she still needed.

A cry from upstairs; Hugh had woken. She looked at her watch. She'd got him down to sleep at four. Five hours wasn't too bad at this age, but Jake was already sleeping through the night. Ros is so lucky to have such an easy baby, Anna thought. And such a beautiful baby. She climbed the stairs and leaned over Hugh's cot, watching him build himself up to a rage, his knees lifting and his fists beating down, as if he was playing on a drum kit. She spoke his name and he paused, trying to locate her face. He is a hard baby to love, Anna thought, but she would admit this to no one, ever. Perhaps after three children she'd just run out of love. Whatever the reason, she had to raise him so that he would never know.

Cara and Jess ran into Hugh's room, their faces red with indignation. Christopher was wrecking their game, they complained. She had to come and see—right now! Anna lifted Hugh from his cot and carried him through to the girls' room where she could feed him and supervise the play.

The doorbell rang and Anna stopped feeding Hugh, asking Jess and Cara to watch him while she answered the door. She wondered if it was Ros and thought it would make sense to give her a key. Behind the stained-glass panes she saw the distinctive shadow of Nick's father. She opened the door and pulled her shirt buttons together, aware of his gaze travelling from eyes to breasts.

'Dear girl.' He stepped inside and leaned forward to kiss her on both cheeks. She felt his smooth skin graze against hers and smelt his immaculate shave.

'This is a surprise.' She gestured towards the kitchen. 'I'll make coffee.' Anna had managed ten years without calling her father-in-law anything, after he had asked her not to call him Professor McNeill, but without giving any helpful suggestion of what else she might use. Nick called him Dad, which she certainly wasn't going to copy.

She brought baby Hugh down to the kitchen and the other children followed. Their grandfather was not an uncommon sight, as he did his duty and visited every few weeks, but he must have seemed to them like a wizard, tall with a head of white hair and usually bearing gifts of extraordinary beauty and expense. The children sat at the table and stared. Anna asked Cara to hold Hugh while she made everyone a drink and opened a box of Christmas shortbread, tipping the biscuits onto one of her Emma Bridgewater plates, instead of handing round the packet.

'Thought I'd call in. Wondered when Harriet was arriving.'

'Late this afternoon. Nick's fetching her from the airport.'

'All water under the bridge, we'll be fine,' Hugh senior answered Anna's unspoken question.

Hugh bent forward and peered at his latest grandchild. 'So, you're calling him Hugh? I'm flattered'.

'We've decided to call him Hughie,' Anna replied, 'since we found out that the girls were calling him Hugh the Poo.' Cara covered her mouth and giggled through her fingers.

Jess raised her hand, thinking that sitting around a table meant that school rules applied. 'Grandpa, do I have a granny?'

Anna listened to her father-in-law explain that he and grandma had quarrelled, and she now lived far away with her new husband. The children had heard this before, but they listened politely.

'But on Christmas Day,' Jess added, 'are you my grandma and grandpa?'

'Yes, we are,' Hugh senior nodded, 'but we're just friends, we're not married to each other.'

'Present,' Christopher said, neatly summarising Jess's real concern in a single word.

Nick's father laughed. 'And we will give you all separate presents, as usual.'

The doorbell rang again, and Anna opened the door for Ros and Jake. Hugh stood to shake Ros's hand when she came into the kitchen and Anna watched his imperceptible, and almost certainly unconscious, appraisal of the girl's body. Ros must have felt it too, as she turned her face from his attempt to kiss her cheek, resulting in an awkward moment of poorly timed body movements.

'So, you're the young lady that helps Anna out?' he asked.

Anna, sensitive to critical comments on her blog that she was training Ros to be her unpaid au pair, replied, 'Of course she's not.'

'We help each other,' Ros interrupted, removing her scarf, and taking the kettle over to the tap.

'I'll leave you ladies to it.' Nick's father remained

standing. 'Got a meeting in an hour. What time d'you want me on the day?'

Anna walked with her father-in-law into the hall. 'Come at twelve for drinks. We'll eat at one.'

The children ran to the stairs, Cara first, Jess running behind and Christopher wailing for the girls to wait for him. Cara stopped on the bottom step and turned to her audience. Christopher struggled to halt his momentum after this unexpected change of direction.

'I know,' Cara proclaimed, 'let's play at divorce. I'll be Dad, you can be Mum, and we'll fight over *him*.' She pointed at Christopher.

Anna drove to the surgery with the baby, leaving Ros in charge at home. It was ridiculous, she thought, for anyone to accuse her of having anything other than the best intentions towards Ros. The criticism had hurt, there was no denying it. On top of everything, having Harriet to stay was terrifying, especially with Nick in his present mood. She hoped she could rely on Nick and his father to behave. They could do with another guest, someone who wasn't family, to break things up.

Anna carried Hugh into the surgery in his car seat, yoo-hooing to the receptionist to watch him while she went back to the car for their presents. She didn't mind doing this every year. Nick would never think of it, and she knew how much the staff appreciated the gesture. She scanned the three bags, checking the bottles of wine for the partners, chocolates for the nurses and health visitors and biscuits for the receptionists and that new young doctor, who wasn't a partner yet. Anna heaved each bag through the sliding glass doors, and pink and out of breath, she joined the small group admiring Hugh.

The new doctor, Jenny, stood on the edge of the circle, trying to catch sight of the baby over the bent heads that cooed and clucked around him.

'It's ages since I've seen you.' Anna smiled at her. 'How are you?'

'I'm fine. Struggling to learn the job but it's all okay.' Anna noticed that Jenny had turned quite pink—well, it was hot in here.

'What are you doing for Christmas?' Anna frowned, remembering the crisis last year with Jenny's mother.

'I'm staying here. My father's gone to Thailand to visit my mother's family. He wanted me to go with him, but I couldn't. I'm the new girl, so I have to work the day after Boxing Day.'

'But you must come to us.' Anna felt triumphant, having found her guest. 'We would love to have you. Nick will be so pleased.'

'No, I can't, really, it's not possible. But thank you.'

'I won't take no for an answer. Unless you're going somewhere else, you're coming to us. Twelve o'clock on Christmas Day. And don't bother with presents. Everyone's got quite enough.'

CHAPTER 12

There was something wrong, a row between Anna and Nick about Christmas.

'It's nothing. Couples always have rows. We'll soon put it behind us.' Anna had explained. Ros agreed with Anna that Nick had behaved quite unreasonably; of course, it made perfect sense to invite one of the doctors who had nowhere else to go for Christmas Day. Privately, she was grateful to have avoided being the guest, whose role was obviously to be the lightning conductor for family hostilities.

The tension in Anna's house felt greater because of the quiet, calm presence of Nick's mother, Harriet. Ros found her scary; she was seventy-five at least but with a fashionable haircut and a scarf tied so simply around her neck it belied the elegance with which it was worn. She seemed to want to talk, and Ros felt uncomfortable with her probing. Anna had always asked her questions, then answered them herself. Harriet was different, she waited for answers, her eyes never straying from your face. She had a strange accent too; it sounded half American and half Scottish, but when Ros thought about it, the words were Scottish, and the accent must be Canadian.

Anna was obviously trying to avoid her mother-in-law by being 'too busy' and the girls sat with their grandmother for a while, but since she wouldn't allow the television on, they found other things to do. Christopher tried staring at her with his thumb in his mouth, but when Harriet reached over to pull it out, he ran to find his mother. So Ros had been left alone to entertain her. Once, Harriet had screwed her crinkled eyes and said, 'Don't I know you? Haven't you been on the television?'

Ros laughed and then shook her head, forgetting that since the very idea ought to be ridiculous, there was no need to deny anything. It had been a mistake to act as if there was something to hide. She muttered an excuse that she needed to help Anna in the kitchen, and there she emptied the dishwasher, sorted wet clothes for the tumble dryer and peeled potatoes for supper, without being asked.

Anna lifted her pink-rimmed eyes from stirring home-made mincemeat and stared at her.

'Goodness me, Ros, surely she's not that bad!'

Ros grimaced, but since the jobs were done and she risked being sent back to keep Harriet company, she decided to leave.

Walking home, she wheeled Anna's old single buggy in front of her, with no regrets about missing the Christmas Eve chaos at Anna and Nick's. As for the day itself, she didn't care about Christmas, not since her mother's baby died and everything went wrong. Actually, Ros thought, it had already been wrong but the special 'wrongness' of her family had been well hidden before then. She could have gone to Roy and Theresa's, but since she'd walked out of their house on her eighteenth birthday and seen the relief in their eyes, she knew they would prefer to spend this Christmas alone, after four tough years of having to share the day with her. Roy and Theresa were her specialist foster carers, assessed as having the skills to deal with her unique 'problems' and because of the circumstances, Ros had to be their only foster child. These assumptions infuriated her, even at fourteen, so there was no way she was going to make it easy for them. Sometimes, she saw them looking at her when they thought she couldn't see, and had watched their confusion and too often, their resentment. To give them their due, Ros conceded as she stumped along, they had supported her through school, not because they cared but because they were easy with the system. They didn't even have to try; the things they knew about education coursed through their veins like blood, or the air they breathed into their lungs.

Ros turned the key in her door and smelt the faint odour of mildew that hung around the flat. Jake was asleep, so she left him where he was. She lit the gas fire listening to it hiss and pop as the flame caught. She made a mug of tea, pulling her sleeves down over her wrists and leaning forward as she sipped, until her knees and eyelids were scorched. Anna had presented her with a basket, covered in cheerful gingham cloth: 'I normally make these up myself but a bought one will have to do this year.'

Ros pulled back the cloth and checked inside. There was a small Christmas cake, some mince pies, a packet of tea—Earl something—some honey, marmalade, and a half bottle of whisky. Nothing worth eating, Ros thought. She removed the whisky and covered the basket, tightening the bow around the cloth. In her fridge she found half a carton of milk that didn't smell too good.

She carried Jake, still in his buggy, down to the shop, Anna's basket dangling painfully from one arm. Mrs Lapinsky was drawing down the shutters outside.

'Ah, Rosemary, we're closing early but Josef's still inside. He'll see to you.'

Josef peered at the basket as Ros thumped it down on the counter, flexing her elbow with relief. 'How much would you give me for this?'

He shook his head. 'No market for it after Christmas.'

'Take a look inside, it's quality stuff.'

Josef untied the ribbon and peeled back the red-and-white-checked cover. She listened to his heavy breathing as he examined the packs and jars.

'Five pounds,' he said at last.

'Six and you can keep the basket.'

Josef sighed. 'I was expecting to keep the basket.' He looked at his watch. 'Okay, six pounds. Can we all go home now?'

Ros staggered back up the stairs, weighed down with shopping as well as the buggy. From the kitchen she ignored the sounds of Jake waking as she emptied her bags: Coco Pops, milk, crisps, a roast chicken ready-meal, frozen peas and roast potatoes, a giant bag of Haribo and a bottle of ginger ale to go with the whisky. She was ready for Christmas. After all, it was just one day.

But the quiet afternoon dragged, and after doing her best to keep Jake happy with his almost three-month-old repertoire of fun games, she decided to go and give Emily her present. It was still only three o'clock; their mother would be at work for at least another two hours and knowing her, after-work drinks with friends would be more important than Emily waiting for her at home. As she walked, Ros checked behind to see whether she was being followed, reasoning with herself that her stepfather hadn't yet been released and his little acolyte had no idea where she lived.

Ros pushed open the gate into her mother's tiny front garden. Since Emily was here it was okay to use the legal route. The doorbell didn't work, so she rattled the letterbox, turning around again and looking back up the street.

At last, Emily opened the door. She was still in pyjamas and her hair stuck up at the back, just as it had when she was a baby. Her eyes widened when she saw her sister.

'You can't come in. Sean will be home any minute.'

'I'll leave through the back door as soon as we hear him.'

Emily stood back to let her sister through and in the sitting room the girls stood, unsure what to do next. Emily put the television on and slumped into a chair with a sigh, pulling a cushion against her chest. Ros could smell sour, day-old sweat from her sister's body.

'I've brought you a present.' Ros reached into her bag

and pulled out a large, soft package. 'Open it now, so Mum doesn't know.'

Emily hesitated, her eyes shifting between the door and the parcel.

'Okay, give it here then. I haven't got you anything.' She tore at the wrapping, her eyes wide. 'Oh yeah ... that's cool. Thanks.'

Ros knew she had chosen well. Her sister placed the bag next to her on the sofa and gently ran the palm of her hand over the tiny mirrors and beads stitched into the fabric.

'How's school?' Ros sat down, facing Emily.

'It's rubbish. I hate it.'

'School should be fun. What subjects do you like?'

Emily shrugged. 'It's crap. They're all crap.'

'There must be something you like.'

'What are you, a teacher? You sound just like one.'

'I used to enjoy school, meeting friends, joking around.'

'It was all right for you. At my school everyone knows ... everyone hates me.'

Ros interrupted. 'What if we meet every week, not here but in a cafe? I could help you. Maybe we could look at your homework.'

Emily's eyes narrowed and she pulled a strand of stringy hair from behind her ear and into her mouth. She sucked it, then studied the sticky, darkened end.

'Mum says you did the worst thing to us and then you got everything. And now you've got a flat and a baby.'

'That's not true. I have been given things, but I lost everything too. I can share with you everything I've learnt and there's Jake. You can help me with him.' They both looked at the baby, stirring from a deep sleep, his mouth searching for his fists, eyes screwed up as if deciding whether it was worth making a fuss.

They heard the front door open and froze. In two steps their brother, Sean, six foot three at least, his cheeks unshaven but his head shaved, filled the doorway of the sitting room. He frowned in the thin daylight, a wary uncertainty flickering across his mouth and eyes. His lips drew into a sneer. At last, he knew her.

'What's that lying cunt doing here?' He spoke to the wall behind her head, folding his arms.

'I'll go, Sean.' Ros stood up. She was shaking but she slowed her movements, tying her scarf around her neck as if Harriet had been giving her lessons. 'It's not Emily's fault. I persuaded her. She didn't want me to come in.'

Sean stared at the wrapping paper on the floor and kicked it with his foot, as if it was alight.

'Go right now, before I call the police. If you ever come back here, then it's—' Sean punched a fist into the palm of his hand.

Ros waited on the front step, on the other side of the slammed front door, listening for sounds from inside. She had to know that Emily was safe. But there was nothing; no shouting or crying, just the blare of traffic from the junction and the wail of a faraway siren.

Ros took the first bus, any bus. She felt water on her cheeks and realised she was crying. Tears were rubbish, she'd given up on them years ago but perhaps it wasn't over. Seeing Sean again had really messed her up. When she'd last seen him, had faced a frightened boy across a courtroom, he'd been small and pale, his voice a trembling whisper.

Now he was a man. Stupidly, she'd put Emily at risk and worse, she'd left a note in the bag. Why had she taken such a risk? Ros wiped her eyes with the back of her hand. She'd been told so often that actions had consequences, but even she could see that this action was going to bounce back in ways she couldn't begin to imagine.

When the bus groaned to a halt to drop off passengers, Ros lifted Jake from the pushchair and kissed his cheeks, blowing a raspberry into his searching mouth.

'It's just you and me babe,' she whispered, 'I've blown it.' The woman next to her smiled at the baby and turned stiffly, her woollen coat restricting her movement.

'Is he yours or are you looking after him for your mother?'

'He's mine, almost three months old.' She turned Jake around, so he could smile at the lady.

'It's best to have them young. You've got more energy.' The woman laughed and grasped the handrail in front of her so that she could look straight at Ros. 'You all ready for Christmas?'

'Yes, just got a few more things to get,' Ros lied. 'I've got quite a houseful coming. I've never cooked a turkey before.' This might be the truth one day.

The woman nodded. 'I'm going to my daughter's. Said I'd drop into the market to get the veg, but I've left it a bit late.'

Ros agreed, as if this was something she knew about. After that, there was nothing more to say. She looked out of the window as the bus trundled from stop to stop, watching the rows of interwar housing become Edwardian villas, then rows of terraces, offices and cut-price hotels.

Ros followed the rest of the passengers into the city centre. She quickly overtook the lady who had chatted to her and turned to wish her a merry Christmas. 'And you duck,' the woman replied. 'Gas mark five for three hours and only stuff the neck end.'

Ros felt better. She'd had a fright, that was all. Nothing had changed, not yet. The people around her were ordinary and safe and there was bustle and music from the bands on the streets. The money in her purse had to stretch until after the holiday but she could spend a little.

Ros pushed the buggy through the crowds as the Salvation Army band trumpeted peace and joy above the umbrellas. She hurried out of the rain into the shopping centre and bought some patterned tights from New Look—a present for herself. It was lucky, she thought, that Jake was indifferent to what he would be given tomorrow.

She found a cafe that promised free toast with coffee. In a corner two girls sat with heads bent over bracelets spread across their table. It was Sukhi, from her old school and Chelsea, who'd been at her party. Ros sat down and watched, remembering that Chelsea had lived with her dad and his second wife in Derby, but her mum was in Leicester. They felt her watching, looked up and called out, gesturing for her to come over. Ros waved back and made signs for, 'Did they want a drink?' Luckily, they shook their heads. She put two slices of bread in the toaster and pushed Jake over to their table.

'What are you doing?' she asked, settling into the sofa opposite.

'Sukhi's bought presents for about a million cousins. We're trying to decide which cousin gets which bracelet.'

'I thought your family didn't celebrate Christmas.' Ros remembered Sukhi's grandparents, ancient bookends at either end of a white leather sofa, greeting the girls after school with a courteous incline of the head. Grandma would rise on bowed legs, swatting at imaginary flies with the edge of her shawl, and sway towards the kitchen to make glorious pakoras and samosas for her hard-working granddaughter. Grandpa would flick his hands at them.

'Homework,' he always said. 'Homework.'

'They don't celebrate it, like, religion and everything,' Sukhi said, 'but I still have to buy presents for everyone. And my parents are really stressing because my dad decided to invite all the neighbours for drinks tomorrow morning.'

'But they don't drink.' Ros remembered a pointless search for alcohol in Sukhi's house.

'Only because my dad's an alcoholic. Why do you think they're stressing? My mum's got Grandma on overdrive in the kitchen and my dad's been to Waitrose twice already this morning.'

A waitress brought her tea and Ros spread the toast with jam. Chelsea was watching her eat.

'God, you're lucky. You're so thin and look at what you pack away.'

'You should try breastfeeding.'

Sukhi looked horrified, but it was Chelsea who spoke for them both.

'Yuck. I can't imagine anything worse. But hey ... sorry we left without telling you the other night. You were sound asleep, and we couldn't miss the last train.'

Ros shrugged. 'That's okay. I didn't mind. What are you doing tomorrow?'

'I have to spend the day with Dad and Sally.' Chelsea made a gesture as if she was trying not to vomit. 'Then back to Mum's in the evening to eat another dinner with everyone watching to make sure I swallow every mouthful.'

Ros wondered if Chelsea's battle with food had tagged along behind her to university. She had always thought that Sally was okay, not at all the witch that Chelsea made her out to be. She was a soft, pink woman, slightly blurred at the edges, like soap that had been left in the bath. Chelsea's dad followed her every movement with his eyes, like an old, sad dog.

'Are you seeing Mother Theresa tomorrow?' Sukhi asked, remembering the unkind name Ros had used for her foster carer at school.

'No, just me and Jake, in the flat. I was asked, but I didn't want to go anywhere.'

'Oh my God!' Sukhi shrieked, 'you are coming to my house. I need you there. You must. Please.'

'No, I can't. The last time I spoke to your parents it was about exams and universities. They'd be embarrassed by me and Jake.'

'I can see your point,' Sukhi agreed, 'but they're so shallow I'm sure they'd pretend to be all modern and accepting ... at least until you'd left.'

'But if it had been you ...' Chelsea interrupted.

'If it was me ... if I'd had a baby, my mother would still be crying in her bedroom and Grandma would have booked her slot at the crematorium.'

'Or they'd have forced you to marry.'

Ros stopped eating; a piece of toast suspended in front of her open mouth. Sukhi stared at Chelsea, astonished.

'Oh shit!' Chelsea covered her mouth with her scarf. 'I'm sorry, Sukhi, that so wasn't funny.'

CHAPTER 13

Nick listened to the sounds from downstairs. It was only seven, but Anna was up giving the children breakfast. They had been woken at five by Jess and Cara, keen to show them what Santa had left at the foot of the bed—a choice selection of tat he had wrapped himself only five hours earlier. Cara had whined that he was commenting with his eyes shut and complained to Anna when he said he had extrasensory perception and knew what the toys were, without having to open his eyes.

He turned over and pulled the pillow over his ears, burying his face into the duvet. His movement stirred up Anna's rich scent and he thought about making love to her last night; the first time for about six months. He'd forgotten how tender and generous Anna could be, how the soft folds of her body responded to his touch. Last night, she'd been tearful and silent as they'd wrapped the children's presents. They'd shared a bottle of wine, as was their habit on Christmas Eve, and as she relaxed, he recognised the signs of an imminent 'talk'. So he kissed her. It was the best way with Anna. She couldn't talk *and* kiss and she liked kissing better. They'd made love in front of the fire, which had set them back with the present wrapping but had certainly improved everyone's mood this morning. He'd heard Anna singing as she fed Hugh and he felt quite relaxed, even smug about the day ahead. How European of him to have his wife and lover under one roof on Christmas Day. The thought of Anna and Jenny eating lunch at the same table was faintly arousing but hearing his mother's bedroom door close in her irritatingly careful way, Nick sighed and kicked off the covers. It was time to become the genial host.

Nick stood by the fire, an elbow resting on the mantelpiece, almost dislodging the frosted glass baubles nestling amongst the artificial garland of holly that snaked along its length. Jenny was yet to arrive, and he wondered if she'd changed her mind, but his father was here, and so far, there had been no friction between his parents. Nick looked across the room, his father and mother were at opposite ends of the settee having their longest conversation on record, Anna snoozed in an armchair as she fed the baby and the children had been stunned into silence by the novelty of their grandfather's ridiculously expensive gifts. Things weren't too bad, all considered. Compared with his own father, alone at seventy-five and with one child he barely spoke to, he was doing fine. Nick squeezed and turned the cork on the champagne and released it with a sigh. He poured a small amount into five glasses and waited for the froth to subside before he filled them, then passed the glasses around, leaving Jenny's on the tray.

Nick raised his glass.

'To my family.' He took a deep swallow, feeling rather than tasting the wine in his throat. He tipped down the rest in a single gulp and re-filled his glass.

The doorbell rang. Nick finished a second glass on the way to answering it. He could see Jenny's shadow outside and opened the door, pulling Jenny into his arms, and kissing her fully on the lips.

'Nick!' she wiped her mouth with the back of her hand. 'Someone might see us.'

'No, they won't.' He spun her around playfully. 'Come in and have some champagne. It's wonderful you're here. I'm sorry I was grumpy. I was being bourgeois.' He said this with a long emphasis on the vowels. 'We're adult enough to carry this off.' Nick took Jenny's coat and steered her into the sitting room. He cleared his throat and Anna woke, looking rumpled and briefly deranged.

'This is Jenny Wallis, one of the doctors in the practice.' He introduced his family in turn, although the children barely raised their heads from their new toys. His father squeezed himself unnecessarily into the corner of the settee, so that Jenny would sit next to him. Anna rose, heavy and unsteady, and tucked a strand of her messed-up hair behind her ear. She passed the hot and rather damp baby to Nick.

'Welcome, Jenny, make yourself at home. My father-in-law will find you a drink because Nick must change the baby. I'm afraid I have to disappear and do battle with the lunch.'

'Can I help?' Jenny asked.

'No way!' Anna said and laughed. 'This is my escape. I can go into the kitchen, drink champagne, listen to music and leave the children in your capable hands.' She looked around, screwing up her eyes. 'Where *is* my drink?'

Nick ended up changing both babies, as Christopher's ripe nappy could no longer be ignored. By the time he came downstairs, Jenny was talking to his parents, and he could only watch her smile and tilt her head, as if meeting them was the best thing that had happened in her life so far. He gulped the last of his third glass of champagne and imagined a fantasy life; his parents together, Jenny as his wife and one baby, a little girl. Jenny looked so beautiful. He felt his throat tighten and he knelt onto the carpet to help Christopher with his new fort, in case someone, his mother no doubt, noticed that his eyes were wet.

He heard Jenny ask Harriet why her husband hadn't joined her and raised his head. Good question, but one he hadn't dared to ask. That was what guests were for. He and his father leaned forward with interest and waited for her reply. Harriet cupped her knee with her hands.

'Tom's father was stationed here during the war. He fought at Dieppe and was killed. Tom's still bitter about it, many Canadians are. He believes the Canadian regiments were used as cannon fodder in a war that wasn't anything to do with them. And he was left without a father.' Well, that told us, Nick thought. The conversation flagged, his mother having deadened all other topics, in her usual style.

As the smell of roasting meat drifted from the kitchen, Nick realised that he was hungry and a little drunk.

'I'm hungry,' Jess whined, speaking for them all and she ran off to find her mother. Moments later, Anna appeared with Jess on her hip, holding two bowls of crisps. She stood over them and counted aloud around the adults.

'One, two, three, four,' wagging her finger in turn.

'There are four of you here to look after the children. I shouldn't have to deal with everything. Now, can one of you fetch the rest of the nibbles from the kitchen? I'm going to give Christopher his lunch while I make the gravy and then I'll put him to bed. After that we'll eat.' She put Jess down and picked up Christopher, who was sucking his thumb and pulling on his ear.

Harriet followed Anna out of the room and Nick rose unsteadily from the carpet. He stumbled and held onto a chair to regain his balance, glancing at Jenny and hoping she hadn't noticed his stagger. She was still talking to his father, so he interrupted, offering them more champagne but was waved away, like an irritating insect.

Nick sat down and stared at the fire, the champagne bottle still in his hand. He felt the cool of its base through his trousers and poured himself another glass. He hadn't liked the way Anna had spoken to them, being told off with that wagging finger. That's how marriages ended up, he thought, each partner reduced to a set of annoying habits. Try as you might, after a while it was all you saw.

Harriet returned from the kitchen with a tray of canapés. 'Anna wants you to set the table,' she remarked as she offered him the tray. Nick pushed four into his mouth at once and tried again to catch Jenny's eye, but his mother put the tray down in front of Hugh and Jenny and said she would give him a hand, after she'd checked on the baby.

Nick tossed the mats onto the dining table. He would make sure Jenny didn't sit next to his father. Of course, being Jenny, she'd be soaking up everything she could from an international plastic surgeon with a specialism in burns but what would she say if she knew about his nice little sideline making faces tighter, tits bigger, bums smaller. Nick huffed on a glass and rubbed at it with a napkin. What would she say if she knew his father couldn't look at a woman without imagining how he might improve the original? At least God didn't think he was a plastic surgeon.

Harriet came into the room and started to help by turning the mats the right way up, so that snowmen and elves grinned and waved their way around the table. Nick placed a matching paper napkin at each setting. Where did Anna buy this crap?

His mother spoke to him without looking up from laying out the forks and knives: 'Anna works so hard, doesn't she? You have a gorgeous family. You're very lucky.'

Nick followed behind her with side plates.

'It's a shame we don't see more of you.'

'I've been thinking about that.' Harriet circled with the pudding spoons. 'Tom is an old man. He's eighty-six. To be honest, that's another reason he doesn't travel. His long-distance flying days are over. Why don't you come to us? Florida's great for kids. What about next Christmas? The climate is at its best and Hughie will be a year old. You don't have to stay right with us. The complex has an apartment that visitors can use.'

'Sounds good,' Nick said, but without enthusiasm, wondering when being old actually started. It was like driving in Scotland. The North kept being signposted, no matter how far north you went. No doubt Jenny thought he was old. He thought his mother was old. She thought Tom was old. When was old? He put the serving spoons in the centre of the table while his mother laid out the cork mats for the vegetable dishes.

'Yeah, thanks, I'll talk to Anna about it.'

Harriet stood admiring the table, her hands on her hips. 'That looks lovely.'

'It looks like a children's party.' He remembered the decorations at Jenny's. What would she think of this?

'Don't be an old curmudgeon, Nick. Ah, there are the crackers!' His mother reached for a box on the sideboard. 'I just wanted to mention, while we're alone ... that girl Anna's friendly with, she seems familiar to me, but I can't place her.'

'She's too bloody familiar, the same as dozens that come into my surgery; tattoos, piercings and babies.'

'I find her very guarded, but Anna is obviously fond of her.'

'I think Anna's training her up to be an unpaid mother's help and the girl benefits from Anna's largesse. At the moment it suits them both. It is a bit strange, but I wouldn't mention it to Anna. She gets very touchy about Ros.'

'I picked that up, that's why I raised it with you and not her. I wanted to check everything was okay, that's all.'

Anna seemed to be the only one who could wear a paper hat with any style, Nick thought as he looked around the table. It had slipped to a rakish angle over one eye, which suited her flushed cheeks and tousled hair. Jenny had slipped hers under her placemat. His father, he was pleased to see, looked like he was wearing one of those paper things chefs used to put on the end of a lamb chop, and his mother's balanced precariously on top of her head, which on a day-to-day basis didn't look large, but a paper hat did nothing for its proportions. No doubt he looked ridiculous, but fortunately, he didn't have to look at himself.

He had managed to sit next to Jenny, keeping his mother to his left and Jess and Cara between Jenny and his father. There had been a tense moment when his mother had asked Jenny if she was seeing anyone, but her blush would have been easy to confuse with modesty. Nick had squeezed her hand under the tablecloth, and she had returned his pressure but quickly pulled her hand away. Cara announced that she was seeing someone, which distracted the adults. Nick noticed his mother's eyebrows lift when it became clear that Cara had a better understanding of what this meant than they might have assumed.

There was a pause in the meal while Anna fed the baby between the main course and pudding, a pause filled by Jess reading aloud all the jokes from the crackers. Her new reading skills were not quite adequate, and Cara kept correcting her. The jokes weren't funny to start with but read phonetically and without any comic timing made each one feel like a small death. Nick made sure the wine circulated around the table—a mellow red supplied by his father. The adults' over-enthusiastic laughter unfortunately encouraged the child to continue.

Anna suggested the girls get down, since they didn't like Christmas pudding. Nick thought that if he'd asked them to do that he would have been in trouble, but he was relieved the performance was over. After the ceremonial waste of quality brandy on a supermarket Christmas pudding, his father and mother insisted that they clear away and Jenny jumped up to help, so that he and Anna could 'spend some time' with the children. Since Christopher had woken, Nick decided to leave that singular joy to Anna. He slipped upstairs to lie down for just five minutes, since he'd had such a bad night. When he woke it was dark and the bedside clock said five o'clock. His head was pounding, and he desperately needed some water. In the bathroom he filled the tooth mug twice with ice-cold water, swallowing in deep gulps, and splashed water over his face. He hadn't bothered with the bathroom light and leaned against the sink, studying his reflection in the mirror. The angle of light from the open door accentuated the shadows under his eyes and the growth of beard on his upper lip and chin. His hair looked as if it needed a wash, and his shirt was rumpled. He thought of having a shower, starting the day anew, but this seemed an indulgence since he'd already abandoned everyone, particularly Jenny, for over two hours. He poured another tumbler of water and emptied in a sachet of Alka Seltzer. He looked at his watch. Only six hours to go.

Downstairs, Anna and his mother were asleep, heads lolling and mouths open. The children, including Hughie propped up in a nest of cushions, were lined up in front of what sounded like *The Lion King*. Nick thought he heard a soft giggle from the kitchen. He crept across the hall, instinct rather than suspicion making his steps slow and soft.

Good God, his father was about to kiss Jenny! Nick froze, bile rising in his throat, as his father's hand circled her back, and he bent his head over hers.

'What's going on?' Nick shouted. 'What are you two playing at?'

The would-be kissers jumped apart.

'Come on Nick, just a bit of fun under the mistletoe.'

Nick pretended to scan the room. 'Mistletoe? I don't see any mistletoe.'

'We're pretending. It was a joke. It's Christmas.'

Jenny said nothing. Her expression was hard to read but Nick thought he saw irritation, boredom and impatience. He felt aware of how he must look, how his breath must smell, how petty and miserable he must appear. His father mumbled an apology and skirted the kitchen table on his way out so that he wouldn't have to push between Nick and Jenny. Nick reached across and lifted Jenny's hands, loose and damp, in his grasp.

'I'm so sorry,' he whispered.

Jenny said nothing. She looked down and swung their joined hands together and apart, together and apart.

'I'm just a jealous fool,' Nick sang, his voice tremulous, dredging up a lyric from somewhere. He thought he saw a quiver of a smile on her lips.

There was a sound behind his back, a footfall, a tread, barely perceptible. He looked over his shoulder. A shadow in the doorway; there and then gone. Something about the shadow; its politeness, its uncertainty, its need to do the right thing, made him certain it wasn't Anna. It could only have been his mother. His mother had seen him holding hands with Jenny, heard him sing to Jenny. He tipped back his head and groaned.

'Fuck.'

Jenny released her grip and glanced at the kitchen clock. 'I'd like to go now, to phone my father in Bangkok. Please thank Anna for me. It's been lovely.'

Nick helped her with her coat and scarf in the hall.

'It'll be okay,' he murmured, 'we're okay, aren't we?'

'Yes, of course, we're fine,' she replied, 'don't worry.'

He watched Jenny's brake lights turn onto the road and thought about the words she'd said and the way she'd looked. They hadn't matched. They hadn't said the same thing at all.

Christmas Day ended, as they always do, in an overheated room watching television programmes that had been advertised since early November and would be repeated in the summer, when the snowflakes and glitz made the programme seem as if it had been filmed in a different universe. Nick's father left after a light supper and once the children were in bed, Anna suggested a walk.

'Come on, you'll feel better for it,' she harried him, 'let's take advantage of having your mother here to babysit. Hughie can come in the sling.'

Nick agreed. He wasn't nervous about being alone with Anna as there was nothing in her tone to suggest that the real purpose of the walk was to have something out. They trudged the empty streets, looking into houses where the curtains had been left open. The blue flicker of the television was all that could be seen from most homes, but some families were still sitting around tables, with candles and hats and laughter. Nick felt envious, sure that everyone, except him and almost certainly Jenny, had enjoyed their day. But he remembered to be gracious.

'Thanks, Anna. You worked so hard, as you always do. It was lovely.'

'You seemed pretty miserable for most of the day.'

'Yeah, I was. I drank too much too early and having my parents there and a new baby and someone from the practice ... it made the day a bit unreal.' Nick glanced at Anna, hoping she might apologise for over-organising the occasion, for inviting Jenny.

But Anna neatly batted the responsibility back to him: 'It was really about your father, wasn't it? You were jealous that he hogged Jenny's attention, annoyed at what he spent on the children, and he upstaged you with the wine as well. You must let it go, Nick. You'll never win this competition with your father and anyway, only one of you is playing.'

'What do you mean?'

'Your father isn't competing with you. He's just being

himself. He doesn't notice that you're angry with him all the time. You may as well drop it.'

Nick felt his temper rise with the unfairness of this wholly unreasonable accusation. He could not have wasted over thirty years in a pointless rivalry. Anna was completely wrong. She didn't know his father like he did.

'You didn't see him trying to kiss Jenny in the kitchen.'

Anna laughed. 'Oh, for heaven's sake, the old fool. Mind you, I wouldn't be at all surprised if Jenny found your father attractive. She probably likes older men. I've always had her down as a daddy's girl.'

Nick stopped walking and snapped at Anna, 'That was a really unfair remark.' He turned on his heel and headed for home, his hands pushed down into his coat pockets. He didn't care whether Anna kept up with him or not. In fact, he didn't really care if they stayed together. All that mattered was being with Jenny.

CHAPTER 14

Anna sat at the table, the kitchen lit only by a low light from under the cupboards, trying to hold Hughie with one hand and type her blog with the other. It was ridiculously early, and the house was silent, apart from the ticking of the radiators beginning to warm. Anna found it hard to find words to describe her family's Christmas because it hadn't been a success and she wasn't sure why. It wasn't as if she hadn't planned every detail, and the food had been delicious, but no one seemed to care. The mood was wrong, everyone had seemed trapped in their own self-interest. And she could not understand what had caused Nick to flare at her like that; his rage had seemed to come from nowhere. Even yesterday, he had avoided the family whenever he could, preferring to hide in his study. It wasn't like Nick to bear a grudge, mainly because he quickly forgot anything he might have said or done that would have hurt someone else. Grudges were her territory, if she was being honest.

She swallowed some tea from her Best Mum Ever mug and decided to come clean with her followers and admit that she might have tried too hard with Christmas. This acceptance, this new honesty, brought relief and a new satisfaction. There was no shame in going wrong sometimes, mothers didn't have to be perfect. This could be the theme for her blog next year, not exactly Chaotic Mummy but Good Enough Mummy. After her admission to her followers, Anna typed furiously about how she would do some research on shortcuts and time-saving tips for harassed mums and promised to post them throughout the year. Satisfied, Anna closed her laptop and felt, rather than noticed, a movement by the kettle where Harriet hesitated, holding her dressing gown at her throat.

'Can I make some tea?'

'Of course, go ahead.' Anna flapped her hand towards the kettle, maddened by her mother-in-law's unnecessary politeness. 'Why are you up so early?'

Harriet made the tea and brought her mug to the table, answering the question she clearly had not heard above the roar of the kettle: 'This dratted jet lag is making it hard for me to sleep.'

Anna tried to laugh but it came out as a snort. 'You should try living with a new baby,' she said, before she remembered that Harriet was unlikely to have forgotten being a mother to Nick.

Harriet moved the mug between the tips of her fingers and spoke slowly, as if she had rehearsed her words. 'Christmas was lovely Anna, but I'm worried about you. Are you lonely?'

Anna made a stronger attempt at laughter but hated the giveaway break in her voice when she replied, 'How can I be lonely? Look around you Harriet. Did I look lonely on Christmas Day?'

'What about you and Nick?' Harriet persisted, 'I can see that things aren't right between you and there's simply too much for you to do. I'm not much help I know. I never was any good as a parent so it's unlikely I would make a success of being a grandmother. Next year don't try too hard. Why not come to our holiday home in Florida? I spoke to Nick about it, but I don't think he listened to me.'

'Four kids on a plane doesn't feel like relaxation to me but thanks for the offer, Harriet. And don't worry about us, I mean me and Nick, underneath we're strong and we'll be fine once the two little ones are a bit older.'

Anna waited for Harriet to agree, but instead she said, 'A marriage can fade away. If you wait too long to fix it, sometimes it can't be repaired.' Harriet sipped her tea, sighing as if she had something more to say but had thought better of it. Anna felt tired of this unwelcome advice and was about to announce that she had to wake and dress Christopher when Harriet spoke again: 'Do you think Hugh is all right?'

Anna looked down at the baby in her arms and said, 'He's developing slowly but I think I saw a ghost of a smile yesterday. I know I need to spend more time with him … perhaps if I try to play with him more, he'll catch up.'

'I meant Hugh, my ex-husband. It wasn't easy seeing him again on Christmas Day, but after all the usual pleasantries he barely spoke to me, even after all this time.'

'We don't see him often ourselves and of course Nick has never been comfortable with him.'

Harriet interrupted. 'I'm not sure what I expected. I hoped we might talk, if only about our shared grandchildren. For some reason, I was looking forward to seeing him.'

'And it was a disappointment?'

'Yes, it was. And if I may speak frankly, I feel a bit in the way here. I'm not any good at playing with the children, Nick won't speak to me, and you have plenty of help from that girl.'

'I couldn't help noticing how you kept staring at Ros yesterday. Is there a problem?'

Harriet shrugged. 'It's nothing. I thought I knew her, that's all. Please apologise to her if I made her feel uncomfortable.'

'You can tell her yourself. She's bound to show up later.'

Harriet drained her tea and crossed the kitchen to make herself another.

'That's what I'm trying to say, Anna. I'm missing Tom and my home and I'm tired, so I'm going to change my flight and leave today. Don't worry about taking me to the airport, I'll get a taxi.'

It was the first working day after Christmas and Claire had asked to see her. It was easy to guess why. Sean would have told their mother and now she was in trouble. It could be worse, Ros thought, she might have been caught stealing stuff from her mother's kitchen rather than trying to give her younger sister a present. That wasn't a bad thing, surely?

The office was empty, apart from Claire, frowning at her computer screen and tapping forcefully on her keyboard. She looked up, saw Ros waiting, and held up five fingers. Ros wondered whether Claire would stick up for her and remembered the many times that Theresa had barrelled into school to give the pastoral head the hairdryer treatment about the rights of looked-after children. What strange words those were, Ros thought, with their implication that a child would be cherished, not just cared for. Theresa always wore a black business suit with a grey silk blouse, the size of her breasts amplified by the lanyard she never removed for these meetings. She was a senior partner in a law firm, one that specialised in equalities, and she didn't avoid reminding the teachers of this. In the car, since Ros was always sent home for the rest of the day, Theresa would tell her how much her professional fees were per hour and the total cost to the firm of every school visit. Ros knew that gratitude was expected, and it was true that she couldn't fail to be impressed by Theresa's force and her arguments, but deep down she knew that Theresa didn't care about her, she simply wanted to be right.

Ros sat facing Claire and noticed that she didn't open the laptop she always used to record their meetings but waited with her chin in her palms, resting her elbows on the table.

It felt as if something was expected, so Ros spoke first:

'I'm sorry I went to my mother's. Was she really mad at me?'

'She was on the phone as soon as we opened this morning. Remind me Ros, why did you want to come back to Leicester? You were very well settled in Derby.'

Ros couldn't answer this question in words. It had been a feeling, one so strong that only action could help. She leaned forward to remove Jake's hat as he lay in Anna's pushchair, soundly asleep.

'I don't know. I've done it this time, haven't I? And there's something else you need to know. Before Christmas I was followed and attacked. It was a boy, not much older than me. He said he was working for my stepfather.'

Claire squeezed her brow between her thumb and index finger and opened her computer. As she logged on, the silence was broken by the intermittent roar of the fan heater, as the room warmed then rapidly cooled.

'By the way, it was Emily who told your mother, not Sean.'

Ros was aghast. 'But why would Emily tell on me?'

'She's still a little girl and she's had a bad time. She needs her mother. To protect her, and you, we'll come up with a plan. There's still two weeks before UCAS forms have to be in, so let's get on with applying for a university place in September. Once we know where you've been accepted, we'll move you to that city. Another fresh start Ros, one well away from your family.'

'How soon do I have to go?' Ros asked.

Claire frowned and tilted her head from side to side. 'I'll have to run this past my manager, but I think your mother will be happier if she knows you're moving on. As long as you promise never to go there again. As for the other matter, we'll report the assault to the police straight away. Your stepfather is due for release but asking one of his buddies to beat you up isn't going to impress the parole board. I can take you Ros, we'll go to the station right now, in my car. If we act quickly, by tonight he'll have had an unwelcome meeting with the police and the prison governor.

'So, you think I'll be safe ... for now?'

'That's my judgement but we'll see what the police and my manager think. Now, wait here while I get my coat. Don't worry about Jake, I have an infant seat in my car.'

So she has a baby, Ros thought. Who is looking after her baby today?

CHAPTER 15

Nick waited in the cafe attached to his gym, looking up every time someone swung through the door. On this February morning, the low ceilings and grey, mock-leather sofas should have seemed unwelcoming, but Nick felt only excitement. This was a great idea, he thought, the last place he was likely to meet Anna, or Jenny, for that matter. A while back he had worked out that an illicit meeting in plain sight was less suspicious than trying to find a hidden corner. He'd meant to give this thing up, stop paying his membership, but Jenny had been distant since Christmas and seemed to be avoiding him. He'd even admitted that he loved her, but she never said it back and usually tried to change the subject. As for Anna, he wondered when it was she'd last spoken to him about anything other than arrangements, when he hadn't felt like another problem to be managed—years probably. Then the message from TreC32 had dropped into his inbox. Thirty-two, with a partner of ten years and two young children. Yeah right, he'd thought when he'd read her profile, but it was all true. She was thirty-two but looked younger and for some reason she was interested in him. Since her boyfriend worked away, he had hoped they could get together at her house, but it turned out that she had principles as well as good taste. From their first meeting Tracey had made it clear that she expected to be treated well. Nothing less than luxury hotels and expensive presents would do. So far, she had been worth every penny.

Tracey shone her wide smile across the room, her eyes finally settling upon his upturned face as she scanned the cafe, reminding him of a young Julia Roberts. It had made sense for Nick to pay for her gym membership and she was wearing the kit that he'd bought; tasteful but expensive. That outfit will raise the reps of the men on the machines upstairs, he thought. She leaned over and kissed him, her hair falling across his upturned face.

'Going to a class?' Nick asked, trying to fix his eyes on hers rather than her cleavage.

Tracey slumped down into the seat opposite, the cushions emitting a sigh, and crossed her legs.

'Yes, I've got Extreme99 at eleven. Shall we have a coffee?'

Waiting to be served, Nick heard the coffee machine grind and hiss its way through the complicated orders of the members ahead of him in the queue. Looking around, he wondered why he had avoided gyms in the past, thinking that everyone would be slimmer and fitter than he was. Truly, most people here could have passed for his patients. He glanced over at Tracey and watched her finger swipe furiously across her phone. It was the one thing he felt unsure about, the fact that she was still active on the site, whereas he had been so overwhelmed by his luck he had immediately made his profile inactive. He'd expected her to notice and do the same, but really, she *could* do better. If he raised it, she might think he was being unfair or even needy. He couldn't risk the conversation, not just yet. Anyway, she might have been looking at her emails; he was being ridiculously suspicious.

Nick carried their coffee to the table and Tracey slipped her phone into her gym bag. She leaned forward and gave him her full attention as he passed over her skinny latte with an extra shot. Her intense gaze was the first thing he'd noticed about her, apart from the obvious. Whenever he spoke, she fixed her eyes upon his face, unlike everyone else whose attention seemed to slide away the moment he opened his mouth.

'I need to talk to you about next week,' Tracey said, 'I'd forgotten it was February half-term. The kids are off school and I've no one to look after them. We'll have to cancel the hotel room, I'm really sorry.' She turned her mouth down in a caricature of regret, but her eyes were smiling.

Nick remembered that he'd chosen the cheaper, no cancellation, option.

'Have you tried to find a babysitter?'

Tracey laughed. 'Have you any idea how much a babysitter would charge for four hours minimum, daytime, for two kids?'

Nick searched in his wallet and counted out fifty pounds.

'Will this help?'

Tracey rocked back against the slippery cushions and pulled her knee upwards towards her chest.

'When was the last time you paid for childcare during the day? It will be double that.'

'I'm afraid that's all I have with me.' Nick felt he must seem unreliable, a disappointment even.

Tracey must have noticed because she leaned over the table and rested her hand on his knee.

'We'll find a way, Nick. We need to have our special time together. By the way, I think I saw a cashpoint outside.' She dipped her little finger into the froth on her coffee and licked it, her eyes never leaving his.

February is the worst month of the year Anna thought, looking down at the garden from her bedroom window. It seemed as if the sky had drained into the garden like a grey colour wash on an artist's palette. The bones of plants stood frozen and alert, the children's swings hung tangled and lopsided from the frame. Nothing moved. The only sound in the house was the constant murmur of the central heating and her own voice. She leaned into Hughie's cot and lifted him out. Carrying him over to the window, he seemed floppy and slow to waken, but Anna was not someone who worried about such things. Christopher was now at nursery for two days a week; part of a plan that had arisen from her determination to make a fresh start in the new year.

But the winter had been bitterly cold and there had been ice on the ground since January. With Christopher out of the house she found that if Ros chose not to come, she risked spending long hours on her own with Hughie, who wasn't the best of company. It had been almost impossible to go out and she had bought Ros a decent pair of walking boots, since public transport had become quite unreliable. The girls' school had closed twice already, once when the teachers couldn't get in because of a snowfall and once when the boiler had given up. She hated the daily school run on treacherous roads and found that she resented the extra trips to the nursery.

Anna felt frozen out of the world and her marriage. Nick wasn't communicating and it seemed as if she could get nothing right. There was no question of repeating the lovemaking of Christmas Eve. He came to bed late, hid in his study, and was often out working odd shifts or spending several evenings and weekend hours at the gym. It might be possible to put things right if she only knew what was wrong.

Maybe there was nothing. Perhaps they'd simply made the wrong choice of partner. When they'd met, Nick had seemed interesting and a little exotic, but that was from a very narrow field of potential suitors. Of course, it turned out he was neither. She must have seemed ambitious and vivacious, and she was neither. He hadn't known how much she'd wanted children of her own, to experience the life of her pupils' mothers and do a better job. When she'd met Nick, she'd been in a rush to start a family but couldn't recall if she had told him. As with all self-imposed deadlines, hindsight made it seem ridiculous. She should have waited. There might have been someone else for her. As for Nick, she had no idea what he'd wanted from life; she had never asked.

Every day she waited for Ros. Sometimes it was ten, sometimes eleven o'clock, but she almost always came, and Anna was grateful for that. Her early fever of planning for the year had involved Ros's life too, although this had not been shared, except on her blog. The comments had been positive, even if some had implied that Anna might consider giving Ros some space, whatever that meant. She'd printed out some details this morning and she smoothed them out on the kitchen table. They had to act soon if Ros was to get a place in September.

'But I've already applied for university.' Ros glared at Anna, as if she should have known this, without being told.

Anna carried on, as if Ros hadn't spoken: 'Some universities provide full day care for students' children. Because of your situation, I mean having no family, being a single parent and a care leaver, you would be eligible for all sorts of support.'

'I already know all this. I have a personal adviser.'

'What have you chosen? Something vocational, perhaps law or social work? You won't have lost any time, as many of your age group will still be on a gap year.' Anna ploughed on, quoting her followers' advice from the blog, as if their words couldn't be wasted.

Ros looked exasperated. 'Anna, I don't want to be a social worker. Haven't I seen enough of that? The same goes for the law.'

'What about teaching? At least you'd have school holidays.'

Ros gave a snort of derision. Anna felt criticised and her frustration rose. 'What are you going to study then?'

'Classics. That's all I'll consider.' Ros pulled a cushion against her chest and folded her arms over it. Her cheeks were flushed.

'But you haven't got the right A levels for classics.'

'How do you know what A levels I've got? You've never asked.'

'You have psychology, I do remember that.'

'Psychology was my fourth subject. It doesn't matter what A levels I've got, but I do have Latin and Greek.'

Anna was cornered. She sighed and rubbed her eyes, her plan to sit with Ros and contact some universities now abandoned.

They sat in tense silence, studying the sleeping babies lying side by side on a quilt, and heard the logs shift in the grate. Anna felt defeated, and Ros's mockery of her own life choice had stung.

At last, she said: 'You seem very sure of yourself ... of the decisions you're making.'

'I'm not short of guidance, Anna,' Ros replied, 'I've never been short of that.'

'I haven't seen you studying any classical literature ... or borrowing any books from the library.'

'Everything I had was left behind with my carers. I've just had a baby ... I live nowhere near a library. I shouldn't have to explain.'

This conversation can go no further, Anna thought,

remembering that she hadn't been able to read anything either since Hughie was born.

'No, of course not. I'm sorry. But if you do want to join a library...' Anna's voice faltered under Ros's glare.

She remembered there was a prescription to fill for one of the girls. Something could still be saved of the day if Ros was willing to stay behind while she visited the pharmacy at Nick's practice. Afterwards, she could pick up Christopher a bit early from nursery. That would be a real help.

Anna inched her estate car down the drive, fearful that the brakes wouldn't grip. She cursed Nick for forgetting, once again, to throw down some of the sand she had rescued from the children's sandpit before he left for work. The heavy car slid onto the road, unresponsive to her tap on the brakes but everyone was driving cautiously, so she came to no harm. Damn Nick, damn this sodding frozen world, she thought. How much more pointless could things get?

Ice quickly formed on the windscreen, even though she had cleared it only minutes before. She turned the heaters on to full power and drove hunched over the steering wheel, peering through a gap in the frost, the car roaring with hot air.

Anna reached the surgery and parked, staring with unseeing eyes through the rapidly misting windscreen. 'Classics!' she snorted. 'How ridiculous.' She locked the car and decided not to look in on Nick. He wouldn't welcome a visit from her, and she certainly didn't want to see him. A few elderly patients sat in rows, coughing and wiping reddened eyes. Anna walked past them to the pharmacy, where she waited for Cara's prescription next to another elderly man, who every few minutes trumpeted fluid into a generous handkerchief.

On her way back through the practice she was greeted by the manager. Helen Astley was the kind of tall woman who dressed in black and wore exceptionally high heels. Anna, tall herself, had to look up to return her smile.

'I would have expected you to be swathed in clouds of glorious perfume,' Helen said, sniffing the air for dramatic effect.

Anna was confused. 'I'm sorry, I don't know what you mean.'

'The perfume Nick bought you for Christmas. I saw it on his desk. I wish someone would buy me Guerlain.'

Anna was about to deny this, to tell Helen that Nick must have intended the perfume for someone else but in an instant, she understood. Of course, it *was* intended for someone else. Nick was having an affair. He was having an affair! She felt herself stumble against Helen's arm.

'Woah.' Helen caught her. 'Are you okay?'

Anna steadied herself and breathed deeply.

'It's nothing, just getting over a middle ear infection.' She spread a smile across her mouth, feeling her lips stick to her dry teeth. 'The perfume is gorgeous, but I can't smell much right now. I wouldn't want to waste it.'

Helen organised her features into a look of concern, practised over years of dealing with grumbling patients.

'Are you okay to drive home? Should I call Nick?'

'No,' Anna said with too much force. She cleared her

throat. 'No, please don't. I'll be fine. You know what he's like. He hates to be disturbed when he's with a patient.'

'But he's not with a patient. He's in a meeting with Jenny Wallis.'

Thank you, Anna thought. Now I know. Everything makes sense.

From behind a curtain, Ros watched Anna drive away. When she knew she wasn't going to be interrupted by an impromptu return, she carried the babies upstairs to Hughie's cot and put them down, head to tail, each move executed with the practised care required to keep a baby asleep. In Nick's study she logged on to the computer, but it was password protected and when she tried his desk drawers, they were locked. The local authority had finally removed her internet, but at least when she was here, she had access to their internet on her phone. Ros sat on Nick's revolving chair and checked her mobile. She felt her stomach tighten. At last, there was a message from Emily. She must have found the note left in the pocket of the bag that Ros had risked so much to give her. Emily's message said: 'Sorry I told on you. Let's meet up Saturday at McDonald's. The clock tower one. What time?'

Hughie began to make his usual sounds, like an old engine starting up, which meant that both babies would soon be awake and hungry. There was no sign of Anna. Emily's message had loosened a knot inside her and this lifting of her mood brought some guilt about her earlier behaviour towards Anna and her snooping in Nick's room. She lifted and changed both babies and set about their lunch with better grace than usual. Anna didn't accept current advice on mixed feeding before six months, so Ros warmed an inedible-looking goo that Anna had left in the fridge and spooned it into the babies' open mouths, side by side in their highchairs. Hughie struggled to support himself and looked horribly uncomfortable, so Ros lifted him onto her knee and fed him there.

Ros heard Anna's key turn in the lock and the front door slam. She felt relief, as Hughie had started to grizzle for his mother, sucking on his fists. Ros guessed what he wanted, and she certainly wasn't going to do that. She heard Christopher calling her name from the hall. 'Oz, Oz,' he bellowed. She loved Christopher, the way he lived life in colour, his enthusiasms extreme, his despair absolute. She couldn't wait for Jake to become a little boy who charged at life head on.

'I'm sorry we're so late.' Ros noticed that Anna's skin looked pallid as she pulled off her hat and gloves and threw them onto a kitchen chair. 'There was a problem at the surgery, which made me later than I'd thought for the nursery. Then I had to speak to the manager. There's been a complaint about Christopher. Another parent is saying he bit her little girl.'

Ros turned her hand into a crocodile and made biting movements around Christopher's neck. He squealed and hid under the table.

'Don't encourage him.' Anna sat down and rubbed her forehead.

'Are you okay?' Ros was peering at her.

'I'll take Hughie upstairs if you don't mind, I need to lie down for a bit. Can you give Christopher his lunch?'

'Is this about my choice of course at university? I'll talk it over with you if you like. I'm sorry I didn't tell you.'

Anna looked puzzled. She waved her hand, dismissing her previous enthusiasm for Ros's future like a bad smell.

'Oh. I'd forgotten all about that.'

With Jake watching, Ros and Christopher played his favourite game, which was to pull all the cushions off the furniture onto the carpet and jump between them, while Ros reprieved her earlier success as a crocodile. But Anna was on her mind and as the time approached when the girls would need to be collected from school, she made a mug of tea and tapped on her bedroom door. The room was dark, but Ros could see the light from the landing reflected in Anna's eyes.

'Do you want me to get the girls? It's just that if I'm walking, I'll have to leave now. It would be easier if I didn't have to take Christopher and Jake, if you could manage?'

'I'm getting up now.' Anna swung her legs over the edge of the bed and leaned forward, resting her knuckles on the mattress. 'Stay if you can. It'll be easier if I go alone.'

'I'm sorry about earlier.'

Anna gave a wan smile. 'This isn't about you, Ros. I'm afraid to say that Nick and I are separating. He'll be moving out tonight.'

Ros walked home along the quiet, empty streets thinking about Nick and Anna. It was hard to imagine what could have happened that was bad enough to take four children away from their dad. Ros had little experience of relationships, but she knew about the kinds of things that destroyed families and felt pretty sure that none of those was going on. She didn't want it to happen. Anna's home had become a sort of base for her and Jake and whatever her faults, Anna cared and thought about other people, even if you weren't there. That didn't often happen, especially when people were paid to look after you. Ros didn't want anything to change unless she made the changes. She was happy with things just the way they were.

CHAPTER 16

Nick left Jenny's at nine. His car was covered in a thin layer of ice, and he resented having to dance around spraying de-icer and scraping at the glass, while his hands and feet developed incipient frostbite. After being with Jenny he liked to get into his car and speed away. It was uncomfortable thinking that she might be watching. Did he look a fool? What would she be thinking, looking down on his thinning hair?

Finally, he was able to get into the car and start the engine. He glanced back and thought he saw a shadow at Jenny's window but there was no wave. Driving home, he picked a little more at his anxiety. The more he needed to be with her, the more uncertain he felt. It was as if he irritated her, but she was trying to cover it up. She smiled at him but not so broadly. She listened to his problems but sometimes he thought he saw her eyes grow distant. Worst of all, when they had sex, he thought she touched him as if he was someone else, and having named the thought, he found he couldn't let it go.

At home, he didn't immediately recognise his suitcase in the hall. It was only when he had hung up his coat and scarf and stepped back, almost knocking it over, that the incongruity struck him. He lifted it by the handle. It felt heavy. Anna must be using it to take stuff to the charity shop. It was pretty thoughtless of her to leave it right in the middle of the floor.

Anna sat alone in the sitting room, the television off. This wasn't unusual, as she often read in the evenings, peering at him over the top of her new reading glasses as if she couldn't quite remember who he was.

'What's that suitcase doing in the hall?' he asked, knowing he sounded more irritable than he intended.

'It's yours,' she replied needlessly, folding her arms.

Nick knew he was in trouble. He adjusted his tie in the mirror above the fireplace to try and settle the panic he could see in his twisted features.

'What's this about?' He sat down and leaned forward, his clasped hands dropping between his knees.

'You and Jenny. I've worked it all out. I want you gone.'

'It's over.' The moment he said this, it was true.

'You're lying. You've been with her this evening. I can smell that you have.'

'I ended it tonight. It is over. I'm so sorry I've let you down ... we can work this out.'

'I want you to go now.'

'Come on, Anna. What about the kids? We're better than this. We've got too much to lose.'

'I want you to leave.'

'But where will I go?'

'That's your problem. Go to her. Tell her you've changed your mind.'

Nick looked down. 'I don't think she'll want me.'

He heard Anna get up and he waited for the arm around his shoulders. When it came, the blow to the back of his head was unexpected.

After being struck in such a ridiculously overemotional way, Nick knew he had achieved, if only temporarily, the moral high ground. Not even Anna could send a man out into below freezing temperatures with possible concussion. His dizziness allowed him access to the spare bedroom and his own things, which he nevertheless had to retrieve from the suitcase in the hall. He had left Anna curled into a corner of the settee, her shoulders shaking with what he assumed were tears. Perhaps he should go back downstairs, right now, and comfort her. It might be possible to stay, to talk things through in the morning. But as he pulled his neatly folded things from the suitcase, he found a photograph of the children tucked into a sweater. Anna meant him to go. She wasn't a woman who played games, who escalated conflict so that she could then retreat into compromise. It was decided. He must live apart from her and the children.

The certainty brought some comfort. Nick slid into the chilled bed and stared at the ceiling, watching the unfamiliar pattern of passing headlights from the window of this unused room, at the front of the house. He drew the duvet up to his chin and caught his mother's scent, the last occupant of the room. For a second, he wondered why Anna hadn't got around to changing the sheets. Nick thought about his mother's sudden departure, the night he came home to find her absent. Anna had been puzzled, worried even, but Nick knew his mother. Harriet had seen him with Jenny and felt she had no choice but to carry the secret away.

It will all be fine, Nick thought, as he drifted into sleep. Not long ago, he had dreamed of being with Jenny. Perhaps he could make it work. If not, he would live alone. Like father, like son.

CHAPTER 17

Ros waited outside McDonald's. The granite paving looked sugar-coated as sun pushed through watery clouds. She always woke early, and her icy bedroom wasn't somewhere to linger, but most sensible people knew that bed was a better prospect on a freezing Saturday morning. There was a possibility that Emily might choose not to come. For ten minutes, she hopped from foot to foot outside the glass doors and kept her jacket wrapped tightly around the baby, having decided against the pushchair. The strings on her knitted hat swung from side to side as she jumped, and Jake reached out and pulled one into his mouth. The sun gave up and the fog deepened; only the base of the clock tower was visible and the lights from the stores opposite looked hazy and welcoming.

After waiting for fifteen minutes Ros went inside and bought a hot chocolate. The grey, tiled floor and muddy brick walls formed a seamless landscape with the outside and there was little difference in temperature. Under an oversized lampshade, she and Jake huddled together for warmth like young chicks in an incubator. She chose a seat where she would be able to see Emily approach and from where she could monitor the few transactions at the counter. She blew on her scalding chocolate and watched the two other customers, both night workers wearing yellow jackets, the badge of the working man. One had a large nose and thinning hair swept back from his forehead, the other was younger with thick, dark hair and a wide nose that looked broken. They chewed heavily through their breakfast; the younger man flicked through a newspaper, the older man stared unseeing, his eyes focused upon the world inside his head.

She watched the cafe workers stand whispering by the counter. The conversation was intense; one stared while the other bit on the edge of her nail. They both looked so young, much too young to be at work. Ros wondered what it must be like to live like them, to be sixteen and with school friends, a job and at least one parent. She watched them so hungrily that she missed Emily's arrival. Her sister looked different, yet it was only two months since they had almost been trapped by Sean in her mother's living room. Her hair was pulled away from her face into a tight ponytail that swung against one ear. She wore dark eye make-up, and her lips were red. Earrings dangled over a chequered scarf and her black skirt was tight and short across her thin hips. Long legs covered in electric blue tights disappeared into crumpled leather boots.

'You look fabulous,' Ros said. When did she change? How had the child become a woman?

Emily shrugged. 'It's just normal. I always look like this.'

Ros went to the counter to buy a Coke and a burger. She looked back at her sister, who was texting furiously, and felt a discomfort that was probably jealousy. I wouldn't know, she thought, how to make myself look like that. She was wearing an old jacket of Anna's, stout walking boots, a thick jumper, and jeans she'd had for years. She paid for the food, seeing in Emily and the girls that served her everything she'd lost. An unexpected and sudden resentment gripped her chest, her head, her fingers, and she fumbled with the change, dropping coins onto the counter. She had to get rid of this feeling, to push it away. Meeting Emily mattered, and anger would spoil it.

She put the tray down and mumbled about going to the toilet. Emily barely glanced up from her phone. Ros splashed her face, bare of any make-up, and leant against the sink breathing deeply. She lifted her head and read the cleaning rota. Sue had checked the toilets at eight and at ten, and they would be checked again at twelve. Ros went into a closet, shredded toilet roll onto the floor and threw water from the taps onto the tiles. That would give Sue something useful to do.

Emily ate, still texting and Ros waited, unsure where to start. 'Did you get a bus in?' she tried.

'Mm, mm.' Emily shook her head. 'Mum dropped me off. She was going in to work.'

'You didn't tell her you were seeing me?'

'Duh brain, why would I tell her that?' Emily tapped her forehead and turned back to her phone, taking another mouthful of burger.

Ros felt herself tense, knowing that once again she'd crossed the line. What if her mother had decided to park and walk Emily to McDonald's, to check who she was meeting? Wasn't that to be expected from a parent who cared? She'd promised Claire she would never try to see her family again, a promise now broken, and she'd be moved on immediately if Claire found out. Oddly, Claire knew she was seeing Anna but didn't mind. Ros hadn't asked but she suspected Anna was thought to be a 'good influence'. Cynically, she also believed that Claire's job was easier if she knew Ros was at Anna's. Everything in her past had led her to this conclusion; people at work always look for ways to cut corners, even if their work is looking after children.

'How is she, our dear mother?' Ros wished the nasty taste of sarcasm hadn't crept into her voice.

Emily stared at her before she answered. 'She cries sometimes.'

'For that piece-of-shit husband? The one in prison?'

Emily shook her head and put down her unfinished burger, wiping the corner of her mouth with her finger.

'She cries for the baby. He'd be almost seven now. We miss him.'

Ros had a flickering memory of a blonde baby, not unlike Anna's. He'd been a pretty, smiley child and she'd loved him. She lifted Jake from his papoose, held him close and kissed the top of his head, smelling the shampoo she used for them both. She said nothing but waited for Emily to continue.

'We don't visit my dad in prison. She says he can't come back to us when he's out. We're making a fresh start.'

'What do you mean?'

'We're going to leave Leicester. Mum says I need to go to a different school. And we don't want Dad to find us when he's released. Sean's not coming with us. Can I have another Coke and some fries?'

At the counter, Ros checked how much money was in her purse. There was just enough. She would have to manage until Friday with what was in the flat and anything she could borrow from Anna. Emily's news made her feel even colder than before. She'd held on to a silly dream that somehow, through Emily, she could build a bridge back to her mother and Sean. But it was nonsense. There was no way back.

Still, she persisted, 'Does Mum ever talk about me?' Ros sipped at the chocolate to stop her lips from trembling.

'Sometimes. She talks to Nan when she thinks I'm not listening. You wouldn't want to hear what she says.'

'What does she say?'

'Hannah, I said you wouldn't want to hear it.'

'Don't call me Hannah.' Ros looked around.

'Okay, *Ros*,' Emily emphasised the name, 'she says you take after your father. I mean yours and Sean's father. He was violent, right?'

'Yeah, mine was violent, yours was an abuser. Does that make you an abuser?' She stood up. 'Can you hold the baby? I have to go to the toilet.'

In the bathroom, she picked up every scrap of the toilet paper she had spread on the floor like confetti and scrunched it into a ball, using it to wipe up the water. The paper disintegrated and stuck to her fingers, and she peeled it off in strips and dropped it into the toilet bowl. Her mother was quite wrong, as always. She was nothing like her father.

'I'm sorry, Em, I was out of order,' Ros said, helping herself to one of Emily's fries. 'I'm glad you're going to a new school. In September, or maybe before, I'll be moving away too. I've applied for university.'

She could see from Emily's face that this meant nothing but saying it aloud helped. It was a plan, a way forward. 'Did you bring any homework for me to look at?'

To her surprise, Emily nodded and pulled a tattered exercise book and a French/English dictionary from her bag, the one that had been a gift from Ros. The girls bent their heads over the exercises and in an hour, they were done.

'Let me know how you get on,' Ros called to Emily from the door. 'Leave me a message.'

'Can we meet next Saturday?' Emily turned around and walked backwards. 'Homework's easier with your help.'

'Of course, same time same place.' Ros gave Emily a final wave and pushed through the Saturday crowds into the shopping centre.

CHAPTER 18

The next Saturday brought the first warmth of spring and Ros decided to walk into town. In John Lewis, surrounded by lovely things that one day she might be able to afford, she saw a couple going up the escalator, holding hands. For over a week she had heard every detail of Anna and Nick's separation, but it was still shocking to see Nick with the other woman, the 'little bitch'. She decided to follow them, to have a better look, and seeing Jenny heading alone towards the women's toilet, skipped ahead of her to create a chance meeting.

Nick waited for Jenny outside the restrooms. He paced the corridor then sat down in one of the thoughtfully provided chairs, giving a rueful smile at another man, also waiting. He felt like a time traveller, as if he had been lifted from his old life and placed into one that must belong to someone else. Of course, some parts were the same, like his work, but even there, everyone knew and seemed to think that he and Jenny were already 'an item'; the words weren't his but Helen's, lifted straight from her world of confessional talk shows. There was a cold atmosphere of disapproval and whispering and even his patients seemed to know, as if the news had been passed to them along with their appointment time.

It had felt hollow, waking on a Saturday morning, and making plans with Jenny over tea in her dark, cramped kitchen, instead of being bounced awake by Christopher and shouting at Cara and Jess to get ready for their dance class. He and Jenny were not a couple, she'd made that clear enough, but here they were doing 'couple' things, buying a new kettle, deciding what to eat that night. Should they stay in or go out?

Nick thought about the morning he left Anna when he had looked in on the sleeping children. He had pushed a damp strand of hair from Cara's brow, and she had turned over and muttered 'Daddy' and then he had walked out of his own home before dawn. He had a key to the practice and had surprised the caretaker by being at his desk, writing up patients' notes on his computer, before six. The caretaker scanned the room, his glance taking in the suitcase in the corner, and left Nick alone after a cursory greeting. The caretaker was a taciturn man but his wife, who cleaned the practice, would not have hesitated to share the gossip.

When Jenny arrived at work there had been a moment of awkwardness when she hadn't immediately agreed to take him in. His stay in her home was in her words, 'only until he found a place of his own'. She had been sweet, pleasant, he couldn't complain, but he knew that only three months ago he would have been welcomed with more enthusiasm. Jenny had argued, quite fairly, that he needed somewhere he could take the children, had made it all too clear they were not to come to her house. They weren't 'together' after all, so she shouldn't start playing the role of stepmother. He could only agree with all this common sense, but he'd hoped for a little more emotion. This afternoon they would visit some estate agents and see what he could afford. Nick wondered what Anna might have planned for him today.

Nick checked his phone but there was nothing from Tracey. Of course, he'd contacted her to let her know about his changed situation but other than a sad-faced emoji, she hadn't replied. Their last afternoon together had been the best ever but she said he'd spilt wine on her dress and would need fifty pounds for specialist dry-cleaning. It was champagne actually and a good one. He couldn't remember spilling any, but her dress was obviously a one-off designer item and who was he to argue about how much those things cost to clean? One thing that amazed him about Tracey was her superior knowledge of the whereabouts of cashpoints.

Ros listened to Jenny's footsteps enter the cubicle next to hers, the lock slide shut and the inevitable bathroom sounds. When she heard the flush, Ros came out of her cubicle, folding open her pushchair and strapping Jake into the seat before she washed her hands, watching Jenny in the mirror. She was small, with a wide face and hazel eyes, turning her hands slowly under the running tap, deep in thought. Jenny lifted her head and caught Ros staring.

'I don't know how you manage to do that,' she said.

What did she mean? Ros faced Jenny who was now bending over Jake.

'I don't understand. Do what?'

'Manage to go to the toilet with a baby and a pushchair. It must be difficult.'

'Oh, I see. Normally I'd use the mother and baby room, but it was busy.'

Jenny stood and gave her a wistful smile. 'I hope I'll find these things out for myself when I have a baby of my own.'

That's not very likely, Ros thought, watching Jenny leave. She'd heard all about Nick's vasectomy, booked the same day Anna had told him she was pregnant again.

Jenny came out from the women's toilets shaking her hands as if they were still wet. Nick stood to greet her; she smiled up at him and he took her damp fingers in his. They wandered through the electrical section, where Nick was distracted by the laptops, and ended up in the cafeteria. Jenny only wanted a coffee. He felt irritated when women didn't eat. It always seemed as if they were trying to make everyone else feel guilty. To make a point, he ordered sausage and mash and apple crumble and custard. They found a table by a window that looked down over four lanes of traffic. Nick watched the cars stop and start, stop and start, left then right, left then right, like a dance.

'I said we're eating tonight.' Jenny raised her voice.

'Sorry, I wasn't listening.'

'You won't be hungry.'

'It's comfort food,' Nick replied, his mouth full.

'Do you need some comfort?' She frowned but her eyes seemed sympathetic.

'I certainly do.' Nick looked across at Jenny, but over her shoulder, someone had seen him and was waving. Damn and blast, it was that silly girl, Ros.

Nick formally introduced Ros to Jenny as Anna's friend and explained: 'Jenny's kindly putting me up until I find a place of my own.'

Ros pulled off her gloves and sat down. 'I've already met Jenny in the toilets. Hello again.'

Nick stood. 'Do allow me to buy you a coffee.'

'That would be excellent.' Ros reached for her purse. 'And could you get me a jacket potato as well, with cheese and baked beans?'

Nick waved away Ros's money, although none had been offered, holding up a hand as if he was directing the traffic below.

'My treat.'

Ros looked at the woman Anna called the 'home wrecker' and in turn, the home wrecker stared at 'the scrounger'.

Jenny spoke first. 'I'm glad to meet you properly. I've heard such a lot about you.'

'Me?' Ros looked surprised.

'Yes, Nick's told me what a great help you've been to Anna.' Jenny leaned forward and lowered her voice. 'Whatever you've heard, I didn't plan this.'

'I guessed Anna had kind of forced things. That's just like her. She makes up her mind and then ... wham.' Ros tapped the table for emphasis.

'But she will take him back when the dust has settled?'

'Couldn't say.' Ros shrugged. 'She might, she might not.'

Nick waited in the line for the second time, wondering why he seemed to spend his life in queues buying coffee for women. Cakes, scones and pastries marked his dismal progress along the counter and the sweet scent of vanilla and cream made him feel nauseous. Once he had ordered and paid for Ros's lunch, Nick could see Ros and Jenny's heads bent together as he carried the tray through the tables and decided that he must end the encounter as soon as possible. He placed the tray in front of Ros but didn't sit down.

'It might be useful for us to exchange telephone numbers, Ros, in case you need to contact me about anything.' Nick pulled out his phone and while the exchange happened, Jenny pulled on her coat and bent to look into the pram, where Jake slept.

'You have a lovely baby,' she said. 'You must excuse us. We have to go and meet some estate agents.' She held out her hand and Ros took it. Again, Nick made his flat-palmed gesture of farewell.

Ros watched their backs disappear into the crowd, their awkward movements betraying the unfamiliarity of being together in public. She understood that feeling. When your life has been a secret, coming out into the open feels raw, like having no skin. For a moment, she almost felt sorry for them. She reached across for Nick's untouched pudding and pushed a spoon into the thick, yellow custard. Tonight, she would just eat toast.

CHAPTER 19

Anna woke with a start. Someone was downstairs. Her ears strained, listening to the soft sounds of an intruder quietly and carefully opening and closing cupboards. Her memory said that whoever was downstairs had used a key to get in; she was sure she had heard it turn in the lock. She slid from the bed and padded across to the window. Nick's car was parked outside. Of course, Nick would choose this time to come. He would have hoped she was still out on the school run.

Anna heard Nick's quick footsteps pad up the stairs and her stomach turned over as he opened her bedroom door. It was hard to say who was more shocked. For a few seconds Nick stood quite still and then he opened the wardrobe, pulling shirts from their hangers. She could see from his open bag that he had already taken some books and framed photos from downstairs.

Nick spoke, addressing the rail of suits. 'I'm sorry, I didn't know you would be here. I thought it would be easier. Your car wasn't in the drive, otherwise I wouldn't have come in. Why are you here?'

Anna returned to the bed, dragging the duvet across her chilled feet. 'Your father took the girls to school and Christopher to nursery. I haven't been sleeping well. Can we talk ... please?'

'My father? I might have known he'd turn up. Did you tell him about us?'

'Of course. He didn't seem surprised. Everyone seems to have known about your affair, except me. He said he'd try to help out more, whenever he can. Nick, I know I asked you to go, but maybe we can sort it out?' Exhaustion made her voice tremble, and it was an effort not to sound whining or pleading. 'We can't leave things like this.'

'There's nothing to sort out,' Nick said, almost crushing a sleeping Hughie as he sat on the other edge of the bed. 'I had an affair with Jenny, and I'd like to be with her. That's all there is to say. Of course, we need to talk to lawyers and so on, but nothing will change financially. And I doubt if my father knew about Jenny, although he might have guessed. Given his own record he'd have recognised the signs.'

'How long have you been seeing her?' Anna hated how much she needed to know this and a million other details which kept her awake at night.

'That doesn't matter now.' Nick shook his head. 'I only came to collect some things. When I get my own place, I'll pack up the rest.'

'I haven't told the girls. They think you're away. You're leaving them, not just me. You must explain it yourself. I don't think I could do it and leave them liking you.' Anna began to cry; silent, shredded sobs that could only be seen in the lift and fall of her shoulders. Nick waited for her to finish. 'How will I manage Nick? How can I cope on my own with four children?'

'I'm still their father, Anna. Of course I'll do all that I can. I'll come tonight at seven to talk to the girls. It's possible we could have the children this weekend to give you a break, but I need to speak to Jenny first. I can't stay with you because of them.'

Nick looked down at Hughie, fretfully sleeping next to his mother and his expression showed a momentary tenderness. 'I don't feel much for this one, Anna. He doesn't even look like one of ours. It feels as if I had no real choice in his creation. The decision to have him was yours alone. Perhaps we might have muddled through if it wasn't for him. He kind of blew us apart.'

Anna felt a hot rage, as if her own hidden feelings about Hughie had been spoken aloud.

'How can you blame him? His being here is just as much your responsibility as mine.' Her rising voice made the baby stir.

Nick turned away to zip up his holdall. 'I can't hang about. I have a surgery at half past nine.' Without looking back, he walked out of the room.

Anna threw back the duvet and ran after him, screaming: 'He may not look like one of yours, but you'll damn well pay for him for the rest of your life.'

The front door crashed shut behind Nick, the brass letter box reverberating with the impact. At once, Hughie began to scream, and the doorbell rang. Crouched on the landing, her head pressed against the newel of the staircase, Anna begged, 'Leave me alone.'

Through the glass panes of the door, she could see the shadowy but unmistakable outline of Jane Clark. The doorbell rang again. She wasn't going away.

'Damn, damn, damn.' Anna picked up the angry baby from her bed, ran downstairs and swung the door open.

Jane Clark blinked. 'I'm sorry to intrude. I called on the off-chance you'd be at home. Is everything okay? Dr McNeill practically knocked me over.'

'Sorry Jane, I didn't mean to startle you ... you may as well come in. As you can see, I've got my hands full.' Hughie's face was red and contorted, his fists clenched in rage.

Jane followed Anna into the kitchen.

'Is there anything I can do to help? Hughie seems so much bigger and stronger than the last time I last saw him. That's a really healthy cry.'

Anna sat in a chair and tried to feed the baby but despite several ferocious attempts, he pulled his head back, wailing in frustration.

'I'm so tired.' She leaned her forehead against the cradle of her hand. 'I haven't slept for days.'

'What about some coffee?' Jane suggested. 'Let me make it.'

'You may as well know,' Anna said after a few gulps, 'that Nick has left me. In case you hear any gossip.' She found it hard to keep her voice steady, to stop the downturned corners of her mouth from trembling.

'To be frank, there has been some talk for a while. It's Jenny isn't it, the one he's gone off with—the trainee they had in their practice last year?'

Jenny, Jenny, Jenny. How could she have missed it? Nick had never stopped talking about her. Jenny was perfect, clever, the best trainee they'd ever had. Their affair had been open knowledge. How could he?

'The bastard,' Anna said aloud. 'The bastard,' she repeated softly and turned her head so that Jane wouldn't see that her eyes had flooded with tears.

'We all think so too if that's any help. Tell me, what support have you got?'

'Ros comes almost every day.'

'That's why I dropped by,' Jane interrupted, 'I'd heard the gossip and wanted to make sure you were okay, but I really wanted to ask you about Ros. Jake's about to be signed off, so to speak, by his social worker and I've been asked to do a report for the case conference. I've got no concerns, but I wanted to check with you whether there's anything about Ros I'm missing? I know you've been keeping an eye on her. It goes without saying, this conversation has to be kept between us, but I'd never forgive myself if I hadn't asked you and then he came to harm.'

'She's great with Jake,' Anna replied, wiping her nose with the back of her hand, 'it's almost as if she'd already had experience with babies. There's nothing to worry about. She's a good mum, Jake will be fine.'

'That's reassuring, thanks Anna. I wouldn't have asked, but we've known each other for so long.'

Jane made the signs of leaving, standing to drain her mug and pulling on her coat but hesitated at the kitchen door. 'It might be an idea to bring Hughie to see me. Come to my next clinic—no need to make an appointment. Stay there.' She flapped a hand at Anna, 'I'll show myself out.'

That evening, supper for the children was a haphazard affair in front of the television. Hughie's unsettled mood continued, and he demanded to be fed almost every hour. Anna was upstairs, bathing both boys, when Nick arrived. Again, he used his own keys. Through the open bathroom door, she could hear him talking to the girls, his deep voice rising and their lighter voices falling in response. She put the babies, clean and bathed, into their cots, both restless and whimpering, hoping for a few minutes grace to deal with whatever was happening downstairs. She slipped into the bedroom and dragged a brush through her hair.

Downstairs, Nick walked through the door from the kitchen holding Cara and Jessica's hands and they met in the hall. Jessica looked at her mother solemnly and said, 'Daddy's going to live with someone else, but he's not leaving us, he's leaving you.'

Both girls glared accusingly at Anna and Nick looked uncomfortable.

'I'm sorry, that's not how I meant it to sound. I didn't want them to feel abandoned.'

'Daddy says we can come and stay with him at the weekend. Can we Mum?' begged Cara.

Anna held her breath. She wasn't ready for this ... it was too soon. Her mind grasped at an idea that might make their horrendous plan unworkable. 'What about Christopher? Surely you should take him too.'

'Come on.' Nick shook his head. 'I'm not saying "never" but let me get my own place first. There isn't room at Jenny's for three children.'

'Can we go, Mum, please, can we?' the girls chanted.

Anna heard the word 'yes' slip from her mouth as she exhaled. She had just agreed to spend a weekend without her girls.

'If it's okay,' Nick said, 'I'll get my solicitor to put something in writing. Maybe I could have the kids ... I mean these two ... every other weekend? Let me know if anything happens that you really can't manage. Otherwise, I'll see you on Friday evening.' Nick kissed each daughter in turn and left.

Cara and Jess were cheerful before bed, planning what they would take when they went to stay with their father, packing and unpacking an imaginary suitcase made from a cardboard box. Anna was occupied constantly by the boys, the small baby irritable and screaming and Christopher hot and fractious. She walked around with one baby or another on her shoulder and tried to talk to Cara and Jess when she could. Much later, when both girls had been in bed for several hours and their voices had long since died away, Cara tiptoed downstairs. Would Anna come and see Jess? Her tone was apologetic, adult, implying with a sigh of resignation that she had done all she could.

Jessica's face and pillow were damp, her eyes bright with pinpoints of light. Anna crouched by her bed and listened. The problem was simple. Last week, Cara had told her that there wasn't really a tooth fairy, it was Daddy who took the tooth and left money. So, the tooth fairy wouldn't come any more, would he? Anna told the child that Nick's job had been to help the tooth fairy, who was very busy and that it would be okay for Mum to do the same. Cara rolled her eyes at this fiction but when Anna winked at her, she returned a small nod of understanding.

Finally, the house was quiet, and Anna fell into an exhausted but fitful sleep on top of her bed, unwashed and fully clothed. She dreamed she was a child at home; heard the jangle of her parents' old telephone ringing at the end of a dark and echoing corridor cluttered with old coats, wellington boots and sacks of seed potatoes. The dog was barking in the kitchen, and she smelt his sour, earthy coat; an odour which permeated the whole house. The ringing went on and on. Why didn't her mother answer it? Her mind struggled past the dream; her bedroom, the ringing, were here right now, in the present. It was her landline, the one by the bed, and whoever was calling wasn't going to give up.

'You've been on the phone a long time.' Jenny looked up from her book, as Nick leaned over to kiss her forehead.

'It was my mother.' Nick pulled at his tie and flopped down on the bed.

'How is she? I loved meeting her at Christmas.'

'She's moved to Vancouver for the summer with her awful husband. I refuse to call him my stepfather. It's bad enough having my father prowling around my family without her prying into my affairs.'

'Hadn't you told her?'

'No, and now she's heard from Anna's mother.'

Jenny cradled a pillow against her stomach.

'She must have been angry.'

'Of course she was. Angry with me for leaving the kids, angry with me for being like my father. Angry, angry, angry. What will your father say?'

Jenny picked at a thread on the sheet.

'I'm not planning to tell him anything. He doesn't need to know. You'll have your own place soon. Let's see how it goes. I don't want him to think I broke up your family, at least not until I'm sure we're staying together.'

'You've got it all worked out, haven't you? Little Miss Perfect.' Nick tried to joke but his tone was sullen.

Jenny threw the pillow at him. He caught it and groaned, rolling over and pulling it tight across the back of his head.

She lay down beside him and lifted the pillow away. Nick turned towards her and traced her eyelids and lips with his fingertips.

'There's something else. After I spoke to my mother, I rang Anna. I'm afraid I lost my temper.'

'Why did you?'

'Because her mother had telephoned my mother. I felt they were all ganging up. Nag, nag, nag.'

'So you took it out on Anna? That wasn't fair.'

Nick knew this was true, so her words stung. 'Okay, okay ... I was wrong. I'll apologise when I see her at the weekend.'

'What if you're like that with me when I annoy you? Will you shout at me?'

'You'll never annoy me.' Nick put his hand on Jenny's waist under her tee shirt. She leaned away to switch off the reading light and his fingers trailed across the top of her silk shorts.

'One more thing.' Nick pressed himself full-length against Jenny's back and his words murmured through her hair and across her ears and neck between his small, soft kisses. 'I said we'd have the girls this weekend. Is that okay with you?'

'This weekend?' Jenny sat up, forcing Nick to roll away. 'But I said I didn't want them here. Where will they sleep?'

'I had to give them something; I was taking everything away. Do you understand?' Nick reached to find her hand in the dark.

Jenny ignored his touch and folded her arms under her breasts.

'I wasn't ready for any of this. You never discuss anything with me.'

'If you have an affair with a man who has four kids and then get found out, unexpected things happen.' Nick weighed each word, the emphasis betraying his exasperation. 'There isn't a road map.' He lifted both hands in an empty gesture and let them drop. 'Can you imagine how it felt to tell Jess and Cara I wasn't going to live with them any more?'

'It must have been awful.'

'Absolutely awful,' he repeated. His voice became gentler, more reasonable, 'We can use the weekend to find a place. The girls can help me choose. It would be good to involve them. It won't happen again, I promise.'

They lay side by side in the dark, listening to the occasional shout as students made their way home from the bars that lined the main shopping street nearby. A siren wailed its lonely cry, at first close then distant. Nick turned onto his side and touched Jenny lightly on her breast. She turned her back to him, but he pressed himself against her again, kissing her neck and slipping his hand inside her pyjamas, tracing the sharp ridge of her hips with his palm. His fingers dipped into the hollow below.

'Don't,' Jenny muttered, 'I have to get up early to work on a court report. I planned to do it at the weekend but now ...' She didn't finish her sentence.

Nick rolled away and folded his hands over his stomach. What he hadn't told Jenny was that Anna was taking the babies to see her parents while they had the girls. There was nothing wrong with Anna's plan; on the surface it was eminently sensible, but she'd said it with a 'so there' tone, which he probably deserved. He knew Anna well enough to guess at the rest, the unspoken bit, 'Don't expect me to stay at home to back you up if anything goes wrong'.

He stared at the ceiling, trying to focus on anything that might distract him from his arousal. Light from the streetlamp crept through a gap above the curtains. The pattern of fine cracks in the plaster could have been a spider's web. Everything has a price, he thought, and it was obviously payback time. If the girls were homesick or unwell, he and Jenny would simply have to cope.

CHAPTER 20

Ros lay awake listening to Jake's night-time sounds, hoping he would sleep. Things were very difficult. Anna swung between rage and despair when they were alone, dramatically transforming into fierce, bright-eyed capability when the older children were around. Ros had no experience of helping with the distress of an older woman, or anyone for that matter. She could remember her mother's rages at her father. He never raised his voice, he just hit her with his closed fist. After Ros left home, when she was forced to leave, she had only caught a glimpse of her mother's pain in the courtroom, but she could do nothing except watch and stay frozen and still. At Whiteoaks, new children had screamed in their rooms, cared for only by their key person. Eventually, they would emerge pale and subdued, to watch television or eat supper with the others. There had been no emotion at Roy and Theresa's, only a determined calm.

She did her best, which was to listen, make cups of tea

and look after Christopher and the girls whenever she was asked. There was nothing she could say, and she really didn't want to touch Anna, although she guessed that maybe Anna needed that sometimes. Anna's friends had started to drop by and were terrifying. They seemed to fill all the available space, hurrying in from their important jobs, with grey suits and loud voices and expecting Ros to make them coffee and a sandwich, as if she were the hired help. It was obvious that they preferred to be alone with Anna, as they avoided talking about Nick until she left the room.

When these friends visited, Ros would have preferred to leave, to go home or into town, but she knew they'd only stay for half an hour and then Anna would be alone. So she would slip into the kitchen and empty the dishwasher or cram wet washing into the tumble dryer and wait until Naomi, or Olivia or whoever had slammed their way out of the house, leaving only their perfume, the silence, and the weight of grief behind them.

Ros propped herself onto her elbow. She thought she had heard a light footstep on the walkway outside her window and stopped breathing to listen. There was nothing. She allowed her chest to rise and fall but her heart drummed painfully. It must have been a neighbour returning late.

Again, a sound—a trainer sliding on wet metal. Her letterbox clattered. She heard a thud as something fell, then footsteps ringing on the metal stairs, a smell of burning. She flung open her bedroom door. Flames tracked across the linoleum down the dark hall, following the petrol seeping from a burning rag. She dragged her duvet from the bed, threw it over the fire and lay across it, using her weight to suffocate the flames. Her nostrils burnt with the reek of fuel and the acrid scent of singed polyester. Above her head the hall was full of smoke. Ros heard Jake cough and ran to lift him from his cot. In the sitting room, she closed the door and flung open the window. Holding Jake tight, she rubbed his back and watched strands of smoke weave out of the open window into the night. From the street below she heard a tuneless whistle.

For the rest of the night Ros had lain awake, tense and cold, curled on the armchair with Jake wrapped in her coat, forced to listen to the piping taunts of her attacker. If it hadn't been for the baby she would have run down and torn him limb from limb. Through the long, freezing hours, anger churned inside her like a gathering storm. Once the smoke had cleared from the room, she put Jake down and slid across the floor to the window. The piping, tuneless whistle had stopped but she was afraid he was still watching. On her knees, she reached up and closed the window, roughly pulling the curtains across the blank panes. She lit the fire, gradually stripping off layers of clothes as the fear left her. Her fingers and toes ached as the blood returned to her numbed skin. She fed Jake in the armchair and slept.

The damage was less than she expected when she peeled away her duvet. There was a hole in the lino below the letterbox with burn marks spreading out from it like charcoal rivers and some smoke residue blotched the walls like rag stencilling. She dressed Jake in his warmest clothes and strapped him into the buggy, leaving him in the flat while she carried her burnt duvet and the oily rag used to start the fire down to the bins. She wasn't afraid that her attacker would still be waiting for her, not if he'd given up his taunting vigil only a few hours ago.

'But this is awful.' Claire shook her head as Ros told her what had happened. 'Do you have any idea who might have done this? Could it have been the same man who attacked you before?'

Ros twisted the lowest stud on her earlobe.

'I'm sure it was. He stood under my window, whistling the tune he used before ... the last time he followed me. He wanted me to know it was him; that he'd come back for me.'

'That's good.' Claire folded her arms across her chest. 'I mean it's not good he attacked you, but it means we might catch him. I didn't say anything before now, so as not to frighten you, but the police thought there was a small risk he might try again. We thought you would be safe because he didn't know where you lived, and your address is only known to me and my line manager. They might want to lay a trap for him at your flat. Will you be okay to go back if there are policemen there?'

'But the point of the harassment is that I stay scared, always looking over my shoulder, never knowing where he is. He'll just disappear again, so we'll never be sure when he's coming after me.'

Claire hesitated. Between them they had always

struggled to find a name they could use for Ros's stepfather, given the harm he had caused to so many.

'Your mother's partner has had his sentence extended by a year because of the previous attack, which he admitted. He may still want some revenge, or his little friend could be acting alone. I think he'll be back. Let me check out a few things.'

Claire went to make some calls. Left alone, Ros waited, looking around at the functional room with its strip lights and table that had seen better days. A high window ran the length of the ceiling, letting in the only daylight. From beyond the door, with its standard pane of frosted glass, she could hear telephones and the murmur of conversation. Her hair smelt of smoke and she needed a shower.

Claire returned with an older woman.

'Ros, this is Sally, my line manager. We've spoken to the police, and we need to check your flat to make sure it's suitable for you to return. We'll arrange a taxi to take you to Anna McNeill's while we sort something out. Tell her about the fire but nothing else.'

'We have some news,' Sally added conversationally, as if sharing gossip about a mutual friend, 'your mother has decided to leave Leicester.'

'I know,' the words were out. Too late.

'Oh Ros, you've seen Emily again.' Claire sighed and rubbed her forehead. It was a statement, not a question. Claire looked at Sally. 'It makes things easier I suppose.'

'Makes what easier?' Ros asked.

'We've decided to move you on. Staying was a risk, but we hoped it could be managed. We have no choice, Ros, you keep breaking the rules. Also, you're no longer safe. It's the right thing to do.'

'But I can't leave now.' Ros felt panicked at the thought of letting Emily down, of failing to turn up when she'd promised, but she couldn't use a prohibited meeting with her sister as a reason to stay. Instead, she grasped at the only other possible excuse she had to remain in Leicester. 'I can't leave Anna.'

'Mrs McNeill will manage perfectly well without you.'

'You don't understand. Nick has left her. She has no one else.'

Sally seemed to find this funny.

'Honey, she managed for years before you came along. She has friends and family to help her. Now, this university thing is a good idea. Claire contacted a few admissions tutors, and with your grades, several can offer you an unconditional place in September.'

'Here's a list of the universities who've agreed to have you.' Claire handed Ros a piece of paper. 'Look it over, talk to Anna if you want, but you must pick one. As soon as you can.'

As Sally turned to leave the room, Ros noticed her try to catch Claire's eye. They'd planned this, Ros thought, they were simply waiting for the moment I went wrong. She slouched down in her chair and tried to look indifferent, while Claire made notes on her laptop. Moments later, Sally put her head around the door.

'Good news—the flat is perfectly habitable. A police team is heading over there now, dressed as decorators, but only one of them will leave. The other two will stay overnight and we'll also have a couple of unmarked cars watching from the street. Are you okay to go back there tonight? If we catch him, it could be years before he's released. With luck you'll be able to live your life without ever having to think of your mother's husband or his friend again.'

Ros nodded. Speech was impossible since she was afraid that her anger might turn the words into tears. She had found her sister and she had made a friend. How could they make her leave now?

'Make sure you're back in the flat before dark. Is that okay? I don't think you'll sleep but you might need more bedding. Can you borrow some from Mrs McNeill? And here's a tenner for milk and biscuits. Those coppers will get through a lot of tea tonight.'

Claire reached out, tried to take her hand over the table. 'Come on, Ros,' her tone was pleading, 'it's not so bad. We won't move you straight away, so there's plenty of time to help Anna through this crisis. Just don't see Emily. Promise me?'

Ros ignored her and crumpled the list of universities into her pocket. She pushed Jake's buggy through the door that Sally held open for her, staring ahead. In the taxi to Anna's, all she could think of was how much she hated them.

It was hard to listen to Anna. Too many words tumbled out at once about Nick having the girls for the weekend and her impulsive decision to take the babies to see their grandparents in Newcastle. It was difficult to interrupt but finally, as Anna drew breath, Ros told her about the fire in the flat.

'I'm afraid I left the damp duvet too close to the fire. Jake had been sick on it.'

'But that's awful, Ros. I assume you've got smoke alarms?'

'Of course, that's what alerted me. The thing is, I need to borrow a single duvet.'

Anna was immediately diverted and insisted that only new bedding would do. She knew just the place—a cut-price warehouse she'd always meant to visit.

'The parking's great, Ros and there's a cafe. It can be an outing for us.'

Anna pored over togs and complicated fillings, trying to interest Ros, while Christopher jumped on and off the display beds. An assistant pointed to a sign that said the beds were not for sitting on, never mind 'using them as a trampoline'.

'He's one and a half, he can't read,' Ros said sharply.

'But you can,' the assistant argued.

Ros was about to open her mouth and release a stream of choice swear words when she remembered her counsellor droning on about recognising the source of her anger and directing it where it belonged. She smiled at the girl and said, 'Of course,' pulling Christopher by the hand towards his mother, while he screamed and pointed back towards the beds.

They paid for a duvet and a cover with matching pillowcases. Ros argued that she didn't need pillowcases, but Anna couldn't cope with the idea of a cover that didn't match its pillowcases. Ros gave in, recognising that this shopping trip had brought something of the old Anna back to her.

They went for tea and scones in the cafe, where Christopher practised the new skill he was learning at nursery—spreading butter and jam. Ros told Anna a story about how she had a new fireguard, now Jake was able to roll around the floor, and it was useful to dry her washing. She gambled that this would give Anna the opportunity to lecture her on fire hazards, which would take her mind off Nick and the 'little bitch' for a while longer, but after a few mouthfuls Anna became quiet and stared into a distant corner of the warehouse, crumbling the scone with her fingers. Christopher held up his hands for Ros to wipe.

'Why isn't Nick taking Christopher for the weekend?' Ros risked breaking into Anna's misery.

'Oh, come on,' Anna rallied, 'we are talking about Nick remember. He made an excuse about lack of space, but can you imagine him and what's-her-name with Christopher for a whole weekend. Besides, I want him with me.' Christopher gave his mother a buttery smile.

'I think Nick should take all the children, even Hughie. That'll give you some weekends free. You can go out, meet another man.'

'Don't be ridiculous,' Anna said, but Ros could see that she was pleased.

'Come with me to Newcastle this weekend, my parents will love to meet you and Jake.' Anna was always confident that her enthusiasm for crowding mismatched people together was shared by others. Ros shook her head. How could she explain that she couldn't leave Leicester without permission? There was also the matter of Emily. They'd agreed to meet again at McDonald's on

Saturday, and she intended to be there, whatever Claire and Sally had said. She'd grown up in the care of people not too different from those two advisers and had learnt that once a punishment had been agreed, you could break the same rule as much as you liked and nothing worse would happen. They might move her earlier than planned but that wasn't as bad as letting Emily down. Anyway, how would they know? There weren't enough resources to watch her all the time.

Since the two older children were having tea with friends—a well-meant offer from a mother who imagined that having spent all day with only babies for company Anna would enjoy several more hours without the company of her daughters—Ros gratefully accepted the offer of a lift home, given the cumbersome bedding.

At the flats, Anna parked and stared up at the dark walkway and blank windows. Ros hoped she wouldn't expect to be asked in, as it would be hard to explain the presence of the 'decorators'. She lifted her bags and the buggy from the back of the estate car and released Jake from the extra car seat that Anna had fitted for him. Anna turned the engine and they waved, promising to meet tomorrow.

Ros took the stairs at a run, so that momentum would propel her and everything she had to carry straight to the top. She dropped her shopping and the pushchair, and with the hand that wasn't holding Jake, searched in her bag for a key. She hesitated before turning the key in the lock. There were no sounds from inside and not even a fraction of light was visible through the glass panes that fanned like a half-orange across the top of the door. Perhaps they were sitting in the dark. The hall smelt of paint and when she switched on the light, she noticed the linoleum had been replaced with something that was meant to look like tiles. She paused and listened. No one called out.

'Hello.' She spoke hesitantly into the silence. Listening again, the only sound was the hum from the refrigerator. Ros pushed open her bedroom door and switched on the light. It was empty. She threw the bags onto the bed and walked down the hall to the living room, expecting to be startled by two quiet adults. Again, the room was empty. Beyond were her tiny shower room and the kitchen, both of which could barely accommodate one small person, never mind two. Regardless, she checked them. It was quarter to five. She tried the number for Claire, but the phone rang pointlessly, on and on.

At first, she only felt puzzled. She had enough residual confidence in the police to close the curtains and put on the lights, to start the evening routine of food and baths. They wouldn't let her down. After Jake's feed, she played with him, encouraging his new reaching skills, and then left him propped under the baby gym Anna had found for her in the Oxfam shop. Looking down from the tiny kitchen window onto the shuttered shops, Ros felt the stir of loneliness. Not the feeling that most people call loneliness but the sort she knew well, as if you were at the bottom of a well and no matter how much you called out, no one came. It was already nine o'clock. The police weren't coming. There wasn't anyone she could ring except Anna, and she would have all the children in bed by now. Whatever happened tonight, she must face it alone.

She sat straight-backed in a chair by the bedroom window with her hands folded on her lap. Tucked between her feet was a can of chopped tomatoes, a present from Anna who had tried to teach her how to make spaghetti bolognaise. She had moved Jake's cot into the living room. The bedroom curtains were closed but the window was open a fraction, since the weather had finally turned towards spring. The room was dark. She thought of her future with Jake, just the two of them and her academic career, teaching clever students who wanted to learn. She thought about the boy who had chosen to act like her stepfather's hand, reaching out from prison to take her future away. The counsellor was right, it was about focusing the anger, understanding where to strike for maximum impact. She waited and listened.

A footfall outside. A scrape as the window eased upwards. A trainer sought the floor, followed by a knee bent away from her. She lifted the can, held it high above her. A hand on the curtain, the back of his head. The crump of chopped tomatoes meeting skull. His body hit the floor, twisted. She bent down and tied his hands with a pair of tights. She rolled him onto his back and undid his belt, pulling his jeans and underwear down to his ankles and tightened the belt around them. He groaned, said something about 'Gemma'. She rolled him over into the recovery position and went into the kitchen to find her nail varnish.

She heard them coming; police cars and an ambulance making a satisfying cacophony as they hurtled from the ring road to the parking lot below. Their lights illuminated the bedroom curtains, still drawn, off and on like a magic lantern, and the metal staircase rang with the weight of their feet, pounding up towards her. She opened the door and showed them her victim. The paramedics managed to rouse him, and he vomited across her carpet. A policeman spoke into a phone then gestured with his head that she should follow him to the living room. He glanced into Jake's cot and smiled at the sleeping baby then sat down on one of the wooden chairs at the table by the window. She heard the joints strain under his weight.

A policewoman put her head around the door and confirmed that her search of the area had found nothing. He asked her to put the kettle on and make them all a cup of tea. Ros noticed her momentary hesitation. She guessed that the policewoman wanted to refuse. He should make his own tea, she thought.

They were alone again.

'What was that all about, pulling down his jeans?'

'Humiliation.'

'That's a bit sick, isn't it? What was it you wrote on his backside?'

'It was cunt. CU on one cheek. NT on the other.'

'You'd already floored him. What was the point of writing that? And with nail varnish?'

'He needed reminding of what he is. It won't come off easily, so he'll have to live with it. Unless you guys have some remover.'

'It will be removed in hospital and the incident recorded. His lawyers could have you for assault.'

One of the paramedics put her head around the door.

'He's stable. We'll take him to hospital now. He's under arrest?'

The policeman nodded and spoke once again into his phone. She waited for him to finish.

'A police car will follow the ambulance. We know him, he's wanted for a string of offences.' He turned back to Ros. 'We can't pretend it didn't happen.'

She shrugged. 'It doesn't matter. Nothing will happen to me. Just give this team a call.' She passed him a card. He picked it up and frowned as he read Claire's details.

The female officer carried tea from the kitchen, slopping liquid over the table as she put the mugs down with a controlled ill-temper. Ros smiled but didn't look up. She placed herself between Ros and the other officer, facing the window, and when Ros finally raised her head, the woman was sipping from her own mug, staring out of the window. Ros saw a pink strip of sky above the rooftops, split by a thin layer of cloud. Jake stirred in his cot and the policewoman startled, putting her free hand onto her chest.

'My God, there's a baby in here!'

Her colleague passed her a form.

'You could start filling out the incident record. I'm going down to the car to make a call.'

She sat in his vacated chair and took another gulp of tea.

'He thinks I'm his bloody secretary.'

Jake began his morning-hungry cry, one that couldn't be ignored. Ros lifted him from his cot and kissed his head. He was safe now, they both were.

'Do you mind if I change him and give him a feed, otherwise you won't get any peace to do your form?'

'It seems we owe you an apology.' The male officer had returned to the flat. He tried not to look at Ros's breast as she fed Jake. 'Plain clothes were meant to be here last night.' He turned to his colleague: 'There'd been an incident the night before, an attempt to set fire to the place.'

'We should have been told.' The policewoman didn't look up from her notes.

'Yeah, sure but we're just the local bobbies remember? This is only *our* patch.'

Ros found that her shoulders were shaking. She bent her head over Jake to hide the trembling. She felt the woman put a hand across her bowed neck.

'It's delayed shock, love. You've had a terrible time.'

'I need to call your doctor.' The policeman knelt in front of her. 'You do have a doctor?'

Ros shook her head. She was registered with a practice of course, because of Jake, but she had never had to see a doctor herself. But then she remembered. She did know a doctor. She pushed her mobile across the table.

'Ring Nick McNeill, he's a doctor.'

He didn't refuse to come, even though it was only seven in the morning. He didn't complain that she wasn't his patient. This was a Nick she hadn't seen before; a confident man free of guilt and duplicity. He was here in her flat, where Anna had never been, with his bag and firm, dry hands. The police officers listened to him, stepped aside to make room for him. In this flat, Nick had respect.

Her mobile rang as she packed her small bag, so that Nick could take her to Anna's. She saw that the call was from Sally.

'I'm so sorry, Ros.' She sounded frantic. 'A different team were supposed to arrive at four, but they'd been given the wrong flat number. When the key didn't fit in the lock, they went back to base. There was an emergency elsewhere in the city and they were called away. We weren't told you were alone.'

'I sorted it.'

'If I'd known I'd have come for you straight away. This shouldn't have happened. You must have been terrified.'

'Okay, Sally. I have to go with Nick now.'

'You're going to the McNeill's? I'm so relieved. You must not be on your own. I'll ring you later today about new accommodation. We have somewhere you can move into almost immediately.'

'That's fine Sally. I'll see you tomorrow.'

'You were very brave. We're proud of you.'

'Yeah. Me too.'

In the car, Ros stared at Nick. There was something she needed to say but wanted him to speak first. Nick studied the traffic ahead, one finger tapping on the steering wheel, but he must have noticed because in the end, he said just one word. 'What?'

'Thanks for coming for me but ...'

'But what?'

'Don't tell Anna the police were there. Things are more complicated than it looks. I can't cope with her prying.'

Nick gave her a quick, questioning glance before returning his gaze to the congestion ahead. 'No problem.

I know exactly where you're coming from. We'll just say there was a break-in and naturally, you were shaken up and called me.'

Ros relaxed. She could trust Nick, not because he cared but because her life didn't matter to him at all. She could see that his mind was already elsewhere, as he began his tuneless whistle and the annoying finger tap on the steering wheel.

CHAPTER 21

Anna drove through the dark to her parents' home in the north. The worst of the Friday night rush was over and after passing Sheffield the motorway became open and clear. She felt a surprising elation at the freedom of a journey without Nick; being alone with two babies instead of four children. The route was familiar, and her attention drifted. She had again tried to persuade Ros to come with her, given what had happened. Although she had stubbornly refused, Ros had asked if she could stay there for the weekend, and Anna had agreed. The girl had seemed pale and shaken but confident that she felt safe in Anna's house, which she was, of course. Much safer than in that awful flat.

Anna thought about the blog she'd written last night after the fire episode. She'd tried to make her account amusing, while emphasising Ros's irresponsibility. The truth was she'd been smoking and had tried to cover it up. Her account of the fire had been a lie, that much had been clear, but here's hoping she'd learnt her lesson. There had only been a few responses so far, and those were in total agreement, some even wondering if Anna shouldn't contact Social Care.

Thoughts of the fire and her personal responsibility for Ros had been pushed from her mind by finding Nick on the doorstep, with Ros and Jake, at eight this morning. Nick had explained that there had been a break-in at the flat and Ros had called him because she felt unwell. Ros went straight to bed with Jake, into the room they now thought of as Harriet's, and although she'd rallied through the day, had remained unwilling to talk. Nick suggested Anna might cancel her trip to Newcastle, but she refused, suspecting that he hoped to be freed from his promised weekend with the girls, rather than having any real concern about Ros's welfare. To be fair, he *had* asked about Ros when she dropped off the girls this evening. Perhaps she was too quick to judge. After all, he hadn't hesitated to help Ros.

Since both boys were deeply asleep, Anna decided to drive to Newcastle without stopping. It was almost midnight when she arrived, dizzy and disoriented. Her parents' shabby, faded home smelt as always of wet rainwear and sacking, and she found her eyes leaking tears of exhaustion when she carried the sleeping children from the car into their grandparents' arms. Her mother took Christopher upstairs to the cot she had borrowed from Anna's sister. Her father, uncomfortable with unnecessary emotion, sat with her by the fire in silence while she fed Hughie.

'He's a fine boy. He seems to feed well.' Her mother Peggy spoke approvingly when she joined them with hot chocolate and sandwiches.

'Too well,' Anna said through a mouthful of cheese and pickle, 'he never stops.'

'And how are the other children?' Peggy asked taking small bites from the edge of a sandwich she clearly didn't want.

'I was a little worried leaving Jess behind. She seemed a bit clingy, but she does have Cara ... as well as her dad.'

She guessed that Peggy wanted to ask more about Nick but was afraid to introduce his name into the conversation in case Anna wept again. She felt she ought to help her out, tell her more about Nick and Jenny, but it could wait.

'I'm sorry I rang Harriet,' Peggy said at last, obliquely approaching the matter of the separation.

'I'm glad you did.' Anna tried to sound reassuring. 'Goodness knows when Nick would have got around to telling her. He worries too much about what she thinks. He's still a little afraid of her.'

'I should have been down to see you. I wish I could do more to help.' Peggy lifted the tea towel that she still held in her hand and dropped it into her lap.

'It's okay, I know you can't get away from here.'

'We may have a bit more time soon.' Peggy glanced at her husband. 'Your dad has news. I won't say anything about it now. Let's wait till the morning.'

In her room, Anna put Hughie to bed, thinking about what her mother and father might have to tell her. She guessed it would be about her sister Kate and husband

191

Jed. After being taken on by Len as a sixteen-year-old, Jed had trained in horticulture and worked alongside his father-in-law, not always amicably. They lived with their two children in a modern house across the road from the nursery and seemed happy. But Anna knew from her infrequent phone conversations with her sister that they had ambitions, if only the parents would retire. It would mean a loss of land to a widened driveway and car park, but worst of all her parents would be asked to give up part of the old house to a restaurant and new sales area. If Kate had managed to persuade Len to agree to even part of this plan, then she was clever indeed.

After February's deep chill, for March, it was warm and sunny in this corner of the walled Victorian kitchen garden. Anna sat with Hughie, sleeping on his back in the large pram that had once been hers and Kate's. She remembered that this was her mother's favourite spot to leave the pram, while she worked alongside her husband in the garden. It had been Anna's job when Kate was in the pram to 'check the baby' and she had been diligent in her duty. She had a memory of peering at her sister over the edge of the pram, a dark-haired child in a pink romper suit with rosebud smocking, and moving the teddy bear just beyond her reach.

Anna stretched her limbs and lifted her face towards the sun, wondering how long she should leave it before ringing Cara's mobile. Too soon and she'd be seen as over-anxious and interfering, but too long might appear neglectful. Her father had taken Christopher to see the caged birds and her mother and sister were serving in the shop. At eleven, her mother appeared with two mugs of coffee. They sat at the old, rough table, which rocked unevenly on the flagstones. Her mother chatted about friends and neighbours that Anna could barely remember, and her thoughts drifted to how quickly her new single status had been accepted. Her parents were practical, not prone to speculation or regret and probably felt their eldest daughter would have to make the best of it, as they had always done. Perhaps there was nothing more to be said. She had a home, enough money, four children and a good education. What advice could they offer her? But she was startled when her mother said: 'Do you think you and Nick might get back together? Lots of men have affairs. It doesn't have to be the end.'

'It feels very final,' Anna said, after holding a silence for longer than was comfortable. 'Even if he wanted to come back, I'm not sure we could. Things weren't good before he left. And then there's the baby, Hughie. I'm not sure I can forgive Nick for rejecting him.'

'Have you met her ... the other woman.'

'Jenny?' Anna used the name to feel the bitter taste in her mouth. 'Believe it or not she spent Christmas with us. I saw her yesterday when I dropped the girls off with Nick.'

'And ...?' Peggy encouraged her to go on.

'And she's small, young, very thin ... dark haired. The opposite of me, I suppose. She's also clever and a good doctor, or so I heard only too often when she was his trainee. Exactly the sort of woman Nick would leave me for. But I suspected nothing.'

'Don't blame yourself. Most women don't know. You were so wrapped up in the babies. Sorry, I shouldn't have said that. It sounds as though I'm saying it's your fault.'

Anna smiled at her mother and wondered if she might be speaking from experience.

'I know you didn't mean that. Nick should have been wrapped up in the babies as well. It's this one that really caused the problem.' Both women looked at Hughie curled against Anna's breast.

'That's nonsense, Anna. Nick's affair with Jenny must have been going on before you were pregnant.' Peggy hesitated and seemed to choose her words with care, 'But is the baby developing okay?'

This wasn't something Anna wanted to discuss. Hughie's progress was none of her mother's business.

'I'm sure he's fine. He's a bit behind because of the underfeeding in his first few weeks. The health visitor wants to see him but I'm sure he'll catch up.'

Peggy pulled on her gardening gloves.

'I shouldn't have said anything. You're right, he's absolutely fine.'

Anna raised a hand to shield her eyes from the sun as her mother's shapely, muscular silhouette weaved through growing fruit bushes to a gate in the far corner. She pushed the heavy pram back to the house to find her father and Christopher.

Her parents had planned a special evening. The table in the rarely used dining room had been cleared of bills and receipts, and flames from a log fire were reflected in the polished wood and crystal glasses, brought out only for birthdays and graduations. The scent of burning logs and furniture polish, combined with the low light, masked the smell of damp, characteristic of this room, and hid the ominously peeling wallpaper in one corner.

There were seven at the table. Kate and Jed's two sons aged three and five were allowed to stay up for dinner with their aunt and their grandparents. Unusually, her parents served wine, so the atmosphere quickly became cheerful. Her father said little. He drank beer rather than wine and smiled around at his family, but his thoughts seemed to distract him. Anna guessed he was waiting for his moment. When the pudding was cleared away and Luke and Andrew had got down from the table to play with the dog, Anna's father stood and tapped on his glass for attention.

'I've thought long and hard about what I want to say tonight. First, I'm as proud as any man can be of my two daughters. But there's a young man at this table I'm every bit as proud of, as if he were my own. What's happened to Anna and Nick has made me understand that loyalty and sticking with things is not something you should ever take for granted. Peggy and I have talked, and we want you all to know that we will take partial retirement in six months' time and from that date, this house will be Kate and Jed's and they will run the business for us. We'll be glad to see the back of this damp old place. Nothing would give us greater pleasure than to move across the way to your centrally heated box. We'll still help out in your garden centre if you'll have us.'

Len sat down and enjoyed the stunned silence that followed. Kate clapped her hands and hugged Jed. Peggy cried and the two little boys, aware that something from them was required, ran around the table pretending to be aeroplanes. Anna smiled at her sister and her mother but felt separate. She had no part in this. She watched her nephews, their squabbling and play fighting, and thought about Christopher and Hughie. Not long ago she had expected to share their future with their father; to be together with Nick, enjoying the energy and enthusiasm of small boys. Her throat tightened with self-pity.

'I'm ready to retire,' Peggy said to Anna over her shoulder, as she filled the kettle in the kitchen. 'I'm too old for this. I can't tell you how glad I am that your father made a decision at last. But things won't be easy between him and Jed. We're in for a difficult few months.'

'Come and stay with me when it gets too much. You'll be free at last, to come and go as you please. It has its advantages.'

Peggy turned to face her elder daughter. 'I wish things had worked out differently for you.' Anna said nothing but Peggy continued. 'We haven't cut you out. We'll sort things out legally in the next few months.'

'Thanks for telling me but I'm not bothered about my share. Kate and Jed deserve the nursery after all the work they've put in. I have a home and Nick won't let me starve.'

'Once men have another wife and family, they're often not so keen to support the original one. Women need to be independent these days.' Peggy tapped on the table to make her point.

'I am thinking of going back to work.' Was she? The words came as a surprise but once spoken seemed to require more detail. 'I have a young friend who might be interested in being my nanny. The children adore her.'

Anna and her mother were interrupted by the sounds of conversation drifting through from the sitting room. Peggy began laying out mugs onto a tray and Anna took this chance to find her sister alone, clearing the dining table. There was something Anna wanted to ask.

'Kate, did you use my situation, I mean what has happened between me and Nick, to get your way here?' Anna asked her bluntly.

Kate didn't look up from stacking dirty plates.

'Of course I did. It made sense. Is there a problem?'

'No,' replied Anna. 'I just needed to know.'

Anna read Nick's text early on Sunday morning. Jess had a bug, and he was taking her home. Could she possibly consider setting off now? Anna was already up and dressed, since Hughie had woken her at five, and it took only a few moments to throw their things into her overnight bag. She scribbled a note for her parents and propped it against the kettle. It was a relief to leave. Her daughter needed her.

Driving home, Anna thought it unlikely she would see her family more often, even though it was now possible. Her reluctance to visit hadn't, after all, been about Nick and his work or the size of her family, although Nick had always been unwilling to help her father. His barely concealed boredom, as he wandered around her parents' house, had been embarrassing. The distance between me and my family is real, Anna thought, and it's because I don't fit in. It hadn't mattered before because she and Nick had made a family of their own. But now she was adrift and her parents, with Kate and Jed, were a unit. Out of duty and love her parents would try to include her but the truth was, she was on the outside.

At half past eight Anna stopped at a service station just south of Leeds as Hughie needed to be fed and Christopher was shouting for juice. She hadn't thought about how she would negotiate a stop on her own, with two babies. She unloaded the double buggy and a man, positioned by the entrance selling breakdown cover, gallantly held open the door as she ploughed towards him. The entry into the baby changing room was too narrow for the buggy, so she had to unload the children. With Hughie propped in the crook of one arm, Anna only just caught Christopher by the back of his dungarees before he ran off and he gave a high-pitched squeal of protest. Anna propped the door open with her back and kicked the buggy sideways into the changing room. Christopher continued to scream, and passers-by stared. Anna felt heat and sweat prickle up her neck and face and through her hair. The door slammed behind her, and she lowered Hughie into the buggy. More roughly than she intended, she shoved Christopher down into his seat and tightened the harness around him. Turning her back on him, she lifted Hughie onto the changing table, ignoring Christopher's crescendo of rage that bounced around the tiled walls, causing her eardrums to throb. Next, it was Christopher's turn and she worked fast, not looking at his face or speaking to him. With both babies strapped back into the buggy, Hughie turning his head to stare at his brother's fury, she sat on the toilet, her fingers pressed against her brow, elbows resting on her knees.

Getting out of the changing room involved the same rigmarole as getting in. She wanted to run back to the car, but she still had to feed Hughie and give Christopher some breakfast. You can do this, Anna, she argued with herself, you can manage. Other women manage. In the cafe she found a fruit drink for Christopher and gave it to him immediately. The silence fell across her shoulders and temples like a blanket. She bought a large cappuccino, a croissant and a muffin, and went to pay.

'I'm sorry, I gave him the juice first,' Anna apologised to the girl at the till.

'Don't worry,' she replied, 'I could see you were struggling. If you hadn't given him something, one of the other customers would have done it for you. There's a highchair over there.' She nodded towards the tables.

Christopher hiccupped over the injustice of his treatment, mixing juice and crumbs on his tray with wide sweeps of his hand. Anna fed Hughie and sipped her coffee, feeling the adrenaline drain from her body, leaving her weak and shaken. She looked out at the rural scene beyond the service station; unexpected fields and hedgerows framed by a deep picture window. The motorway snaked through a gap in the hills, the cars progressing like beads on a rosary.

She caught Christopher's eye and reached out to stroke his head. He wasn't quite ready to forgive her and drew away. Hughie was already asleep, and Anna strapped him back into the buggy. She lifted Christopher from his highchair and held him close, rubbing his back. He permitted himself to lean into her chest and suck his thumb. Anna finally looked around at the world within the service station. There was enough food to feed passengers on a cruise liner, a television on the wall played twenty-four-hour news, flickering fruit machines satisfied those who needed to gamble and there were shops, toilets, flowers, newspapers ... She closed her eyes; perhaps she could just rest here for a while.

But there was a sick child at home who needed her, so she kissed Christopher again and put him down next to his brother. It will get easier, Anna said aloud, already thinking about her blog and how best to describe this journey for her readers. What mattered, she thought, was what she could do differently next time. That's what she would share.

Easy access to money, that's another convenience these places share, Anna thought, as she pushed her card into the slot and typed her pin number. She peered at the screen and blinked. Puzzled, she read the message again. No funds available. Contact your bank for further information. Anna tried three more times, but the message was the same. She looked around, as if the answer lay in the faces of the men and women streaming past. A man behind her coughed, letting her know that he was waiting.

Outside it was raining and Anna pushed the buggy across the shining tarmac between rows of cars. In her confusion she couldn't remember where she'd left her car and had to track up and down the rows, flicking her car key, hoping to spot a flash in response. As she ran, wind and rain now hitting the babies full in the face, Anna tried to understand how they could have possibly spent everything in their joint account. Her mind searched through recent bills and expenses, but she found no answers. Anna found the car at last, nowhere near where she thought she'd left it, and settled the boys in the back drying their wet faces with a piece of shredded tissue from her pocket. The squall had passed, and she leaned against the car to draw breath. Surely not, she thought. Nick wouldn't do that. But she'd heard it said many times by women living through a toxic separation, she'd listened to their shock and despair: 'He even emptied the account, Anna, so I'd have no money. He emptied the account.'

CHAPTER 22

'Where will they sleep?' Jenny asked Nick as they closed the door behind Anna.

'Not in front of them,' Nick hissed, 'they're not stupid.'

Jess and Cara were standing holding their coats, their faces pale and solemn under the light over the doormat. Nick saw Jenny's eyes glisten and she blinked.

'I'm going up to my study.' Jenny retrieved her briefcase from the floor and pushed past him. Nick and his daughters listened to her footsteps pound up the narrow, hidden stairs and a door slammed.

Cara looked at her father and shook her head. 'She's angry with you.'

He made a grimace. 'Yes, I'm afraid she is.'

'Is she my stepmother?' Jess asked.

'Sort of,' he replied, 'but just call her Jenny.'

'Stepmothers are wicked.' Jess glanced at Cara for reassurance.

'Not nowadays.' Nick bent down, level with her eyes

and unpeeled her scarf. 'Only in fairy stories. Now let's get you both settled and see what we can find on the TV.'

After what he judged to be a safe interlude, Nick hesitated outside the study door and knocked, pushing it ajar the very moment Jenny asked him to come in.

'The girls say they've had tea at home. They're happy watching a kids' film. Why don't you come down and I'll order us a takeaway?'

He saw that Jenny's eyelids were red.

'But where will they sleep?' she repeated.

Nick glanced around, revealing his hope that they might sleep in there. 'Not in my study.' She shook her head.

He heard the soft hum from her computer, measured the neat ranks of floor-to-ceiling books and journals. No, of course they wouldn't.

'I've thought of that.' He spoke a little too enthusiastically. 'If the girls sleep on the floor in our room, you could sleep on the sofa, if you don't want to share a bed with me in front of them.'

'I've got nothing for them to sleep on.'

'I asked Anna to pack their inflatable mattresses and they've both brought sleeping bags. Little girls have a lot of sleepover kit.'

'Okay.' Jenny nodded. 'Let's give it a try.' She stood up from her desk and reached for Nick's hand. 'Let's just survive the weekend.'

'Not survive, Jenny, I want it to be a success. I want my kids to like you, to enjoy coming here. Can we start again?'

At breakfast it was uncomfortable to watch Jenny's barely contained disapproval as both girls refused everything that was on offer. He felt awkward having to admonish Jess, under the critical scrutiny of Jenny's different parenting expectations, when she spat out her cereal after being persuaded to try a mouthful. If Nick thought about his girls at all, it was through Anna's adoring lens and he'd always accepted, as a matter of course, that they were polite, well-mannered and willing children. But here they behaved without regard for Jenny's things and had created mayhem by jumping on the bed and handling her tidy possessions. It was, indeed, an invasion.

It was a relief to get out of the cramped house and into the city centre. They trailed between estate agents, picking out rental properties that seemed suitable. These had to be near the girls' school, have a garden, three bedrooms, all of which made them stupidly expensive. Nick barely glanced at the leaflets Jenny pulled from the displays. He felt irritated that her first question to the agent was always whether the house was 'immediately available'. Unlike his student days, few were furnished. This was going to be more complicated than he'd thought. He'd wanted to move in with Jenny, maybe have the children one at a time, until he'd sorted something out with Anna. Surely she couldn't expect to stay on in a house with five bedrooms?

'People must think we're a family. I've seen them looking,' Jenny said, with what seemed like a rare moment of good humour. They carried their tray laden with apple juice, coffee, and the cakes the girls had demanded, over to the table where the children were waiting. Nick had bitten back the words: 'You should have eaten more breakfast' for fear the girls thought he had joined the 'judgemental' camp.

'Probably my patients,' Nick said wryly, 'or yours.'

'I hope not.' Jenny's mouth set into a determined line and her chin jutted forward. He'd seen that look a lot recently.

'People have to get used to it, Jenny. We can't hide away.'

Nick sat down with Jess and Cara and spread in front of them the bundle of photographs and descriptions of houses. 'Look at these and tell me which ones we should visit this afternoon.'

He turned to Jenny. 'I've been thinking. It would make much more sense to buy a house together. I can't afford any of these.' Nick waved a dismissive hand over the photos the girls were studying. 'And still maintain Anna and the kids. If we sell my house and yours, it would be possible to buy something quite large.' Jenny stirred her coffee and licked the foam from the spoon with the same delicacy as a cat might take cream from the edge of a saucer.

'But that would take months. You need a place of your own right now so that you can see the kids at weekends. They can't keep coming to my house. You promised.'

'This one, Dad, this one.' Jess fought to keep the paper out of Cara's grasp.

'It's too small,' Cara whined. 'Daddy needs three big bedrooms because he has to have Christopher and Hughie as well. Tell her, Dad.' She rested her cheeks in her hands and thumped her elbows onto the table.

Thanks Cara, he thought. He knew it was true, but he'd thought he might get away with having the girls and boys separately every fortnight, giving him two weekends a month to be with Jenny. But of course, it wouldn't work out like that. Why on earth would Anna be so accommodating? He might even be expected to have all four of them, week on, week off. He'd have to find childcare.

Nick reached into his pocket for his mobile and held out his free hand. 'Okay, pass me the ones you think we should visit.'

Squashed into the double bed with Jess splayed out next to him, Nick thought about the house that was his for the next six months. Two thousand pounds deposit, one thousand pounds rent for the first month, all paid in advance. On top of an existing mortgage of almost fifteen hundred a month, utilities on two properties and food and clothing for everyone, he would be bankrupt. Why on earth was the divorce rate so high? How could anyone afford it?

He listened to Jess grinding her teeth and Cara snoring from her mattress on the floor. These two would have to change their bedroom habits or they'd find themselves short of partners. Partners! Add on weddings (probably) and university fees; four rounds of sponsorship for student union bars at three years apiece. He'd have to talk them out of a medical degree. Dear God! When they hand you a baby in hospital someone should point out the giant blank cheque you've just signed. He rolled over to face the wall and Jess kicked him in the kidneys.

They should have searched for longer. He felt he'd been pushed into it. Being furnished had been the deal breaker. Besides, by four-thirty he'd been losing the will to live. The girls liked it because it had a swing in the garden. Jenny liked it because he'd be out of her hair, although she wouldn't have said that. She'd have come out with some perfectly reasonable comment about her place being too small. He was getting tired of reason. Where was the passion?

He wondered about sneaking downstairs and seeing if she was awake but remembered how she'd looked as she'd gathered up her things to spend a second night on the sofa. Luckily, she was short. He couldn't even have tried to sleep on it.

It was funny, but the person he would have most liked to ask about his new house was Anna. He saw her, head on one side, saying: 'It's not you, is it darling?' He wondered what she was doing. She would be asleep in that awful lumpy bed at Len and Peggy's. He probably wouldn't see those two again. That felt strange.

The bedside clock flicked to two a.m. How would they fill the day tomorrow? He'd have to leave Jenny at home to get on with her work and find something entertaining and cheap for the girls. There was the museum, maybe that would do.

Jess groaned and sat up. 'Daddy.'

There was something in that simple filial statement that filled him with alarm. He knelt and switched on the bedside lamp.

'Are you okay?'

'I'm going to be ...' he heard a projectile stream of vomit hit the wall and in its descent spatter on Cara, finally settling in pools on Jenny's duvet, mattress and pillows.

Nick jumped out of bed and lifted the sobbing child into his arms.

Cara woke. 'She's been sick on me!' she screamed.

'I know,' he called from the open door, 'I'll see to you in a minute.'

The bathroom was downstairs, through the kitchen. He felt a trickle of warm liquid on the hand that supported the child's bottom and heard it drip through his fingers onto the oatmeal stair carpet. He stumbled through the dark sitting room, knocking over a wine glass, and waking Jenny, 'What on earth ...?'

Thank goodness there was a tiled floor in the kitchen. At last, the toilet. He propped Jess on the seat easing the sodden nightdress over her head. 'I'm going to be sick again.'

'Wait, I'll get you a bowl.' Nick was back in the kitchen in two strides and snatched a wooden salad bowl from the draining rack. He held it under the child's mouth as she heaved. Jess shivered, her ribs prominent, her veins blue under her translucent skin.

Cara appeared in the doorway. 'I'm covered in sick.'

He heard more fluid trickle from Jess's bowel into the toilet and sat on the floor, still propping the sick bowl on his knees, his back against the cold radiator. Nick looked between the girls' pinched, white faces.

'Hold this for Jess,' he asked Cara, passing her the bowl. 'I'll start the shower.'

The bathroom filled with steam, and he pushed Cara under the stream of hot water. 'Wash your hair, that's a good girl.' Nick passed her Jenny's shampoo.

Cara now sat against the radiator, wrapped in a towel, her hair tousled. They waited for the stream of liquid to empty from Jess's poisoned insides. In between cramps, she cried and trembled, and Nick wrapped her in another of Jenny's towels and kept his arm tight around her shoulders, even though his thighs ached from the awkward position. He could hear that Jenny was up.

'I want to go home,' Cara said, without whining or petulance.

'Me too,' he answered, unsure whether his tone sounded quite as mature.

The bathroom door opened, and Jenny passed him a mug of tea. He saw her glance at her salad bowl.

'I thought I'd leave you to it. There's only room for one adult in here. I've been cleaning up the mess.' Jenny looked at Cara. 'Shall I dry your hair and find you a tee shirt?'

Cara shook her head. 'No thank you,' she replied with formality, 'I'm staying with my father. He needs my help.'

Nick carried Jess up the narrow stairs, his ice-cold feet finding the wet patches on the carpet where Jenny had scrubbed. She was in the bedroom, wiping down the wallpaper. The roses on the wall by the bed were joined together by a new rainbow, made up of shades of brown and yellow. The bed was stripped down to the mattress, an ominous damp patch in the middle. There was nowhere to stand. The room smelt of cleaning fluids and vomit. Cara, who had followed behind, squeezed onto the edge of the mattress and he put Jess down next to her. He straightened his back, easing the tension in his muscles and swept his hand through his hair.

'That's the last time we risk hot dogs at the cinema.'

'I'd no idea one small child could produce so much sick.' Jenny didn't turn to look at him. 'Or so much poo.'

'You didn't have a stint in A&E?'

'Other people were paid to clean up there.'

'Look, Jenny, I've been thinking. I should take the girls home. They need to be in their own beds, close to a bathroom.'

Jenny lifted her head and stared at him.

'And you need some sleep too,' he added, remembering too late the damp patch on the mattress.

'I'll come back as soon as their mother arrives. I'll text her at six.' He looked at his watch unnecessarily, as the bedside clock was quite visible. It was already four-thirty.

Nick crept into his former home, carrying the girls from the car into the hall, both wrapped in one of Jenny's spare blankets. It was tiredness, that was all, but he felt such a palpable sense of relief that he wondered if he would cry. He carried each girl upstairs and surprised himself by finding clean nightdresses in the first drawer he tried. He peeled the blankets from their shoulders, and they lifted their arms so that he could dress them. He pulled back their duvets and slipped each girl under. In a few minutes, they were asleep. He sat at the end of Jess's bed and watched her chest rise and fall under the sweet-smelling nightdress. He stood over Cara and saw her tousled, still-damp hair spread across the pillow. His throat ached. He swallowed and thought he should make himself a cup of something, perhaps a hot toddy. Must be coming down with something, an infection after all, not food poisoning.

Nick walked through the house while he waited for the kettle to boil. In the sitting room, a single baby's sock lay abandoned on the carpet and the girls' schoolbags were open on the floor in the hall, spilling their contents of crumpled drawings and unwashed lunch boxes. He picked up Cara's and smelt rotten lettuce and apple juice. A child's story book lay on the dining room table; a library book, weeks overdue. He tiptoed upstairs with his warm honey and whisky and looked in again on the girls. All was quiet.

In the room he had shared with Anna, he sat on the edge of the bed and sipped, enjoying the burning sensation of the liquid in his throat. He left a message on Anna's mobile and eased off his shoes, swinging his legs up onto the duvet. Leaning back against the pillows, he closed his eyes.

The bedroom door had opened. He heard the scrape of the handle and the brush of wood against carpet. In his dream, someone was watching him. She was standing at the end of the bed. He opened one eye. It was someone small. Cara?

'What are you doing here?' He knew that voice. Nick opened both eyes and struggled to emerge from a deep sleep. She touched his foot. Shook it. 'What are you doing here?'

He pushed himself up and blinked at Ros.

'I could ask you the same thing.'

'You brought me here on Friday, remember? Anna said I could stay for the weekend.'

Only Friday. It seemed like weeks ago. 'I had to bring the girls home. Jess was sick. Anna's on her way.'

'I was terrified, hearing you moving around, after what happened at my place.'

Of course. All the pieces of the jigsaw clicked into place. 'I'm so sorry, I had no idea you were still here.'

'But then I heard the kettle boil and that tuneless humming sound you make. So I knew it was you. I thought Jenny must have thrown you out.'

'I don't make a tuneless hum.'

'Yes you do.'

Nick lay back against the pillow and closed his eyes. 'What time is it?'

'It's eight o'clock. Do you want some breakfast? We should let the girls sleep.'

In the shower he thought about that inclusive 'we', a small word that defined ownership, belonging. His life seemed like a patchwork of broken pieces that had been thrown into the air, being caught as they fell by people who were little more than strangers. At least to him, Ros was almost a stranger. Anna might have a different view.

This was no longer his home—he didn't have to stay. Anna would expect Ros to care for his girls. She had more right to be here than he did. He would have to leave, go back to Jenny. The thought didn't bring any pleasure or anticipation. He soaped his belly, pulling it tight and trying to hold it flat. It was too much effort. He let the muscles go and could no longer see his feet.

Ros had made bacon, eggs, toast and tea and they sat at opposite sides of the table and ate. Jake was propped in Christopher's highchair, watching the silent adults. Nick sipped from his mug and smiled over the rim, as Ros wiped her plate clean with a piece of toast and licked the ends of her fingers. He knew he ought to ask how she was feeling.

'What's funny?' she asked.

'Nothing. I'm glad you've not lost your appetite.'

Ros frowned at him, as if she'd been criticised.

'I'm okay now. I've got a new place. Moving in tomorrow.'

'That's good. I've got a new place too. I'll move in next Saturday.'

'I thought you were living with her.'

He shook his head. 'Mustn't rush things with Jenny. It's best to take it slowly because of the kids.'

'They'll be okay with me now. You don't have to wait. Anna won't want to find you here.'

Nick agreed. Anna wouldn't want him there. He wondered if Jenny would welcome him back. He should try, at least, to help her finish the clearing up. He could offer to take the towels and bedding to the launderette, and she could get on with her work. It would be a start.

They heard footsteps and the girls appeared in the open door. Jess ran across the kitchen and leaned her head against Ros's shoulder. Jake gave a squeal of delight and relief at seeing more children. Ros stroked Jess's hair and peered at Cara, standing at her father's side.

'We need to sort your hair before your mum gets home.'
That 'we' again, Nick thought.

It was a shock when Anna banged on Jenny's door, with needless aggression, Nick felt, late in the afternoon. He held open the door, but Anna refused to come in.

'How could you? I thought better of you,' Anna hissed.

'I'm sorry, Anna, but I had to take them home. Jess was so ill, she needed to be in her own bed. I would have stayed but Ros was there,' Nick pleaded.

'You've emptied our joint account, you bastard. I haven't got any money.'

'No I haven't, Anna, I wouldn't do that. The money must have been stolen. Are you sure you haven't let that girl see your pin number?'

'Ros?' Anna shrieked at him. 'How could you accuse her of theft? That's so typical of you, Nick. You're nasty and suspicious.'

Nick nodded. This wasn't the moment to disagree. He knew that he wasn't nasty, at least he didn't mean to be, but he was suspicious, that was true. Within seconds, his suspicion, no—a creeping fear, told him what had happened to their money. He tried not to look at Anna as he reached into his wallet and passed her everything he found there.

'Here's twenty quid. I'll contact the bank.'

Anna snatched the notes from his hand. 'I'll do it. I don't trust you.'

'There's no need, Anna. Please let me do this. I'll contact them right now.'

Jenny joined Nick at the door, her arms twisted around her waist.

'What's all this about? I couldn't work for the shouting.'

Anna stared at Jenny and said, 'If you think that was shouting, you've a lot to learn.'

Nick leaned against the doorframe and watched his wife stamp towards her car. Jenny had already retreated inside.

Bloody Tracey, he thought. Bloody, bloody Tracey.

CHAPTER 23

It was late May. Even in the part of the city where Ros now lived, there were trees with new leaves that seemed liquid against the sky, and verges hung with hawthorn blossom. She had taken to walking out of the city, into dormitory villages, and beyond into countryside with farms and hamlets. The evenings were long, and she had no intention of joining in the chatting and smoking on doorsteps that filled her neighbours' nights.

Claire had given her no choice but to move into a complex for teenage parents, 'for her own safety'. The warden was the kind of woman Ros hated on sight. Given a choice, she'd have preferred someone like Anna; a woman who made lists and wore unfashionable, flowery dresses, but Jacki wore cut-off jeans and said 'cool' rather too much. Jacki was the kind of woman who had built her career on children's misery, she thought.

It had been made perfectly clear after the attack that while she needed more protection, she was also in some sort of disgrace. Jacki had said something about her having 'revenge issues', which she could only have read in a report. Ros knew it was because of what she'd done to him, pulling down his trousers, and the nail varnish. She didn't regret it but wished she'd had time to prepare a revenge that was subtle, something that didn't make her look like a perv.

Ros avoided Jacki and everyone else, particularly the young men, the 'new fathers' as Jacki called them, as if they were a boy band. But she didn't mind living with other young parents; the tiny flats felt safe, and it was cheap. Startling awake in the night from dreams full of confusion and fear, she felt glad that another human breathed on the other side of a thin wall. But there was no point in making friends right now. In Manchester she would become an anonymous student amongst thousands of others. Friendship could start at university.

Early on, Jacki had tried to persuade Ros to attend sessions at the local children's centre. She could join in with Baby Fun Time, where she might meet other 'cool' people. Didn't she know Jake needed to be with other children? Ros reminded her that she spent almost every day with Anna, who had two boys, both babies. Not disheartened, Jacki mentioned the crèche, where Ros could leave Jake while she attended courses. Ros said nothing about going to university in September although she felt sure Jacki must know. She'd been forced to pick a university from the list and had chosen Manchester simply because she'd never been there. She didn't admit that she planned to do her first year only and then transfer to Oxford. By then it would be nothing to do with them. For six years, Ros had smiled and agreed, but gone on to do whatever it was she'd first decided. Early on, she had learnt it was only the agreement that mattered.

Every morning she would set off for the children's centre but end up at Anna's, or if she knew Anna wasn't there, she would walk for miles.

Nick's father, Hugh, was taking Anna and the children to Norfolk for half-term and Ros was being paid to look after the house, so this morning Ros packed a small rucksack and locked up her bedsit, leaving a note for Jacki to say when she'd be back. Anna had wanted Ros to come with her: 'You'll be such a help,' but Ros had refused. She couldn't explain to Anna that she needed Claire's consent to leave and that would certainly be refused.

On the bus, Ros watched a father playfully kiss his baby daughter and she remembered her own father's rough cheek and his smell, like wet bark. She wondered where he was now, whether he had another partner and more children. If he had ever tried to find her, he would have failed. Hannah's path had gone dead.

In town, Ros stopped to pick up nappies from a cut-price chemist near the market. Looking ahead in the queue to pay, she saw her brother operating the till. She wondered whether to change queues but the line behind her was long and it would have been difficult to manoeuvre the buggy. She would have to face him. What could he do to her in public?

Sean glanced up and flushed crimson as he flicked her items across the barcode reader.

'Do you ever see our dad?' Ros asked.

'No.'

'Has he ever tried to contact you?'

'Fuck off.'

Ros packed her bag and paid, ignoring the stares of the other customers, as if being sworn at by a member of staff was a normal occurrence. She pressed on.

'Where are you going when Mum leaves? Are you staying in Leicester?'

Sean turned his back and began scanning the next customer's purchases.

Ros swung her carrier bags onto the handles of the pushchair and walked away. She had given Sean a second chance and there would be no more.

Anna had texted her to bring cherries, so she pushed Jake towards the market where crowds, anticipating the weekend, swarmed around tables piled with grapes, oranges, bananas, pineapples and early strawberries. She was soon lost amongst the mosaic of colours and the smell of fruit ripening and rotting. Stallholders called out, tempting her. She hovered, feeling the crush might be too dense, and found a stall at the edge piled with shining, purple cherries as large as chestnuts. She bought a kilo. The stallholder gave her a slice of apple for Jake and winked as he said: 'Cherry Ripe, eh?' Ros didn't understand the reference but felt better for his kindness. She smiled back and thanked him, reaching out for her change.

At Anna's, Jess opened the door, stretching up on her toes to reach the latch. The hall was littered with clothes, toys and an open suitcase waiting to be filled. Ros sat Jake down next to Hughie, who lay batting toys dangling from his play gym. She found Anna in the kitchen, her hair chaotic, her blouse mis-buttoned.

'Thank goodness,' Anna exclaimed.

'What do you want me to do?'

Anna pushed the list towards her. 'Anything that's not ticked.'

'What do you want the cherries for?'

'I'm going to make a clafoutis for the freezer this afternoon when everything's done.'

Ros knew better than to question the point of this, but Anna sensed that further justification was required and added, somewhat irritably, 'The cherries won't be at their best when we get back.'

Ros nodded, as if this made sense and picked up Christopher, who was hanging onto her jeans. She went upstairs to help the girls pack their cases. She couldn't imagine how Anna was going to manage the journey, and six days in a cottage, since it hadn't been explained how much of the week Nick's father was staying. Anna had thrown any such doubts back at her.

'It's just a matter of organisation, planning ahead. If I've learnt anything from this separation, it's that. And when to accept help when it's offered.'

Ros felt that these weren't the most important lessons Anna had needed to learn. Slowing down and making life simpler might have been a better place to start. She'd suggested that Anna take someone else with her to Norfolk, one of her friends, but this had been met with a barking howl of derision.

'They're all at work or busy with their own children. It is half-term, Ros.'

Jess and Cara had been told that they could bring one game, one puzzle and one book each, and this had created considerable conflict. Their bedroom was now strewn with all possible choices, and both girls were hot and quarrelsome. It didn't take Ros long to settle the dispute and she left them to tidy up while she changed the bedding in Hughie's cot, so that it would be clean for Jake. Hugh senior was coming at four and then every room, the garden, the plentiful cupboards and freezer would be hers.

Downstairs, the suitcase was almost full, and the kitchen table was set for five with a highchair at each end. The cherries glistened, wet and forgotten in a sieve under the tap, and Anna was buttering a mountain of bread. Ros joined her, silently cutting cheese, slicing tomatoes and lining up the drinks in an assortment of feeder cups, plastic tumblers and glasses. Thank goodness, she thought, there will only ever be me and Jake.

With her mouth full of sandwich, Anna went through the list she had made for Ros; the day the bin went out, where the stopcock, the gas and electricity meters were hidden, what was in the fridge that had to be 'eaten up' and would she remember to do a wash, 'whites only, don't mix the colours'. Ros stopped listening. Didn't Anna remember she'd been helping out since last November?

Nick's father arrived and stood in the hall, jangling loose change in his trouser pockets. Cara and Jess waited next to him; their faces solemn since excitement had drained them of words. Christopher was using the zipped suitcase as a trampoline. Upstairs, Anna was banging drawers and slamming cupboards. Ros said hello to Hugh but didn't want to hang around in case he wanted to chat. He gave her the creeps. She slipped away to be with the babies and found that Jake had fallen over Hughie, and both had decided to take advantage of being prone to have a nap. Ros pulled her mobile phone from her pocket and took a photograph, then moved Jake to one side so that she could take a picture of Hughie on his own.

The doorbell rang. Ros heard Nick's voice carry through from the hall.

'Didn't expect to see you here,' she overheard him say.

'Someone had to take them on holiday. Couldn't expect Anna to drive all that way with four children.' The father's voice was higher than the son's. Was he making a deliberate jibe at Nick?

Ros moved closer to the door and listened. 'Get off that case!' she heard Nick snap at Christopher.

Anna's voice now: 'What are you doing here?'

'Saying goodbye to the children.'

'You said goodbye at the weekend.'

'Not to all of them. That was only the girls.'

Ros heard Christopher crying. He wouldn't have liked to hear his father shout.

Suddenly, Nick faced Ros in the doorway, and she jumped back.

'Oh, you're here too. I might have guessed you'd be hanging around.' He bent over the playpen to stroke Hughie's head.

'I'm looking after the house while they're away.'

Nick stood up, pushing his shoulders back.

'Of course you are. But I could have done that.'

'Nick, we have to go,' Anna shouted from the hall.

Ros bent to pick up Hughie. 'It wasn't my decision. You know that.'

'Let me.' Nick pushed her aside and scooped Hughie from the mat, pink-cheeked, his hair dark with sweat from where his head had pressed against a teddy. Nick kissed the top of Hughie's head and carried him through to join his family, waiting in the hall.

Ros heard the front door slam as Nick left and she felt safe to join the departing group. The father-in-law present, but the father gone; it felt all wrong. She waited, unsure what to do next, until Anna clapped her hands and sent her in search of forgotten teddies and the drinks left behind in the kitchen. Finally, Anna hugged her, and Ros stiffened but tried to pat Anna's wide back, feeling the ring of flesh circling her waist, squeezed out between her bra and jeans.

Ros watched Hugh's Mercedes estate car disappear, pale hands fluttering farewell at the windows. She closed the front door and felt their absence in the silence. They had gone at last.

She made a cold drink and carried Jake into the garden, sitting on a bench and letting him crawl at her feet. He raised his hands to study the palms where some bits of grass were stuck, and then he looked up at Ros, his hands flat for her to see, using sounds that were almost words. Too clever by half, she thought, lifting him onto her knee. They sat for a while, Ros pointing out birds, telling him the names of the ones she could remember.

Emily was coming to spend the night, encouraged to lie to her mother about a sleepover with a friend.

'She'll never find out,' Ros had reassured her. 'She's not careful enough with you.'

Emily had protested. 'She doesn't love me?'

'Not enough. If she'd been careful with us, if she'd been watching out for us, nothing would have happened.'

'You weren't careful with me either.'

'No, I wasn't, but I was just a kid too.'

'I can't remember you being a kid. You've always been an adult.'

Now Emily was in Anna's sitting room and Ros saw their reflection in the panes of the tall, darkening windows; two small girls, half-sisters.

'Come into the kitchen and talk to me while I cook.'

Anna had left a row of Tupperware boxes in the freezer, in strict date order. 'I've planned a balanced menu for the week, so don't muddle them up.' In a pointless but satisfying act of rebellion, Ros chose the one meant for her final night. On the kitchen table the recipe book lay open, and the neglected cherries sat in their colander. She had cooked before, part of her preparation for independent living, recipes like cauliflower cheese and Victoria sponge, things that no one ever ate at home. But at least she knew how a recipe worked. It was just one step after another, like arithmetic. She would give it a go.

The recipe book had been written by someone called Delia Smith. Anna talked about Delia and Nigella, waving her hands towards the shelf of worn cookbooks, and Ros had once believed they might be Anna's proper friends until she finally understood the irony. Emily watched her lay out the ingredients into a neat row on the table, alongside the mixing bowl and the electric whisk, a spatula, and a sea-blue rectangular dish that Anna had told her was 'oven to tableware'. She asked Emily to butter the dish, then whisked the eggs and sugar and folded in exactly the right amount of flour and cream.

'Where did you learn to cook?' Emily asked.

'At Whiteoaks.' Ros tipped the swollen mixture over the cherries. 'They thought we might need to cook for ourselves one day.'

'I can't cook anything.' Emily pulled the recipe book towards her and flicked through the pages. Ros saw that they were spattered with crumbs and grease from Anna's cooking and felt something odd, like being sad but for no reason. They would almost be in Norfolk by now.

She bent to put the dish in the oven.

'You must have cooked at school, in home economics. Or do they call it design?'

'I never have the ingredients, so I just have to sit and copy out the recipe.'

'That's what I meant when I said she doesn't care enough. If you were my child, you would always have the ingredients.'

'I forget to tell her,' Emily defended her mother, 'and in the morning she's gone to work. Is Whiteoaks the place where you lived?'

Ros pulled a chopping board from under the counter, onto the table.

'That's what it was called, Whiteoaks. I lived there until the trial.'

'Did they care enough there?'

Ros turned away from her sister, crouching to lift the salad from the fridge.

'They were okay, they were paid to care.' She spoke into the drawer of the chiller. 'They stopped caring the second they clocked off.'

She turned the tap, cold water roaring into the sink. With both hands, she pressed the lettuce down into the water until bubbles of trapped air caught between her fingers. Her chest hurt. It was hard to breathe. Tears dropped down her nose into the water.

She reached for some kitchen towel to wipe her eyes and lifted the dripping leaves into the salad spinner. Finding the wooden salad bowl that Anna said was from her honeymoon in Tanzania, she threw in the damp lettuce. She searched the cupboards for olive oil and balsamic vinegar, even though she knew that Emily probably hated salad dressing.

'Did you miss us?' Emily turned to look at her with eyes that were pools of dark liquid, like the melted chocolate Anna poured over home-made cake.

Ros sat down again at the table and fiercely chopped tomatoes, peppers and cucumber. The smell reminded her of the market. She noticed that the varnish on the salad bowl was missing in places, giving it the look of an ancient map, like the table in her old flat; the one that was burnt.

'All the time. I waited for you, I waited for her to come.'

'And she never came?'

Ros shook her head and scooped the glistening salad vegetables over the lettuce. The microwave pinged a reminder that their pasta carbonara was hot. She reached for plates from the rack above the kitchen counter and pulled cutlery from a drawer, throwing two knives and forks onto the table. She saw Emily flinch.

'If you were my child,' Emily said quietly, 'I would have come.'

The clafoutis sat in the middle of the table. The blue glaze made a satisfying contrast to the singed brown and yellow of the eggs and cream. The dark cherries lay hidden below the surface, only their backs visible like water mammals diving for food. Ros liked the smell and the sight of the dish against the table. Whether they ate it or not didn't matter. She took a photograph of Emily, posing with a beckoning hand over the pudding, like a girl in an advert.

They finished their pasta and salad and left the clafoutis to cool. Emily ate only a few mouthfuls of Anna's carbonara and picked cucumber slices from the bowl with her fingers, nibbling the skin around the edge like a rabbit before swallowing the translucent middle.

Ros served bowls of clafoutis, spooning over more cream.

'Yuck,' said Emily, 'it's just big lumps of warm fruit stuck in chewy custard.'

Ros tasted hers. She agreed but felt she should try to be mature, set Emily an example. 'It's French,' she explained, as if that made a difference.

'No wonder it's so disgusting. Is there any ice cream or anything?' Emily pushed her bowl aside.

Ros doubted this, but in the freezer she found some organic brown bread ice cream. She offered this to Emily.

'What kind of house is this?' Emily sighed. 'Don't they have any normal food?'

In the morning, after Emily left, Ros wandered the house and in Anna's bedroom her laptop lay on the duvet. She lifted the lid and found that it was still on and in the text that appeared, she read her own name. It was a blog and Ros read each post, scrolling back to the first entry— the day after she had met Anna in hospital.

She felt sick and a wave of something that felt like shame scoured through her body, quickly followed by anger, and then rage. Anna had used her. Reading this blog, it seemed as if Anna didn't like her at all. She had laughed at her, had enjoyed making fun of her and these followers had loved it. All day, Ros paced the house, wanting to knock things over and break everything that Anna valued, and Jake cried too, sensing his mother's unhappiness. Once he slept at night, she ran a deep bath and crouched in the hot water, skin burning, her arms wrapped around her knees, and cried until her neck and jaws ached. Ros drained the bath and felt her rage ebb, leaving only self-pity. No one was coming for her after all, not even Anna. Things would go on, as they always had.

She wrapped herself in Anna's dressing gown and took the laptop into her bedroom. Propping it against her knees, she re-read Anna's last post and clicked 'reply'. She would take her time and would try to be fair, but she would tell the truth. 'This is Ros,' she wrote, 'I want to tell you how things really are.'

CHAPTER 24

Finally, the children were in bed and only Hughie nestled on her lap sucking his fingers, as Anna logged onto the site. Driving back from Norfolk, where there had been no Wi-Fi, she had thought about how to describe for her readers their week away. It had gone better than she thought, since the cottage had been on a site with other families and there had been organised activities every day for children. Her father-in-law had only stayed two nights, but it hadn't mattered, as the children had been occupied and there was adult company if she needed it. In fact, there had been a single dad in one of the cottages with his two daughters, and they'd twice managed to share a glass of wine at a rickety table in the shared courtyard, the bricks warm and mellow in the last of the evening sun. Anna wasn't planning to tell her followers, but the memory made her smile. Inexperienced though she was, she had sensed his interest went further than their daughters' friendship.

Anna clicked the link to her blog and was puzzled to see that there were over two hundred comments. Something had happened; she was being accused of being a liar, a fantasist, deluded even. Scrolling back through the comments, she saw that more thoughtful readers were warning her about Ros, advising her to take care. At last Anna found the post written by Ros and read what she had said. She felt her scalp prickle and heat flooded her cheeks. The words were horrible, unfair and untrue. How could Ros have done this to her, how could she? Anna searched in her bag for her mobile and found Ros's number, furiously texting an angry and outraged response. But she didn't press send. She would have to deal with Ros face-to-face.

Anna couldn't sleep, her mind rehearsing and practising the words she would use, so that the girl would understand how wrong she had been. It was important that Ros apologised. How much contact they would have afterwards depended on how the conversation went but perhaps it was time to end things. Anna rose at four-thirty, raw with lack of sleep, and went downstairs to make some tea. Her laptop sat on the kitchen table, open at the site, and Anna pressed the keys to bring the computer back to life. Reading Ros's reaction again, she began to feel some shame. There was little said by Ros that wasn't true, but it felt like a lie because it was so different from her own version of herself. The Ros that Anna had written about wasn't real either, she was a figure created for the purpose of the blog, so that Anna could develop themes of interest for new mothers. But Ros wouldn't have understood. Anna sat back and sipped from her mug imagining how Ros must have felt reading her words. Immediately, Anna cancelled her blog and deleted all past posts. In her dressing gown pocket, Anna found her phone and texted Ros, 'Can we meet today? We need to talk. I'm so sorry.'

After two days of no reply, Anna drove to the flat where Ros had lived, with the two babies strapped in the back. Leaving Hughie and Christopher asleep in the car parked below the flats, where she could see them if anyone came near, she ran up the stairs and banged on Ros's door. Anna knew that Ros no longer lived here but there was the possibility of a forwarding address from the new tenants. She'd heard much from Ros about her bedsit in the unit, but it was all so negative she'd stopped listening and had no idea how to find the centre. Her knock echoed through the empty flat, but Anna tried again and waited. She wondered why the window was boarded up, since Ros hadn't said anything about a broken window, but perhaps it had happened after Ros left.

Anna unloaded the double buggy and eased both boys into their seats without waking them. She would try the local shop.

'Ah yes, Rosemary,' said Mrs Lapinsky, 'she's been gone for a few weeks. After the police came. So many of them! Cars, sirens, dogs ... happens too much around here.' Mrs Lapinsky shook her head.

That the police had responded in force was news to Anna, but she didn't want to ask too many questions. Mrs Lapinsky had to be convinced that she already knew.

'Awful, wasn't it?' Anna frowned. 'So frightening for her.'

'She was moved to that parent and baby place, for her own safety.' Mrs Lapinsky nodded.

'The thing is,' Anna explained, 'I've forgotten where it is. She did write the address down for me, but I seem to have lost the bit of paper.'

'Sorry, I can't help. Rosemary said goodbye to us and that was it. Gone.' Mrs Lapinsky lifted her arms in a gesture that suggested Ros had vanished in a puff of smoke.

Anna spent the rest of the day searching on her computer for the name and address of parent and baby units in Leicester. There were three, but for obvious reasons, no addresses were given. There was a phone number, which Anna rang, finding herself linked to the main Social Care switchboard. She remembered that the warden of Ros's unit was called Jacki and asked to speak to her, pretending to have forgotten her surname. The operator asked for her name and profession, and without hesitation Anna said that she was a health visitor, Jane Clark in fact.

Jacki answered the telephone and Anna tried to dismiss the unkind image in her mind from Ros's description of the woman, who sounded both sensible and friendly.

'It's Jane Clark here, Jake's health visitor. I need to finalise a few more details for my report. Is his mother there? Can I speak to her?'

'I'm sorry, Jane, they've moved on. Didn't anyone let you know? Ah well, the wheels turn slowly in Social Care.' Jacki laughed, with an ex-smoker's wet growl, followed by a deep cough. Anna waited for Jacki to recover.

'Is there a forwarding address for Ros?'

Jacki coughed again. 'Can't give that out over the phone, even to you. You must already have her mobile number. Why not give her a ring? She went to Manchester if that helps at all. She'll have enrolled with a doctor by now, so you'll find her through your professional contacts if it's urgent.'

Anna thanked Jacki for her help, but Jacki hadn't finished. 'I'm not sure if this is any help for your report but Ros didn't do herself any favours here with the other parents. She didn't mix, and she could be harsh with some of them, especially those she thought weren't very bright. And then there was the humiliation thing.'

'What humiliation thing?' Anna wasn't sure if she wanted to hear any more.

'Can't blame the girl for hitting the intruder hard, anyone would, especially with a baby in the flat. But when he was unconscious, she pulled down his trousers, left him with a bare bum, and wrote on it. It wasn't the first time the lad had attacked her, and it seems that his team are not planning any legal action but before she went, we were trying to sort out some counselling to address her anger, her need for revenge. As you know, she doesn't easily accept help ... not too surprising considering her background.'

There was a pause as Jacki waited for her response. Anna struggled to find the words to thank Jacki for her help, to keep her voice level and professional. Why had she not known this? What was Ros's real background? Jacki was right, Ros's action had been serious and troubling.

'Might not be important,' Jacki concluded, 'but gives you more of a picture.'

Anna knew that she had reached a dead end in her hunt for Ros and ended the call. Finding Ros had become essential; it was no longer about an apology, she needed to learn the truth. She took Jacki's advice and tried ringing Ros's number again, but it rang unanswered and then switched off. Anna sent Ros another text: 'I've heard that you're in Manchester. Please get in touch. I want to apologise.'

Now, she could only wait.

CHAPTER 25

Cara was spending the afternoon doing handstands, which meant that Nick's attempts to read the newspaper were interrupted by a regular smacking sound as her bare feet hit the wall. He kept forgetting not to look up at the sound, so he was too frequently exposed to the sight of her generous belly, porky thighs, and Barbie knickers. There was no doubt about it, the child was fat. He would have to speak to Anna tomorrow.

Christopher ran around the settee, whooping. Nick wondered whether he might be hyperactive, but Anna had tossed the idea aside.

'He's not like that at home,' she lectured, 'he just needs a bit of structure. Why don't you take him out?'

Nick hated the word 'just', particularly when used by Anna. It always had the ring of criticism.

'Of course I take him out. His behaviour is even worse.'

Anna had sighed, her eyes darting back to the car, as if he was wasting her time.

'I'm not going to argue. You have a choice. Play with him here or take him out. Go to the park or something, where he can run around. And don't forget that Madison is bringing Hughie around later, just for an hour or two.'

Nick yawned and stretched. He'd better get moving in case, heaven forbid, he missed the delights of Hughie's 'access' visit.

'Come on you two, let's go to the park.'

Cara swung her legs down from the wall and jumped in front of him, her face pink and shiny.

'Can we have an ice cream?'

Christopher circumnavigated the sofa in the opposite direction, shouting, 'ice cream, ice cream,' like a market trader.

'Of course, we'll have an ice cream,' Nick promised, wondering how they could walk far enough so that Cara might burn off the calories.

It was one of those disappointing summer days, when the sky seemed brown and leaden, yet it felt warm and sticky. The leaves on the trees and ubiquitous park shrubbery hung limp and faded, as if they couldn't muster up the energy to do anything interesting like flutter or turn a golden brown.

In the play area, Christopher rocked frantically on a crazy-looking duck, which seemed to throw itself forward to peck at the wood chips scattered on the ground, then rear backwards as if poisoned. Cara was scrambling up the climbing frame for the twentieth time, those Barbie knickers visible again but from a different angle, bellowing, 'Look at me, Dad,' every time she reached the top. He encouraged her to keep going. The five hundred calories in her double vanilla cone with chocolate flake and raspberry sauce would take some undoing.

Nick stood behind Christopher, wary of the possibility of whiplash injury. He thought of Anna, how foxy she had looked this morning with her hair cut short and dyed blonde. She must have lost at least three stone. Something had happened to change his ex-wife. Before, when she'd dropped off the children, she'd hung around as if she couldn't bear to leave them. Now it was as if she couldn't wait to get away. He couldn't get rid of a picture in his mind of her lying naked on their bed making love to some predatory creep with a paunch and nose hair.

He hoped Jenny would come for dinner and checked his mobile for a text. Nothing. He looked at his watch. Ten past three. Last time he checked it was eight minutes past.

Nick called the children and they walked along the paths that crossed the park, taking the longest route possible. Their pace was slow as he hadn't brought the pushchair. Christopher was creating a lexicon of park-related vocabulary. He would point to an object and Nick had to give the word. Failure to do so resulted in a lying-on-the-path tantrum. So far, they'd covered bandstand, fountain, pond, sprinkler, seagull, dog poo and bench. Cara maintained a stream-of-consciousness monologue, interspersed with brief, hopeful silences, regretfully always broken by: 'Shall I tell you another thing, Dad?' Elderly dog walkers said 'hello' and someone said 'Afternoon, Dr McNeill,' but he had no glimmer of recognition. He particularly noticed the other fathers. They shared a sideways glance that might have said, 'You and me both, mate.'

One of the advantages of living alone, Nick thought, was that he hadn't had to explain to anyone about how he'd been fleeced by Tracey. After the business of creating a new bank account and being sent new cards, all he'd done was move money from a personal account into the new joint account and pretend that there had been a simple bank error, relying on Anna's previous indifference to the account, as long as there was enough money in it. It was lucky that he and Anna weren't rich, and by the end of the month there was never much left. He smiled, thinking of Tracey's irritation at discovering how little there was for her to steal. Of course, he'd tried to track her down, but her gym membership had been cancelled and she was nowhere to be found on the dating site. He could have gone to the police but the thought of them smirking over the details stopped him. Nick knew that was how she worked, what she relied on. He wouldn't be the last. Let the next chump deal with the cops.

Nick drove onto the grey, slabbed car parking space in front of his rented pebble-dashed semi and lifted Christopher from the car. They climbed the steps to the front door, the slope of the front garden supported by cracked and tilted paving with a mottled, pinkish hue. Someone had sprinkled gravel where there might once have been a square of grass. He noticed in the distance the nanny Anna had employed for the school summer holidays and waited for her, reluctant to enter the small, sterile rooms redolent with the whiff of other families. Ros had vanished, and he hadn't bothered to find out why, although he knew how much it had upset Anna.

'Hiya.' She waved at him, as if they were friends. There followed a complicated choreography; the artful dance unknown to those without multiple children. The sequence went like this: the nanny unstrapped Hughie, Cara held on tightly to Christopher because, in his enthusiasm, he was likely to fall down the steps, and Nick hurried back down to lift Hughie out, using a kick to collapse the buggy into submission. The nanny, whose name he couldn't remember, carried the outsized baby bag into the house. What a performance!

Nick made mugs of tea in the kitchen and sat opposite the girl on the carpet, although not cross-legged like her. Cara passed toys to Hughie, who gave each one an indifferent shake, then sucked on his fists. He smiled when he saw Nick and lifted his arms.

'What's Anna doing today?' He hated himself for asking.

'Don't know.' The girl shrugged. 'Seeing friends, I think.'

They finished their tea in silence, avoiding looking at each other. Nick picked up Hughie and carried him through the open patio doors into the garden. It was simply a rectangle of grass, grown too long, with a wooden fence on three sides stained an unpleasant orange. He could smell lighter fuel and burning charcoal from other gardens. Children shrieked, and he heard water splash from paddling pools. He could just see the top of a woman's head and the bounce of the line as she worked her way along, pegging out her washing. Nick walked the perimeter with his baby, letting his lips brush the top of Hughie's downy hair, and then crossed to the centre of the lawn, circling twice around the swing and the see-saw contraption that had been the deal-breaker for the girls. He pulled his mobile from his pocket. Nothing from Jenny.

Checking over his shoulder in case the nanny was spying on him, he knelt on the grass and put Hughie into the commando position. The baby collapsed and began to whimper as his face met the prickling, dry blades. Nick picked him up by his hands to see if he could bear weight, but Hughie's legs buckled under him. Father and son sat facing each other. Nick stroked his chin. He must remember to speak to the health visitor at the practice on Monday since Anna was clearly too busy with her hairdresser, gym and spa treatments to worry about the child's development.

The nanny left with Hughie at five and once Cara and Christopher were in bed Nick went back outside. Being alone in the sitting room when it was dusk felt uncomfortable. The electric light bounced off the white walls, the cream faux leather sofa and glass-topped coffee table. His own reflection was mirrored in the window, even though it wasn't yet dark, and he didn't like what he saw. His face was in the wrong space.

Nick left Jenny a voicemail. She might still come. In the fridge he found peppers and courgettes, and in the freezer drawer, two salmon steaks. It would have to do. He opened a bottle of wine, poured a large glass, and carried everything outside on a tray. He piled charcoal onto his own small barbecue and pushed a firelighter into the coals. Once they were hot, he drizzled oil onto the salmon and vegetables and wrapped them in foil before putting the parcels onto the grill. He creaked back in his cane chair and looked up into the slate blue night. Swallows still darted and wheeled, catching insects, and a bat spun and dipped close to the eaves of the next house. People were starting to go to bed. Lights were on in upstairs windows, and in the frosted bathroom panes of the house at the end of the garden he saw someone's shadow sit down to use the toilet and stand to flush it. He heard the water drain from the cistern.

The coals glowed in the dark. He took a deep draught of wine and refilled his glass. If she didn't come, he'd sink the whole bottle. He noticed that the woman hadn't taken in her washing. From his narrow patio, he could see the sheets hanging limp and wondered if they would smell of smoke in the morning. The letterbox rattled and he remembered there was no doorbell. His foot caught the edge of the barbecue, almost toppling it. He ran through the sitting room, tripping on Christopher's train set, and opened the front door. At last, Jenny.

She shivered as if it was cold, and her eyes darted everywhere except onto him. He hugged her, and she leaned her forehead against his chest, but her arms stayed tightly at her sides.

Nick led the way outside, picking up another glass from the coffee table as they passed. He dragged a chair across the patio and she settled into it, easing her legs into the corner, her hands between her knees. He noticed her tiny feet wrapped in navy espadrilles.

'I hoped you would come. Did you see my texts?'

'I was in the university library all day. My phone is on silent.'

'How's it going, the exam study?'

'Okay.' Jenny chewed on her bottom lip and peered down the garden.

'Do you want some food? I've got salmon steaks and vegetables. They should be cooked.'

She nodded and watched him tip her parcel onto a plate. She ate slowly, separating each forkful and blowing onto it before placing it between her lips, dragging the fork back through her teeth. He finished his in four mouthfuls and watched Jenny reach for the paper towel to wipe her mouth and hands.

It was properly dark, and he could hear theme music, which signalled the end of the BBC news, drifting through open windows.

'I've met someone else.' Her words hit him like a blow to the side of the head.

'Don't do this, Jenny. Don't throw it all away.'

'We have no future. I want more than this.'

'We can have more. I wanted us to move in together, remember?'

'It's too late, Nick. It's already started.'

Silence. He couldn't think of any words that might bring her back. Only ones that dripped with anger and jealousy.

'I suppose he's younger than me. Someone with better prospects. You can take him home to meet Daddy.'

'He makes me laugh. He's kind and generous. I love him. And he's single.'

'And how long has this been going on?'

Jenny stood up.

'That doesn't matter. I only came to tell you we were finished. You must have known.'

He stood too, gripping her wrist more tightly than he meant.

'I gave up everything for you.'

'I didn't want you to. I didn't ask to be a stepmother. It was just an affair. Now, please let me go.'

Nick let her hand fall and slumped back into the chair, his head in his hands. He felt her hesitate then heard the patio door click with polite finality. In the garden, something rustled at the edge of the grass. A cat snaked to the edge of the patio and waited. Seeing no danger from the inert man, it crept under the barbecue to the remains of Jenny's meal. Settling down on all fours, its front paws tucked under its chest, the cat delicately chewed through the salmon, its head on one side. Once finished, carefully avoiding the vegetables and the skin, it sat up and licked its paws and mouth, then washed all over. The man didn't move and, quite relaxed, the cat closed its eyes, only its ears twitching as the man's breath came in soft, shuddering sobs.

At eleven the next morning, when Nick had already been up for five hours with Christopher, Jess was dropped off by her friend's father, where she had been spending the night. He knew the man a little, from years of school fetes and concerts, bonfire nights and moments passed on tiny chairs outside classrooms, when they had waited their turn to speak to a child's teacher.

Nick couldn't remember his name, although he seemed to know his, probably because of all the gossip. Regardless, Nick invited him in for coffee. Any adult company will do, he thought. The man shook his head.

'Can't, mate. I'm off to B&Q. I'm in the middle of tiling the bathroom and I'm out of grout.'

'How are things?' Nick leaned against the doorframe and folded his arms, as if he hadn't heard the man's urgency.

'Can't complain. How about you?' The father grinned and flicked his head towards the open door, lust and envy moistening his lips.

Of course, Nick thought, I'm supposed to be living every married man's dream.

'Fine, fine. Kids are a bit of a handful but it's only every other weekend.'

'Lucky you,' the man said and leered. 'Listen, a group of us from the PTA are rebuilding the adventure playground before the new term starts. Come along to the school next Saturday about nine if you've got nothing else on.'

'Thanks, I might see you there.'

Nick waved as Jessica's friend's dad turned and trotted down the steps. He closed the door and leaned against it. He would be at the school next Saturday. Definitely. He had nothing else planned.

CHAPTER 26

Anna startled. The alarm had failed, and it was now almost a quarter to eight. None of the children had woken her, not even Hughie. She swung her legs out of bed and pulled on her robe, glancing into the babies' rooms. She could see the back of Christopher's head as he sat in his cot lining up his toys, and the top of Hughie's fuzzy hair, his body partially covered by his blanket. He was still asleep. She rushed through to the girls' room, woke them, and ran downstairs to organise breakfast. I wish I'd kept Madison on, she thought.

Anna threw bowls, spoons and packets of cereal onto the table, filled the kettle, then took the stairs two at a time, running back to wash and dress herself and the boys. As she opened the door to Hughie's room her attention was caught by the absence of sound or movement, a stillness. She approached his cot and gently pulled back his cover. Hughie's eyes were closed, his colour exceptionally pale. Rolling him onto his back, she couldn't see him breathe.

'Cara!' she screamed from the top of the stairs, 'call Daddy, quickly. Tell him the baby is ill. Now!'

Anna lifted Hughie's warm body from his crib and began to breathe gently into his mouth, covering his nose and lips with her own mouth even before she laid him onto her bed. She was terrified of damaging his lungs by exhaling too hard, yet desperate to feel him breathe. Again and again, she breathed for Hughie, trying to give him life, seeing his chest rise and fall but afraid to stop, even when she heard the slam of the front door and Nick's heavy footsteps on the stairs. Nick examined Hughie between Anna's breaths.

'Let's get him to the hospital now. The ambulance is already outside. They'll have oxygen. Go as you are. I'll come as soon as I've sorted the kids.'

Anna nodded, tears streaming down her face. She lifted Hughie from the bed and together they descended the stairs, Nick walking just ahead to support her elbow, as if he was afraid she might drop the baby.

Nick watched the ambulance disappear into the morning traffic, its siren wailing. He turned to the faces of the three children left in his care, their eyes fixed on his own in descending order of fear and confusion.

Cara spoke first: 'Our baby's ill.'

Nick knelt to pull the three pale children towards him.

'He was struggling to breathe but he'll be okay. He's with Mummy, so he'll be safe. You two girls go upstairs and finish getting dressed. I'll look after Christopher.'

Jess stopped after a few steps.

'He looked dead to me, Daddy. He was all white and he wasn't moving.'

'Babies can look like that when they're ill, Jess.' Nick picked up the receiver of the landline in the hall. 'Now go and dress.'

His father's phone rang unanswered, and Nick barked an order into the voicemail. He made toast for Christopher and the girls, pacing the kitchen as the children ate, painfully, almost deliberately, slowly. Nick glanced at his watch and reached to pick up the telephone from the kitchen wall. It was already ten. He hadn't let the practice know he wouldn't be in. He must try to get to the hospital, be with Anna, but not with these three. There was no option but to call Jenny, she was the only person left. Her phone cut to answerphone and he left a message, more conciliatory and pleading than the one he had left his father, but no less impatient.

In the bathroom he peeled the tapes from the sides of Christopher's sodden nappy, unchanged since the night before, and felt nauseous at the weight and smell as it fell to the floor between the child's legs. He cleaned Christopher with the shower spray and dressed him, pulling a tee shirt and shorts over his clean nappy and damp skin. There was no choice, he reasoned, but to take the girls to school but he couldn't take Christopher to nursery, he didn't know where it was. To his shame, he couldn't even remember its name. Christopher would have to come to the hospital.

'Aren't you coming in with us?' Cara pleaded when Nick stopped right outside the school entrance on the yellow, zigzag lines. 'We're really late.'

'I have to get to the hospital, Cara. You'll be okay. Look after Jess for me.'

'You're not allowed to park here. We'll get into trouble.'

'I've told the school what's happened. You'll be well looked after.'

'We've got no lunch,' Cara argued.

'You won't starve,' Nick snapped, 'just go inside, now!'

As he reversed in a nearby driveway, in his driving mirror he saw the girls' reproachful stare as he abandoned them, but by the time the car again passed the school gates, they were already pushing their way through the swing doors into the reception area.

Getting to the hospital involved driving past the house. Jenny's car was pulled up outside. He swung across the road making another driver sound his horn, and parked behind her, one wheel on the pavement.

'I need you to look after Christopher,' he panted through her open window. 'I wouldn't ask unless I was desperate. The baby's ill. It doesn't look good. Anna's at the hospital with him.'

'I thought you needed me for a medical emergency. This isn't my business. I told you, we're finished. I have a lunchtime surgery.'

'Please, Jenny, an act of friendship, nothing more.'

She turned off her ignition. 'Okay, I'll do it.'

Nick lifted Christopher from the car seat and handed him to Jenny, along with keys for the house.

'You'll find everything you need inside. If my father turns up—you remember him, tall, white haired—you can go.'

Christopher began to whimper and leaned way from Jenny's grip towards his father, hands outstretched. Nick hesitated.

Jenny flapped her free hand towards him.

'He'll be fine. Leave! I hope everything works out.'

Nick bent to kiss her, but she had already turned to walk away, and his lips met the back of her hair.

'Thank you, Jenny,' he called out, 'I'm so grateful. And when you ring the surgery, can you let them know I'm not available either.'

She turned back and from her expression, he saw that she was about to protest. The momentary hesitation made Christopher try and struggle from her arms and she heaved the heavy, twisting child back onto her hip.

'Nick, just get to the hospital.'

A blur of faces waited for Anna in Children's A&E. She was aware of corridors and voices, the crashing of trolleys and doors slamming. Finally, there was a quiet, dark room where Nick eventually joined her. They sat in silence, side by side.

'What about the other children?' Anna asked.

Her voice sounded different, low and catarrhal, and Nick thought for a moment whether he should lie about Jenny; pretend that his father was looking after Christopher. He found it mattered to him, even in this worst of circumstances, that Anna should still think he and Jenny were together.

'I took the girls to school. My father wasn't contactable, so I had to ask Jenny to look after Christopher. I'm sorry but I had no choice.'

'The girls will hate being at school ...'

'I told Jenny she could leave if my father turned up.'

Anna frowned. 'What do you think is happening to Hughie?'

'They'll be doing everything they can. We just have to wait.'

'I want to see him.'

'We'd be in the way. The best thing we can do is wait here.'

Nick bought tea from a vending machine, but Anna let hers go cold. She stared at a point on the wall, replaying the last few hours. There had to have been a moment when she could have changed everything. Why hadn't she checked the alarm, why hadn't she lifted Hughie as soon as she woke? Was he on his side or his back, had he been too hot?

Finally, she spoke: 'I miss Ros. I need her here. I text her every day, but she doesn't reply.'

'What happened between you two?' Nick asked.

Anna told Nick the story, omitting the most worrying details and he listened, his head forward, arms dangling from his knees.

'I can see why she was furious about the blog,' he said, 'but if you ask me, she's taking it too far with this silence.'

Anna found herself agreeing. Perhaps Jacki was right, Ros could be hard and unforgiving.

A doctor came into the room. Anna could tell that Hughie was alive by the way she smiled. She softly pushed the door closed behind her with both hands and since there were only two chairs, leaned with her back against the wall.

'I'm pleased to say that he's stable, but we need to keep him in. Would you like to see him for a few minutes?'

Nick put his arm around Anna's shoulders, and they followed the doctor across the corridor to where Hughie was lying on a white sheet, the metal sides of the cot raised. The doctor motioned to two chairs, and she picked up the baby, supporting his head and passed him over. Anna held Hughie's heavy, unresponsive body close to her breast and felt an ache to feed him. She stroked the top of his head with her cheek and kissed the curve of his neck below his ear before passing him to Nick. Nick cradled the baby and bent his large frame protectively over the tiny body, rocking back and forth, his shoulders shaking. In that moment, Anna saw that Nick did love his child.

Anna put an arm around him, her head against his and Nick turned to face her, his cheeks wet.

'He's a baby, just a baby,' he murmured.

At last, Nick passed Hughie back to Anna, who held him close until a nurse tapped on the door.

'We need to take him to the babies' ICU. It's just a precaution in case he has another episode.'

They nodded and stood together, passing the baby into her arms.

'I'll stay here with him,' Anna said to Nick. 'You should get home and rescue the others.'

'Where on earth have you been?'

Nick opened the front door to Jenny's shadow, framed in the panes of stained glass. 'There was no note ... you left no note. I couldn't imagine what had happened, you weren't answering your phone.' Nick crumpled into the chair that normally held coats and scarves and things put down and forgotten. He ran his hand through his hair and across the back of his neck. Christopher, released from Jenny's grip, climbed onto Nick's lap, and managed to place his thumb into his mouth while grasping his father's tie. He leaned back into his father's chest and ran the back of his free hand across the coarse fabric of Nick's jacket.

'I had to take him to work. I couldn't cancel my surgery, not with you off as well. One of the partners said to bring him in.'

'You went to work,' Nick said. It was not a question. He frowned, repeating the words as if trying to make sense of them. 'You should have stayed here. I thought you would look after him. We thought he was being looked after, not minded at the surgery. Anna mustn't know, not right now.'

'I did my best. I hadn't expected to be involved with your family in this way. He was well cared for.'

'What planet are you on? My baby nearly died this morning. How do you think I felt when I got home and found that Christopher was missing?' Nick's voice rose.

'You're being unreasonable, Nick. You feel guilty because you should have been here when it happened, with your family. Don't take your shame out on me.'

Nick rose from the chair, cradling Christopher in one arm, the child's head already nodding with sleep. 'I have to go and get the girls from school.' He crossed the hall, vigorously opening the door for Jenny to leave.

'One day,' he said, choosing his words with care, 'when you have children of your own, I hope you will remember this day. One final act of kindness was all I needed, nothing more.'

CHAPTER 27

Anna paced the house. Rain drummed onto the conservatory roof and streamed down the windows. She wandered from room to room, dry-eyed, her arms feeling strangely light, almost as if they would float away unless she kept them folded, too tightly, across her chest. It was as if she had put down a weight; that peculiar sensation of lightness that follows when something heavy is dropped.

Nick was at the hospital, taking his turn to be with Hughie so that she could collect the girls from school. Christopher was at nursery every day, paid for by her father-in-law. The empty house felt unbearable, even for an hour. She ran upstairs to Hughie's crib, tugging the sheets from the mattress, and buried her face in his baby smell. He was out of intensive care, he would be home in a matter of days, so what was wrong with her? If she had a friend, they would tell her, as her mother reminded her on the telephone last night, 'Anna, it's okay to feel weird. You nearly lost your baby and you've split up with your husband, why would you expect to feel normal?' But there was more, something she couldn't share with anyone, something at her core had been undone. She no longer felt certain of herself, who she was, whether she was worthwhile.

Anna lifted her face from Hughie's blanket as a new thought arose from her buzzing, sleep-deprived mind. I've been too busy, she thought. I could so easily have lost him—simply not noticed until he'd passed away from me. I can't even keep a baby safe. And losing Ros feels like more than losing a friend. It's as if a child I'd nurtured all her life had shouted out how much they hated me and walked out. How do women live with a child leaving like that? The not knowing, the emptiness, the shame that you drove them away. Waiting every day for news. I'm the sort of mother who doesn't care enough about her baby so that they almost die, and I used that girl, someone who had been used too much already.

In the hospital that night, sitting beside Hughie's cot, Anna decided to try Ros one more time, to send her another text, telling her what had happened. Perhaps this will make her respond, Anna thought. Ros cared about Hughie, even if she no longer cares about me.

A nurse passed the end of the cot and whispered to her conspiratorially, 'Anna, did you know that your husband is sleeping in one of the on-call rooms?'

Anna slipped her phone into her pocket, worried that she might be judged as uncaring, texting her friends, or scanning Twitter, while her seriously ill baby slept close by.

'Is he really?' she replied, guessing what had happened.

Nick arrived on the ward, the back of his head tousled with sleep, to relieve Anna so that she could be home when the children woke.

'So you've left her?' Anna said.

Nick's first instinct was to lie, to present himself in the best possible light, but then he sank down onto a stool opposite Anna and told her the truth, that Jenny had ended things between them.

'I couldn't face another night alone in that awful house. Even the hospital rooms seemed preferable.' He glanced up at Anna and tried to smile.

'I'm sorry.' Anna leaned across and touched his knee. 'No, I really am. I can't forgive her, but I am sad for you.' In his expression she saw what he was hoping for, to be asked to move back home, but she couldn't say those words. Instead, she patted his thigh and left him alone by the crib, in the half-light of the ward.

At home she felt overcome by exhaustion. She checked on the girls, touching their warm cheeks, and then opened the door to Christopher's room and bent over his cot, rearranging the tangled blanket from around his legs, pausing to listen to his quiet, rhythmic breathing. She waited outside her father-in-law's bedroom, listening to the rise and fall of his snores. Finally, she entered Hughie's room. She did not put on the light but picked up the rumpled blanket from the floor and smoothed it across the mattress. 'You'll be home soon,' she whispered, 'and we'll start again.'

Nick's father took the girls to school. Both Cara and Jess had become afraid of being left, but Anna guessed that they would be more willing to be brave in front of their grandfather. She battled to dress Christopher, as he refused every item of clothing with imaginative variations on the word 'no.' In the end, she took him to nursery without any breakfast after two bowls of porridge had been hurled onto the floor. The staff at nursery were usually resilient and patient and they understood why Christopher was so unsettled. Let them soothe him and feed him, Anna thought. I can no longer manage.

As Anna approached the glass doors with Christopher in her arms, arching his back to escape, she could see the manager's shadow waiting for her. She had no experience of complaints about her children. Even Hughie seemed to be adored on the ward, as he re-learnt how to smile and reach out for toys. In quiet moments alone, whenever she thought about Christopher, she felt sympathy for the struggling mothers she may have spoken to harshly in the past. Her demands had been unreasonable, her expectations too high, remembering those red-faced women, close to tears, while she patiently explained how they should be raising their children.

'And this is how I must look,' Anna murmured aloud, seeing her reflection in the reception mirror, sweating, hot and tearful. She put Christopher down and watched him run into the toddler room. Straight away, he snatched his favourite ride-on car from a little girl, tipping her out onto the floor. The nursery manager, an exceptionally young woman called Rita, led Anna into her office and offered her some water. Anna sat down and sipped from the mug, thinking about how much she would have preferred a strong cup of coffee. Rita, sitting opposite, ran her fingers through her hair and shook it out like a mane.

As if she had read Anna's mind, she apologised for the water: 'I'm sorry. No hot drinks on the premises—health and safety.'

'Of course,' Anna replied, 'that makes sense. I'm guessing you've some bad news for me?'

'We had two more biting incidents yesterday. Other parents have had enough. I'm afraid that Christopher really isn't ready to be at nursery right now.'

'But he's reacting to everything that's happened at home. Give him time,' Anna pleaded. She heard her phone ping but didn't reach into her bag.

'I understand, and we'd like to help, but I don't think nursery is the solution. I'm sorry, Anna, but I think he'd be happier at home with you. Pushing a child out of the home when there's a crisis might seem like a solution but it's one that works for the adults, not the child.'

'I'm not sure I can cope with Christopher at home, with the baby still in hospital.'

'This is a business, Anna. We're close to losing clients. Perhaps you could employ someone to help?'

'Do you mind if I read this message,' Anna interrupted, 'it might be the hospital?'

On her phone, there were two missed calls from Nick and a text. She read that Hughie was being discharged and Nick would bring him home. Yes, she thought, if Hughie is at home I will manage. Christopher should be with me and his brother.

Anna saw the relief on Rita's face when she agreed that Christopher would no longer come to nursery and was grateful for her offer to keep him there for the rest of the day, since they both knew that removing him now would cause a volcanic outburst.

At home, in the quiet of her kitchen, Anna rested her phone on the table, only just hearing the distinctive ping of an Instagram message as she rattled plates and cutlery into the dishwasher. Only one person she knew used Instagram—could this possibly be a reply from Ros?

It was a photograph of Hughie, looking up at the loved person who had once pulled her phone from her jeans pocket, catching a rare smile. There were no words, no text, but Anna studied each detail of Hughie's face and his hair, trying to remember the day when the photograph might have been taken. She held her phone against her chest and whispered: 'I will find you, Ros. Whatever has happened to you, tell me and I will understand.'

Jess and Cara were delighted to find Hughie at home but were old enough to realise that they had to tiptoe around this far-from-well baby. But Christopher was overcome with excitement and launched into Anna's lap, crushing his brother. Nick offered to take Hughie upstairs to his cot while Anna made the children's tea.

Nick remained to help with the bedtime routine and sat with Anna while she fed Hughie. He poured himself a glass of wine and made Anna a mug of green tea.

'This baby is the heart of our family after all,' Anna said, looking up from gazing at her child. 'Everything feels right now he's back. Even the children seem more settled.'

Nick felt the children's mood had every bit as much to do with him being there, never mind Hughie, but he wasn't planning to push his luck with Anna.

'He's always been the centre of the family, surely. Any new baby is.'

'No, he wasn't. Perhaps I'm only talking about myself, but for ages it felt as if he was an intruder, inveigling himself into what we had before. I feel so bad about it now, but I couldn't make the time for him. I resented him.'

'Anna, you were great. I know he had a poor start but that wasn't your fault. We can both make more effort now he's home.'

'It made such a difference having Ros here. I can see now that I came to rely on her and not just for the help she gave me. Here, look at this, she's been in touch at last. She sent me this photo of Hughie.' Anna held up her phone for Nick to see. 'When I saw this, I realised that we've got almost no photos of him. Take one of me now, while you're holding my phone, one of him being fed.'

Nick took the photo and passed the phone back to Anna for her approval.

'We must have hundreds of photos, surely. I remember everyone had their phones out at Christmas.'

'Yes,' Anna said and sighed, 'loads of photos where he's just there with the others but none of Hughie on his own. It's another sign that he didn't matter ... at least, not enough. Take that again, Nick, my boobs look too low, and my stomach is enormous.'

Nick reached for her phone.

'I'm not sure there's much I can do about that, but I'll try again.'

Anna started to protest but the house telephone rang. Nick said they should leave it unanswered, but it was clear that the caller wasn't going to give up. He hurried to take the call in his study and Anna leaned forward, trying to listen. From Nick's stilted tone it was obvious it was Harriet. As she waited, Anna knew that she should try to talk to Nick about their future, that in this moment of relief and harmony, he might be expecting to move back home. But she wasn't ready for that. This calm, compatible evening only meant that they could be good parents, but did she want him any longer as a husband or lover? Since she didn't know the answer, she resolved not to ask the question. No matter how much it hurt, he would have to leave tonight.

Nick slumped down in the armchair next to Anna, biting on his lower lip, his skin mottled grey and pink.

'What is it?' Anna whispered, 'What's wrong?'

'My mother has remembered where she saw Ros. That's not her name by the way. Whoever she is, she was accused of murdering her mother's baby, years ago. A photo was printed in the Canadian press at the time but obviously her identity wasn't revealed here.'

Anna felt the blood drain from her face and a sensation of needing to pee.

'No, not Ros. Harriet must be mistaken. It can't be Ros, it must be someone who looks like her.'

'Harriet doesn't make that kind of mistake. Anyway, she's checked back through the internet and found the article with the photo. She's sent it over to us. I've had a look, Anna. I think we've had a killer in our home, looking after our children. And what about Hughie? There's no obvious explanation for what happened to him.'

'No, Nick, no ... she can't have hurt Hughie. She's been gone for a couple of months. This is a mistake.' In a muddle of fear, guilt and an inexplicable rage against Harriet, Anna felt her heart race and leapfrog in her chest.

Nick stood up, his expression hard. 'That girl has hidden so much from us. You remember the break-in at her flat? That wasn't what it seemed either ... I didn't tell you because she begged me not to. She could have been slowly poisoning our child. Whatever you think, Anna, I'm going to ring the police right now. We have no option.'

'She loved him, Nick. She loved all the children. Ros wouldn't harm a child. I couldn't be wrong about that.'

Anna paused, made a decision. There could be no more secrets. 'But you're right about the break-in, Nick, and there's something else you need to know.'

CHAPTER 28

Around the kitchen table, the courtesies of tea or coffee refused, Anna and Nick faced two police officers, their bulky uniforms sprinkled with drops of rain.

The female officer spoke into her radio: 'Yup, just at the McNeill house now. Yup ... about an hour, I think. Say half ten? Yup ... okay.' Everyone waited for her to finish.

At either end of the table, two women who claimed to have responsibility for Ros's welfare introduced themselves. Nick began by sharing his suspicions that Ros had poisoned their baby; every word spoken as if double-spaced. He needed them to understand; the poisoning had been slow and careful, the effect cumulative, so that only after she was gone would the devastating impact occur, and no one would suspect her. As a result, the child had failed to develop and poor Anna—here everyone turned to look at her, another victim of this monstrous act—poor Anna had blamed herself. Nick saw Anna bend her head over Hughie as she listened to his account. She wouldn't look at him. You *are* to blame, Nick thought, despite my warnings you let Ros into our home. You didn't care what was going on.

'We've moved Ros away, to Manchester. We had to do it, for her own protection. The person you know as Rosalind Carter is actually Hannah Murray ...' Claire paused, anticipating a reaction. There was none. The police carried on making notes, their radios crackling intermittently.

'Sorry,' Nick interrupted the hanging pause, 'I'm none the wiser. Why did she need protecting? Wasn't it my family who should have been protected?'

Sally leaned forward, staring at Nick with an intensity that he recognised as a pointless attempt to make him feel uncomfortable.

'Hannah had committed no offence. She was accused of killing her mother's baby and the media were sure she was guilty, but she was found innocent at her trial. She was removed from her family, school and community and spent almost two years on remand in Whiteoaks, a secure children's home near Sheffield. On her release, she lived with specialist foster carers in Derby because she couldn't return to her family. She was constantly supervised by Social Care and later by us. It was all going well until she got pregnant and insisted on moving back to Leicester, where she's from. She was eighteen, no longer in care and had been found guilty of no offence. We could only advise her against it, we couldn't stop her.'

'Jesus Christ!' Nick's anger flared, and he glared at Anna, who had raised her head to listen to Sally. 'This is the woman who's wormed her way into our family, aided and abetted by her so-called advisers. We left her alone with our kids. Just because she wasn't found guilty doesn't mean she isn't guilty. Even her own family think she did it. I'm as sure as I can be that she's attacked our son. She's struck again.'

'Shut up Nick, don't be so dramatic.' Anna interrupted, keeping her eyes on Sally. 'What do you think? Do you think she might have been guilty?'

'She was left to babysit the baby and her younger sister,' Sally continued. 'Her older brother was at a sleepover all night and his friends could vouch for him. The baby had bruises on either side of his neck that exactly matched Hannah's hand span. The younger child's hands were much smaller and the brother, who's a year older than Hannah, had a cast-iron alibi.'

'But Ros loves babies,' Anna argued, 'she would never hurt a baby.'

'I agree,' Claire said. 'I never thought she was guilty. It's just that no one else was ever charged.'

'The baby's father, Hannah's stepfather,' Sally picked up her story, 'is in prison for sexual offences against boys but there was never any evidence that he had harmed the older brother. Sean was interviewed but he refused to speak. The stepfather was imprisoned before the baby's death, so he had an alibi too. He hates Ros, I mean Hannah, because he believes she killed his child. That's why we had to move her away from Leicester, she was being threatened and even attacked, by his cronies. Of course, she must be given another new identity. People are out to get her, and she could easily be found, even in Manchester.'

'Let me get this straight,' Anna spoke, 'Ros, I mean Hannah, was trusted enough by her mother to babysit two younger children, but that night was falsely accused of killing the baby. She was removed from her home and was never allowed back. Is that what you're telling us?'

'Yes, that sums it up,' Claire said.

'But that's a disgrace.' Anna's voice rose. 'She was twelve for heaven's sake. I can't imagine being twelve and suddenly taken by strangers to a place you don't know—waking up in the morning to a world that's utterly changed.'

Nick shifted his body towards her, his tone impatient.

'Yes, yes, we can all feel some sympathy for Ros's situation but surely our child's fate is more important?' He addressed the police, who sat silently. 'I assume you knew all about this person, Hannah Murray, but were in collusion with these two do-gooders. My wife finally came clean last night and told me she'd found out something about Ros's reaction to the intruder. It wasn't considered normal—something about revenge issues? Well, she has plenty of reason to hate my wife and want revenge. Perhaps this was her way of punishing Anna.' He saw Anna's neck flush.

In that moment, Anna felt only dislike for Nick. Last night, any hopes she had held about sharing the truth and facing this crisis together had vanished in the mire of Nick's self-satisfied outrage. She spoke softly, her calm words masking her anger. 'There's no connection. The timing's all wrong.'

She turned to the group, to explain. 'Ros found out that I'd been writing about her in a blog. I made her seem vulnerable and naive, and of course, she's neither of those things. Reading it made her angry, she's so proud. It's why we haven't spoken for months. If she was poisoning Hughie, and I don't believe she was, it wasn't because of that.'

The female officer looked up from her notes. 'The details of what happened following the attack on Ros Carter are confidential, so I can't share them with you, although it appears that someone already has.' She stared at Claire and Sally, as if the blame lay with them, or at least their department.

'I'm sorry,' Anna whispered. 'It was me. I just wanted to find out where Ros was living, so I pretended to be someone else and spoke to a person who might know. She wasn't discreet, but then she thought I was involved professionally. She told me about the revenge. I tricked her. I wish I hadn't said anything to my husband, it's made him more certain he's right about Ros.'

Nick ignored Anna and turned to Claire and Sally.

'I feel I should sue you two for letting that little bitch near my family. Why didn't you warn us?'

'I can understand your feelings,' Sally kept her voice low and deferential, trained to deal with angry men, 'but for some time we didn't know she was spending so much time here. Ros may not be a killer but she's a skilled liar. Like Anna, I don't think Ros would harm a baby.'

'Poor Ros.' Anna worked a damp tissue between her fingers until it lay in shreds on the table. 'What happened to her at Whiteoaks?'

'We didn't know her then,' Claire said, 'but I understand that she didn't speak for a year. Once she trusted the adults enough to learn, they found she had a fierce intelligence, but I don't think they ever reached her emotionally. I think she had started to make those connections with you and your family. She must have thought it had all been a pretence when she read your blog. It would have broken her.'

Nick, slouched in his chair, picking at toast crumbs on the table, sat up, thrust his hands into his pockets and pushed his shoulders back.

'Oh, boo-hoo, don't waste any more of my time. That girl might have killed our baby, the rest is irrelevant. Your monitoring of her was negligent, bordering on criminal, even if she played no role in Hughie's illness.'

The police stood to leave, pushing their notebooks into pockets. The male officer leaned towards Nick, using his body to block their conversation from the eyes of the group.

'Even if it turns out this Ros Carter had nothing to do with your baby's illness, we'll follow up your concerns. Someone will visit her in Manchester today.'

The phone rang and Anna passed the sleeping baby over to Nick, to answer the kitchen extension. The police hovered at the kitchen door uncertain whether the meeting was over. Anna turned her back to the room and listened. Nick saw her flap her hands at him, miming pen and paper, and he passed over a crayon that was lying on the table, with a page Claire had ripped from her notebook. Anna wrote, leaning against the wall, checked some details with the caller and replaced the receiver. She remained facing the wall for several seconds, then turned to address Nick, but her words were intended for everyone.

'That was the hospital, the Clinical Genetics department. Hughie has a problem … it's an inherited condition.' Anna stopped to read from her notes, frowning as she deciphered the scribble. 'It's called metachromatic leukodystrophy or MLD and it affects a child's development from infancy. We all need to go for tests, even the other children. What happened to Hughie is part of the illness and will happen again. This had nothing to do with Ros.'

Nick's skin flushed and he pushed back his chair, rising to face Claire and Sally, who were already standing, their movements awkward, as if unsure whether they ought to stay, or leave the family alone with this devastating news. He swept his hair back with his free hand and rested a palm on his neck.

'I'm sorry,' Nick said, 'but it seems that we've wasted your time. Understandable in the circumstances, don't you think?'

The police were already in the hall and Nick hurried after them, passing Hughie back to Anna. 'Stop. False alarm.' Nick raised both hands. 'The baby has an inherited condition. I'm withdrawing all accusations against Ros Carter.'

The policeman patted his many pouches, and finding his notebook, scribbled a final entry.

'You were right to call us. I'm sorry to hear the news about the child but at least we're not dealing with an attempted murder.'

Nick watched them crunch down the driveway past the yew bushes dripping with rain. Although it was mid-morning, it was barely light. He leaned his forehead on his arm, resting on the doorframe, breathing in the smell of leaf mould and traffic fumes. He wasn't a paediatrician, but he had enough training to know that this news was bad. Hughie would decline and was unlikely to live for long. The girls ought to be fine, but they could be carriers, and what about Christopher? Nick closed the door, hearing the click of the catch, and went to find Anna.

In the kitchen Anna was still chatting to Claire and Sally, her eyes too bright and her neck mottled. He saw that in her relief, Anna had swung into hostess mode and was trying to persuade the women to stay for coffee. Nick intervened, saying he felt sure that Claire and Sally had work to do, and noticed their relief. They wanted to be gone and he wasn't surprised, but he no longer cared what they thought of him. His responsibility now was to share what he knew about MLD with Anna.

After he heard the front door close, Nick took hold of Anna's shoulders and steered her away from mugs, spoons and instant coffee towards one of the chairs.

'Anna, I need to talk to you.' He sat down next to her.

'I know, I know, we need to talk about this condition, whatever it is. But let me say something first,' she placed a finger on his lips. 'You owe me an apology but most of all, you owe Ros an apology. You wronged her.'

Nick tried to interrupt. 'No, wait,' Anna continued, 'Jake and Hughie are one next week. It's going to be their birthday. This is the right time to track down Ros, and you must do it. You must find her, Nick!'

CHAPTER 29

Ros pressed the button. She was late this morning, since her first lecture wasn't until eleven.

'Hello?' A voice crackled from the speaker in the wall. 'It's Jake's mum.'

The buzzer sounded, and she pushed the door open, backing through with the buggy. Jake pulled away from her as she stripped off his gloves and hat, dragging the string through his coat sleeves so that the gloves were secure for home time. Jake pointed to his peg, identified by a picture of an elephant as well as his name.

'Jake peg,' he said clearly. He pointed to the next one. 'Henry peg.'

He climbed onto the bench and waggled his feet so that Ros could undo the laces of his boots. She could hear singing from the toddler room and a baby crying. There was a smell of damp coats and lunch.

Janette, Jake's key person, pulled the door of the baby room behind her. 'Welcome birthday boy!' She knelt, and

Jake slid down from the bench into her arms. Ros turned away and hung his coat on the peg.

'We've got a cake for teatime, and we'll all sing happy birthday.'

'You don't have to. He doesn't know it's his birthday.'

'We never miss a birthday here.' Janette spoke too loudly, as she always did. Ros guessed it was because she spent all day with babies.

'Okay.' Ros shrugged. 'That's fine.'

She folded the buggy, pushed it under the bench and followed Janette and Jake into the baby room.

'Happy birthday, Jakey!' another adult called out from the floor where she sat between two baby girls, who were inspecting the contents of a treasure basket, their concentration intense. Ros hated the staff calling him Jakey.

He held onto her finger, swinging against her leg, surveying the room. She knew he was considering the scene, weighing up which group to join. Soon he left her for the water tray. He studied the other children, mechanically holding up each arm as Janette put on his waterproof apron. Ros saw him hesitate, then grasp a plastic tub that no other child was using. He pushed it under the water and poured the contents into a sieve held by another child. They stared at each other. Jake smiled and emptied the tub again through the sieve. The other child laughed. Humanity in slow motion, Ros thought.

'We'll have to think about when he'll move up,' Janette interrupted, 'I know he's only one, but he's got more language than many of the kiddies in the toddler room. He needs more stimulation.'

Kiddies was another word Ros hated but she made the effort to smile back at Janette.

'Maybe we can talk about it when I pick him up.'

'Late lecture tonight?'

'No, I should be here by four.'

'You can leave him until a bit later. Have a drink after class with some of the other students?'

Ros bridled when they took an interest. Did her isolation shine out like some sort of beacon?

'Thanks, I'll think about it. I'll see you later.'

Janette touched her arm. 'You okay?'

Ros shrugged. 'Yeah. Just a bit tired. Had to finish an essay for Greek Lit last night after he'd gone to bed.'

'I don't know how you do it.' Janette rolled her eyes. 'When mine were Jake's age I could only concentrate on a catalogue.'

She cackled at her own joke and left Ros's side for a crying baby.

'Bye, Jake,' Ros called to her little boy. He paused and looked for her across the room. His eyes found hers and he gave her his heart-stopping smile. He then added the latest trick from his social repertoire, waving farewell with just his fingers, as Anna used to do.

It was raining as usual, and Ros opened the vast umbrella that had been almost her first purchase when she and Jake had fled from Leicester. She trudged the streets from the nursery through to Oxford Road, walking past Manchester Metropolitan University and Blackwell's bookshop before cutting through the quadrangle to the coffee shop opposite her base, the Faculty of Arts, Histories and Cultures. If she was early for a lecture, she usually went to a cafe on the opposite side of the road, when it was empty of students slopping beer. The high ceilings and Victorian fireplaces made her feel at home. Here she could sit at a scrubbed pine table in the bay window and watch buses surge into the city centre, squealing to a stop outside the Students' Union to disgorge hundreds from Rusholme, Fallowfield and beyond.

She bought a coffee and some toast and sat down to read through her essay. What she hadn't been able to tell Janette was that it was Hughie's birthday too and he was ill. Her chest felt heavy, as if she had a weight strapped to her back. It always felt tight but some days the strap pulled so hard she could barely breathe. Ros wished she hadn't had to run away but Sally and Claire had said there was no option. She was like an inverse scion of royalty; no expense had been spared, no string left un-pulled, to get her out of Leicester and into a one-bed flat in Horniman House and Jake a funded place at a university day nursery.

Across the bar she saw a group from her class. One of the girls noticed her and waved. If she was Jake, she would wave back and gather up her things to join them, but instead she smiled and lowered her head. She hadn't made friends yet. When they were paired for joint work or put together in groups, everyone was pleasant, but she didn't know how to take it further. She couldn't be with them on their nights in the town or sit talking around the kitchen table in a shared flat. A girl in her tutor group also had a baby but had to leave the child with her mother through the week and go home at weekends. When she found out Ros had a flat a few minutes' walk from the university, she'd become distant and sullen.

Anyway, she didn't have time for all that. What nobody except her tutor knew was that she had filled out another UCAS form for Oxford and had to prepare for her Classics admission test and essays, on top of her normal assignments. Anna had been right, she should have tried harder to keep up with her Latin and Greek during those long, empty hours in Leicester.

But what mattered now was to gain a place at Oxford and then present Sally and Claire with the decision. She wasn't refused much, but perhaps having supported her onto a course at Manchester, they might feel they'd fulfilled their obligations to her. She had been given all the resources any care leaver could expect. Another year of university funding was unlikely to be part of the deal.

Ros tore open a sachet of sugar and watched the grains float and then sink below the chocolate on her cappuccino. She tried to remember her baby brother but could recall nothing about him. He had been left in her care and died, apparently strangled. It was obvious who was guilty, but she had said nothing. Sometimes, at night, she had a dream where she was trying to save a baby from drowning, and these had started again since she'd heard that Hughie had almost died.

Everything about her was in the notes from the Life Story work that her social worker had tried with her, apparently so that she could make sense of what had happened. How could she make sense of something that had ripped everything from under her like a tsunami?

Eventually, she'd asked for the Life Story work to stop. It was just prying.

Ros closed her folder. She wasn't concentrating. Anyway, the essay couldn't be improved; she'd used all the sources and had developed her argument soundly towards its conclusion. Another top mark coming her way. She wished she could tell Anna. Anna had loved top marks.

Ros walked through the marble hall of the faculty and climbed the broad sweep of stairs that forked towards different lecture theatres. She took her usual place in the centre of the middle row where she could concentrate fully on every word Dr Barber used, watch how she moved, and notice where she put jokes; how she asked questions. Not too long from now she would be standing there. This wasn't just a degree course; it was work experience. At the end of the lecture, she hung back, allowing her now shoulder-length blonde hair to cover her face as she pushed her notes into her bag. She noticed the other students merging into groups in search of lunch and she waited for them to go.

She was the last to leave the lecture hall; even Dr Barber had gone. It was still raining, the drops heavy and spattering against the paving and she paused on the steps outside the faculty to put up her umbrella. She scanned the distance she had to travel to the library, weighing up whether to wait or to run. A man caught her attention. From the back he could have been Anna's husband, Nick, his hands pushed deep into his pockets, his collar up, head bowed against the wind and rain. He ran up the steps of the postgraduate centre and was gone. Ros found she had been holding her breath and the tight belt around her chest had ratcheted up several notches. She stumbled towards the library, struggling with the sail of her brolly, while the strap of her bag kept sliding from her shoulder. Through the glass doors she let everything drop and she crouched to find her access card. Water ran from her nose into her bag. She used the lift to climb to the fourth floor where her favourite alcove, with views across the university rooftops, was hidden.

Today there was an intruder. Her desk had been stolen. Ros dropped the bag onto a shared table and frowned at the usurper's back. She felt defeated, as if the effort to get here hadn't been worth it. She could have gone home and made a mug of tea, enjoyed the silence of the flat without Jake. It had shaken her to think she had seen Nick, but the man was probably one of the thousands of postgraduate students, imagining they looked as if they fitted in, wearing their hair too long and ill-fitting jackets and jeans from Marks and Spencer. In fact, the desk thief was one of them, and what was worse, he had a cold.

She ate her honey sandwich, brought from home, ignoring the sign that said no food was to be consumed in the library. Silly word 'consumed', she thought, why not use 'eaten'? She felt the tension slide from her limbs, bringing with it a curious heaviness and an urge to sleep. She opened her Greek language text. Some simple translation would help. Despite the sniffing from the abject party in her alcove, the routine mechanics of transforming words from Ancient Greek to English absorbed her and when she next looked up it was dark outside, and the postgraduate student had gone. She could do another hour or go back to the nursery for Jake. Her damp clothes had stiffened on her body, and she felt the need to stretch. The decision was made.

The rain had finally given up and the pavements shimmered with rectangles of reflected light from the buses. Through neon-lit windows, university staff pored over computer screens, finishing their end-of-day spreadsheets and emails. Ros felt the wind separate strands of her hair, dried in clumps after the rain, and shook her head to better feel the breeze. She reached the nursery and was allowed through the doors.

Nick was waiting for her, hunched on the low bench, his knees almost at his shoulders. She saw him but he hadn't seen her. It was still possible to run but there was Jake. She had to stay.

Janette brought Jake out to meet her, curiosity flickering across her face as her eyes darted between Ros and Nick.

'It's lovely to see Jake's daddy. And on his birthday too. Of course, we couldn't let him see Jake, but we thought it would be okay if he waited here, until you came.'

Ros dressed Jake in his outdoor clothes as if Nick wasn't there, her back turned towards him.

Janette sensed that something was wrong. 'I'll tell him to go,' she whispered, 'you stay here with us. I'll call the cops.'

'No, it's fine.' Ros stretched her lips across her teeth. 'I'm perfectly safe if that's what you mean. It's a surprise, that's all.'

Janette hesitated. 'Are you sure it's okay?'

Nick stood up, rested his palm on the handle of the pushchair and looked at Ros with eyes that were dark-circled and lined.

'We're fine,' Ros said brightly, 'we'll be off now. See you tomorrow. And thanks for all this.' She gestured to the party hat that Jake had thrown onto the floor and the bag he held up to her, containing something wrapped in foil.

Ros walked to the Oxford Road, side by side with Nick. Neither of them spoke. She didn't ask him where he wanted to go but took her usual route to Horniman House. At Lidl, she asked him to wait outside with Jake while she bought milk and biscuits. She paid at the till, counting the coins with her fingerless gloves, and saw Nick through the torn adverts on the glass panes, crouching down and talking to Jake.

In the flat she fumbled between the kettle, fridge and waste bin, dripping tea from the used tea bags across her narrow counter. Nick sat on the sofa across from the kitchen area making an effort to entertain Jake who showed him toys, one after the other, dumping them in a pile on Nick's knees.

Ros pulled the chair away from her desk and sat opposite Nick. He cupped his hand around the back of Jake's head.

'He's lovely, isn't he?'

'It's Hughie's birthday, I hadn't forgotten. I meant to text. How is Anna?'

'Up and down.' He pushed out his lower lip. 'We've had some bad news about Hughie. It would help her to have some contact from you, she misses you so much. I've been sent to find you.'

'How did you do that?'

'I'm a doctor, remember? I had Jake's date of birth and was pretty sure you wouldn't have changed his name. I was able to access his health records. Well done for keeping up to date with his inoculations.' Nick saw Ros smile at his weak joke. 'I knew you were a student here and made a guess which nursery he might attend. I was lucky.'

'I thought I saw you on the campus. It gave me a shock'.

'It *was* me. I did a further degree here, so I'm allowed to use the postgraduate centre. I thought I might bump into you but then it rained. I went for some lunch.'

'I had to leave Leicester … there was no choice. I was angry about the things Anna wrote about me but that's not why I left.'

'Claire and Sally visited and explained everything to us both. We asked to meet with them.'

Ros didn't ask why.

'And how do you feel about me now? You didn't like me much to start with.'

'I was furious, more with them than with you. I thought they'd been slack, not warning us about your past. You should have told Anna yourself.'

'And would she still have been my friend? Would you have allowed me into your house? No one does, not even my mother. But you're right, they are slack. I think they felt sorry for me and wanted to help, which made them careless. I've noticed that happens. And I wasn't easy to manage.'

'I felt horrified, at first, that we might have had a child killer in our home, but I've had time to think about it and I know you didn't kill the baby. Anna, of course, was always certain. She's been working on me.'

'I can guess what that was like,' Ros said. She paused, frowned, and cupped her mug. 'I'm not a killer.'

'Then who did murder the baby, Ros? Only you were in the house.'

A silence hung between them, only fractured by the traffic from the street below and Jake's chatter as he played. Ros nodded, as if she had given herself permission to speak.

'Sean, my brother. I heard him come back from his friend's house through the back door. It was never locked. I saw his feet on the stairs. When he came down, I asked him what he'd forgotten, and he said his toothbrush. He didn't tell the police he'd been back, so I knew it must have been him.'

'Why didn't you tell anyone? Your mother or the staff looking after you?'

'I was taken away to a police station and then to Whiteoaks in a van, with a social worker. It happened immediately. Because I was twelve and knew I was innocent, I thought it would get sorted. I was sure that my mum would come for me. But after I'd been there a week, she hadn't visited, and I knew she wasn't coming. Sean wouldn't have lasted, not in that place. He's not clever enough. I didn't understand how long people would think I was guilty … certainly not my whole life.'

'And you've never told anyone about this?'

'You're the first.'

'Oh, my goodness, Ros.' Nick was holding onto the back of his neck as she'd seen him do before, whenever he was rocked by emotion. 'It's time to sort this out.'

'It can't be sorted. Sean hates me because I know the truth. He'll never admit it. My word against his in court if it ever got there.'

'But why did Sean kill the baby, Ros? What possible motive did he have?'

'Come on, Nick, use your brains. Was it likely that my stepfather wasn't abusing Sean? What better revenge than to kill your abuser's child?'

'Perhaps he thought he was protecting the child from future harm?' Nick volunteered.

Ros gave a harsh laugh and tossed her head. 'You haven't met Sean. He doesn't do forward planning. It would have been an impulse. He probably heard the baby whimper and killed him in a moment of resentment. He might not even remember he did it.'

'We have to put this right, Ros, it's not too late. I'm burning with the injustice that's been done to you.'

'Thanks Nick, but who do you mean by *we*?'

'Me, of course, and Anna. Please come back, or at least make it up with her. She knows she was wrong, and she wants to apologise.'

'Are you two back together?'

'Anna seems to think she can go it alone, without me, even with the dreadful news about Hughie, which can wait until another day—assuming there will be another day. I thought if I found you as she asked ...'

'She might have you back?'

He nodded but didn't look up from his clasped hands. 'Here's the deal, Ros …'

'Imogen.'

'That's a classy name. Why Imogen?'

'Oh, I just keep dipping into Shakespeare. It wasn't Rosemary by the way, it was Rosalind.'

'And your second name?'

'Hope. I'm now Imogen Hope. The hope bit is obvious.'

'The thing is, Ros, sorry, Imogen, I know we haven't always seen eye to eye, but I want you to think about whether our home could be your home too. I wouldn't expect you to give up all this,' Nick said and waved a hand to take in the minimal contents of her room, 'but come home to Leicester in the holidays. University vacations are long and can feel lonely.'

'How would I live with you? Would I be a nanny or some sort of helper?'

'No, not at all. You'd be like a daughter, or a niece, or a friend.'

'But you don't like me, Nick, how would it work?'

'Actually, I do like you—you annoy me sometimes, that's all.'

'And you annoy me.'

'Okay that's fair, but Anna loves you, the children love you and I love them.' He looked across at Jake, sitting on the floor between them, eating the biscuits neither of them had touched. 'I could get pretty fond of him too.'

'What if I say yes and Anna still doesn't want you back?'

'That's a gamble I'm prepared to take'.

'Sally and Claire won't be pleased if I move back to Leicester.'

'To be honest, I don't think they'd mind. They told Anna they'd turned a blind eye to your friendship with us because they knew it was good for you.'

'Less work for them, I suppose,' Ros mumbled.

'I think they genuinely care. They've put their necks on the line for you time and time again. You seem to have that effect on people.'

Ros felt a prickle of shame and thought of Theresa. 'That's true.'

'Ros, if you do decide to come home, I think we have to deal with the matter of Sean and the baby's death. How else will you ever be safe? Anna and I will be behind you all the way and I'll persuade my father to fund the best legal team.'

Nick looked at his watch. 'I'd better go. Anna and the children have made a cake for Hughie, and they might have left me a slice.'

He zipped his jacket and put out his hand as if to shake hers. Ros put her hand in his and they stood awkwardly, like delegates at a peace conference.

'Oh, my goodness, I nearly forgot.' Nick reached into his briefcase and handed her a package wrapped in dinosaur paper. 'It's a birthday present for Jake. Anna chose it just in case I found you. Think about what I've said. The girls would be overcome with excitement if you came home for Christmas.'

Ros stood at her open door as Nick disappeared into the lonely whine of the lift and heard it travel down the shaft. She crossed the flat, carried Jake to the window and saw Nick run across the street for a bus, the hood of his walking jacket falling back and exposing his thinning crown. Ros guessed that Nick had no money, given the length of the transaction with the driver as he fumbled with a bank card and watched him stagger down the aisle to find a seat. Nick caught her observing and waved.

Ros put Jake onto the floor and together they opened his present and the foil package from nursery. She split the sweet, heavily iced cake between them and giggled at Jake as they pushed large pieces into their mouths. 'Mm,' she said, wiping her mouth with the back of her hand.

'Mm,' Jake copied her, wiping his hands on her jeans. Ros laughed and felt her lungs expand as she gulped deep breaths of air. Someone had released the vice around her chest.

CHAPTER 30

Anna's satnav announced that they had reached their destination before she saw the sign on the high wall that said Whiteoaks Centre. The building looked anonymous, like an ordinary business but one keen on security. She parked in front of the gates and left the car to press the buzzer, aware of the cameras perched on the wall above, like two black crows waiting to pounce.

Back in the driver's seat, she pulled her belt around her and waited for the gates to open. A judder in the centre of the steel mesh was the first sign that her presence had been acknowledged. The gates inched apart. Finally, there was room to drive through towards a low, modern, red brick building caught in the last breath of afternoon sunshine. Behind the building rose the patchwork landscape of the moors, shades of ochre and taupe lit by sunshine falling through ragged gaps in the clouds.

Her meeting was at three-thirty, when the children would have left the classrooms for their social areas.

She parked, one of only five cars in a car park laid out to welcome at least fifty visitors. The sky beyond the high wall that framed the parking area looked heavy and threatening, while the grey, slate roof of the centre glistened in thunderous sunlight. A minivan waited outside the reception area, presumably to take staff, not children, home to the low, stone villages she had driven through.

A new wind whipped around her ankles as she hurried to Reception. The door opened automatically, and she was contained in a small lobby with a glass paned security panel to her left, which overlooked an office where three very ordinary people were engaged with the usual business of offices. She tapped on the pane and one of the secretaries looked up and smiled. He reached into a drawer for a key and unlocked the window. The panes slid apart, and he indicated an electronic screen where Anna had to sign in.

'You're here for the volunteer interviews, aren't you?' The man passed her a lanyard enclosing her blurred photograph and details.

'Yes, I'm a bit early. Probably nerves but I allowed twice as much time for the journey as I needed.'

'You can't be too careful in December.'

'That's true,' Anna replied, glancing out at the darkening sky.

The man followed her gaze. 'Might snow later.' He shivered. 'I'll make you a cup of tea. If you sit over there,' he gestured to a coffee table and chairs pushed against the opposite wall, 'I'll bring it to you.'

Anna sipped her tea and glanced at her watch. Where were the other volunteers? After half an hour, locks turned in the door that led into the centre and a heavily overweight man with white hair and a grey-and-black beard beckoned. Once through the door, he held out an outstretched hand.

'Steve Miller, head teacher. You must be Anna McNeill.'

'Is there no one else being interviewed?'

He lifted his hands in a gesture of resignation. 'Believe me, we thought we'd gone to heaven when your application dropped onto my desk. Not many volunteers want a placement in a secure children's centre.'

'I thought I'd be facing a panel and lots of difficult questions I couldn't answer.' She felt relief and a tinge of disappointment.

'I think you'll be asking us the difficult questions, at least I hope so. I'll show you round and then you can decide whether you want to stay for a talk with me and one of the governors.'

Steve puffed and wheezed ahead of her through one locked door after another, always securing the door they had come through before opening the next. 'Keeps any trouble to one small area,' he said over his shoulder. Rooms led off from each airlock but there was no sound except for the sigh of closing doors.

'Is anyone here?' she asked, feeling a twinge of anxiety at the possibility of becoming trapped in one of these glass cells with a perspiring Steve Miller. It felt as if the oxygen might too quickly become in short supply.

'Oh yes, they're all here but you may not see the staff today. You'll only meet the kids once—sorry, hope running ahead of expectation—if you agree to help us. Then you can stay for tea, at least I hope you can.'

Anna was shown the primary classroom and felt a familiar sense of satisfaction with the well-ordered room. The displays showed children's work mounted with care and she recognised the well-worn rules for behaviour, or 'respect' as referred to here, that she could talk through with the children. There was a 'golden ladder' where Troy was almost at the top, but Alisha struggled near the bottom. She touched the teacher's desk and wanted to sit there, to feel that sense of anticipation when a swarm of children, tousled from the outdoors, would burst through the door.

She stopped to look at a school photograph; nine children of different ages, mostly boys. She thought of Ros and imagined her small, pale face lining up with this group.

'Oh, they're in uniform,' she announced.

Steve was flicking through workbooks, frowning. 'Yes, uniform for lessons. They change into their own clothes when they go back to their rooms. Just like home.'

'Do they socialise together after school?'

'Not much. We try to keep them occupied with activities. They vary widely in age and interests and most have therapists and counsellors to see and sometimes lawyers and social workers. The lucky ones see their parents. If they're spending time together, we do something organised like cooking or watch a video. By the way, we have youth workers for after school, in case you were wondering. It's important that the classroom role is kept separate, just like for children on the outside. We never leave them alone together. Remember, some of these kids are guilty of society's worst crimes.'

Ros must have hated this, Anna thought.

'I knew someone who stayed here. She wasn't guilty of anything.'

'That's what they all think. One of our main tasks is to help them accept the consequences of their actions, which is something most of them find very hard. That means facing up to their crime and accepting responsibility.'

'I think Ros, I mean Hannah, was different because she was allowed to leave here after her trial. She stayed on in care but went to an ordinary school.'

Steve folded his arms across his wide chest.

'Of course, I can't talk about individual students, but I do know who you mean. It's not unusual for a young person to move back into ordinary society if they're found not guilty. It can be hard on them though. Once you're through all these locked doors, we try to make this place like an ordinary home and school, but the difference is, we have highly trained staff and very small class sizes. Sometimes, home turns out to be a disappointment.'

'Hannah didn't commit any crime. She shouldn't have been here.'

Steve sighed. 'That's probably true of them all, Anna. Can I call you Anna? Not that they didn't commit a crime, but that they shouldn't be here. Most of these kids have been raised with violence, inconsistency, drug addiction, prostitution—you name it. By the time they commit their crime they're at the end of a long path, which led with almost total certainty to their own unforgivable act. They're victims too. All I can say is, many are better off here with us. We feed them, clothe them, educate them, and forgive them. Sometimes, they forgive themselves.'

'She lives with us now, at least in the university holidays. She's at Oxford, studying classics.' Anna couldn't keep the pride from her voice. 'She has you and her other carers to thank for that.'

'We're not supposed to know this stuff, but I'll break a rule and tell the secondary teachers tomorrow. It'll help staff motivation. We only hear about our failures if they commit another ghastly crime.'

'Does that happen much?

'Sadly yes, given their backgrounds, but the figures are much lower than for other parts of the youth justice system. I believe we make a difference.'

'That's why I want to help, why I want to volunteer. I'm ashamed to say that I didn't know places like Whiteoaks existed.'

Steve grinned. 'And from your CV, I hope it won't be too long before you're teaching here. Then you might wish you'd never heard about us. We're due for a visit from you-know-who. I wouldn't put it past them to turn up in the last week of term, when the kids are climbing the walls with excitement.'

Steve shambled on, showing her the withdrawal rooms for 'chill out time', the music therapy room and the art workshop, and led her through the social area, strangely empty of children's clutter.

'There aren't any toys,' Anna said, hoping she hadn't sounded critical.

'They're not good at sharing. Remember, most of them have had little of their own. Anything they did own might be smashed to pieces in a rage, either by the child or one of their siblings. We bring the toys and games out when they want to play and then lock them up. They do tend to destroy equipment rather than share it and it can get expensive. We give gifts for Christmas and birthdays, and they keep those locked in their rooms.'

'It's so sad,' Anna commented as they passed the bedrooms and she wondered if any child had heard her, listening behind their closed doors, waiting for her to leave.

It was a relief to reach Steve's office, where she was introduced to a governor, who was also the caretaker. Sounds of music practice drifted from the area they had just left. Steve went off to find more tea and the caretaker-governor introduced himself. He leaned towards her and whispered, 'That's our student who's got her grade five clarinet exam tomorrow. She's passed two grades in six months. In and out of foster care before she committed her crime but one of her carers was a classical musician. Children are like clay. Every adult who passes by leaves their imprint.'

Anna remembered the 'not talking about the students rule', clearly not strictly adhered to when it was a matter of staff pride.

'That's a very good way of putting it,' she said. 'I was aware of that when I was a teacher, but I haven't thought about it much with my own children.'

They waited for their tea, listening to the clarinet music stop and start. In her mind, Anna listed the thumbprints shaping Cara, Jess, Christopher and Hughie. Testing had shown that Cara and Christopher were free of MLD, Jess was a carrier, but the genetic thumbprint had pressed too heavily on little Hughie. Of course, the children had been affected by her separation from Nick, but now he was living at home, at least in the spare room, they seemed to have forgotten he'd ever left. They had lost their adored Ros too, but she had returned. And she, Anna, was changed; she'd stopped trying to make life perfect.

As Steve had promised, her interview was a conversation. She learnt that she would be one of two part-time volunteers, helping in the primary classroom two days a week, while her partner covered the rest of the week. There were only three children of primary age, one of whom had significant special educational needs and another, the clarinet player, who seemed exceptional. She could already see how she might be able to support their teacher with such a wide range of ability and the children's emotions so unpredictable.

The school governor checked that Anna understood that the youngest children would have committed truly heinous acts, if they had been committed to Whiteoaks. Could she cope with this? Anna nodded, there was no hesitation. She had barely listened to Steve's description of each child, her mind racing ahead, planning activities. Why had she not known that such perfect jobs existed?

The governor pressed her: 'How will you manage your own children, during school holidays Mrs McNeill? The children at Whiteoaks have shorter, more frequent breaks than mainstream schools.'

'My eldest daughter is at Oxford. Her terms are short.' She noticed Steve smile. 'If she can't help, I'll sort something out.'

'Of course, you can't avoid being ill yourself occasionally or one of your children might be sick, but the children here need consistency. We can't ask such questions of prospective teaching staff, but since this isn't a formal interview, we need to check that you have enough support at home. If you join us, Anna, will you be reliable? Can we count on you?'

'Because I have four children, one of them very poorly? Of course, you shouldn't be asking me these questions, but I understand why you are. I'll make sure I have enough back-up at home.'

'So, you'll join us?' Steve sounded astonished.

'I'd be delighted.'

Steve clapped his hands. 'In that case, come and have tea with the kids. You can stay to meet them, can't you?'

Anna sat at a round table with a youth worker and her three primary-aged charges, glad to be spared the raucous banter from the adolescent table, where nothing was spoken but every word shouted, with frequent use of 'fuck' and 'cunt' and those often run together into a single word.

'Be quiet, Dale,' Steve shouted, 'or Mrs McNeill will change her mind about coming to work here.' Dale looked over at Anna and made an 'ooh' sound, which implied she was too precious for her own good. 'That's enough,' Steve bellowed.

The musician at Anna's table cut her cake into small pieces and lined them up in rows across her plate. She studied the cubes, each one a perfect square, with jam in the centre and a dusting of icing sugar on top, as if wondering whether it was worth her while to eat them.

Was the cutting and the order enough for her, Anna thought? She could understand that. The eating would spoil the symmetry.

A tiny boy, with bird-like features, kept up a stream of inconsequential chatter, asking her questions without waiting for a reply. Steve leaned over Anna to fill her teacup and whispered in her ear: 'Mum is a drug addict.' She glanced at her small companion, anxious whether he had heard, but he was oblivious. The other boy in her group, who could have been ten or eleven, had tight curly hair cut so short the many scars that criss-crossed his scalp were clearly visible. He didn't look at her or answer her awkward questions, but when she turned away to speak to the clarinettist, she caught his eyes watching her just as she turned back. So he's interested, Anna thought, that's a start.

She left at six, and having drunk at least five cups of tea, she stopped at a pub in the first village to use the toilet. The wind had dropped, and a fine sprinkling of snow dusted the pool of light around the streetlamps. She ordered a drink, feeling an obligation to the landlord who stared moodily into the log fire of his almost empty bar. Anna rang Nick so that he wouldn't expect her soon. She hadn't thought about what there was to eat at home, but it would do him no harm to rummage in the freezer. She didn't say she'd got the post; like the children in the centre, she wanted more time to hold onto her prize, just for herself.

Pulling out her volunteer's terms and conditions, which she had already signed, she turned it over and started to make a list on the back. She wrote 'Disclosure and Barring Service, Resources: Gifted and Talented'. Below these she added, 'Specialist childminder/helpers' and put a star against it. Leaning back, she chewed on the end of her pen, letting the glow from the logs warm her cheeks. Ros would be home next week, and she could decorate the Christmas tree with the children. Christopher would be so pleased to see Jake.

Hughie and Jake had turned two last month. What would Hughie have been like if he hadn't been hit so hard by his condition? There was so much he couldn't do, and he had already lost some skills. But he was a happy child, easy to care for, and she felt no guilt about leaving him. She swallowed her drink and re-read her contract.

'You can change your mind,' Steve had said, used to disappointment in the hiring of staff, 'just give me a ring.' Anna knew she wouldn't.

Her mind was buzzing, full of plans for the term ahead. Steve had said she might teach there one day and once she felt confident, she would apply whenever a job came up. Nick was back with her, not much changed but trying hard to be a better father, if not a better husband. It was to his credit that he'd admitted he was wrong to accuse Ros and had cared enough about Anna, if not about Ros, to find her. Ros had agreed to report her brother and the investigation was in its early stages but already looked promising. One of the boys at the sleepover, now a man, had been formally interviewed and had remembered Sean leaving the party and his return.

Cara, Jess and Christopher travelled their own unique paths with health and energy. She could only watch and guide. Anna drained her glass and pulled on her coat, wrapping her scarf around her neck against the frost outside. She waved cheerfully to the landlord as she left. This was her life.

CHAPTER 31

Ros sat with Hughie on her knee, flicking between channels on the TV. Jake and Christopher were playing a game, where they had dragged the metal bin from the kitchen into the hall and were dropping toys through the banister to see which toy made the loudest bang when it hit the lid. The boys screamed with laughter at each new crash of sound and tumbled down the stairs together, searching for new missiles in the playroom. It made Ros happy to see them together, as if they had never been apart, and she decided she'd only ask them to stop if their noise made Hughie startle. She looked down at the child, smiling in his sleep, content to be held by his favourite person. The trouble with this family, Ros thought, is that no one has time for him, except me.

She checked her phone. It was the girls' last day at school and Anna had asked her to babysit so that she could finish her Christmas shopping. Inevitably, Anna had wasted precious time making lists and had fussed over her scarf, but Ros hoped she might still have a couple of hours alone. At least, not quite alone. Nick had been on the late shift last night, so wasn't due to do a surgery until this afternoon and he was still in bed upstairs. Perhaps she should try to keep things quiet, find a cartoon for the boys to watch, given how drunk Nick had pretended not to be last night.

Too late, Nick padded down the stairs and grabbed the dinosaur that Christopher was planning to launch from the landing.

'No!' Nick wagged a finger. 'Stop this game now!'

He leaned against the doorway, unshaven, his hair plastered flat on one side of his head and sticking up on the other. 'Want a coffee?'

Ros listened to him in the kitchen, the chink of mugs, the slamming of cupboard doors. The thing is, she thought, Anna never seemed to be able to remember Nick's shifts, but Ros had learnt them by heart and knew there were times when he wasn't at work, or at home. But she wouldn't say anything to Anna. What was the point?

Nick carried two mugs into the sitting room, and slopped milky coffee onto a side table, as he tried to set Ros's drink down. He wiped the spill with the sleeve of his dressing gown, then kicked the smoking logs in the grate with the toe of his slipper, sparking them into life, before tossing on two more. He sat down opposite her and sipped his coffee, staring ahead as if in a waking dream, until a new crash from the hall brought him back to the present. He screwed his eyes and grimaced.

'How are you finding things here now that you're back home?' he asked Ros.

'It's great Anna's found a job, but I wish she wouldn't talk to me about Whiteoaks. Why can't she understand? It's the last place in the world I want to talk about. She's excited about it, but I'm not.'

'What would you prefer to talk about with Anna? Not me I hope.' Nick rested his head against the cushions and closed his eyes.

'Well, my course for a start. They're all so clever, the other students, and I'm older than most of them. They open their mouths and all these words come out that I can't understand. And they're so confident.'

The boys had gone quiet, so Nick eased himself out of his chair.

'I'd better check on them. I'll be back.'

Ros heard Nick scrape the kitchen bin back across the wooden floor of the hall, followed by his raised voice, from further away. He returned with a pack of eggs in his hand.

'This was going over next.' He held up the carton. 'I've banned the game and they're both sulking in the playroom. We have a few minutes.'

'I've brought home a lot of work,' Ros complained, picking up the important topic of her course. 'We might have long holidays but I've two essays to do.'

Nick pushed his hands deep into the pockets of his dressing gown as he leaned back into the armchair and closed his eyes again.

'Don't let Anna take over too much of your time. Make up a work plan and show it to her. That's a language she understands. And you're every bit as bright as the other students. Take a couple of terms to watch and listen, then you'll realise they're talking rubbish.'

Surprised by Nick's comment about Anna, Ros adjusted Hughie in her arms and sat up to reach for her coffee. She swallowed two mouthfuls, weighing up what to say.

'Anna doesn't pay attention to your schedules or your plans.'

Nick raised an eyebrow, but his eyes stayed closed.

'She chooses not to notice.'

'I notice.'

'I know you do. I see you watching me.'

'You sound a bit fed up.' Ros changed the subject.

'Yeah, well.' Nick sat up and rubbed a hand across his bristled chin. 'Maybe you're not the only one who's feeling a bit used. Am I ever to be allowed out of the spare bedroom or am I just an extra pair of hands? And don't answer that or we'll be here all day. It's too long a conversation. I'd better go and shower.'

Ros wandered into the hall, still holding the sleeping child, and went in search of Jake and Christopher. A white envelope lay on the mat below the front door, and she bent to pick it up. It was addressed to her and looked formal. With the weight of the child in the crook of one arm, it involved an awkward movement to open the envelope, but she couldn't wait, even if she woke Hughie. The detective in charge of her case, she read, wanted her to attend a meeting at Claire's office. Tomorrow.

Ros took Nick's advice and prepared a study schedule, which she showed to Anna after dinner but then felt guilty, since Anna immediately insisted she start work on her essays, when she'd hoped to watch a film with the girls. Once the children were in bed and Nick was still at work, she tried to speak to Anna about the letter, but Anna was preoccupied, working at the kitchen table doing admin for the local MLD support group, of which she was the chair. Anna lifted unfocused eyes from her computer and patted one of the kitchen chairs.

'Let's work together, it's more companionable,' she'd said, but Ros made them both a mug of tea and crept away to her bedroom to watch her own television.

The next morning Anna dropped Ros at the office. She had found a possible childminder and had decided to induct the woman by leaving her in charge of all five children, while she went food shopping. When Ros protested, Anna had argued: 'It's only for an hour and Cara's there to help. If she can't cope, then she's no use to me.'

When Ros entered the office, Claire was already sitting in the interview room with KathyRawnsley, the detective working on the reopened case of the murder of her baby brother. The mugs on the table between them gave away the conversation they'd had without her, and Ros felt angry and excluded, wondering when things would ever change.

She sat down in the empty chair, trying hard not to behave like a sullen teenager, and refused a drink. DS Rawnsley smiled across at her, but Ros had always found her disappointing, with her caution and failure to be impressed, and chose not to return the smile. If you had to pick someone who was the exact opposite of Anna, Kathy was it.

Claire swept the mugs away and Kathy asked if she could use the ladies, so Ros was left alone to study the tired Christmas decorations in the adjoining offices, knowing that they were finishing their chat about her in the kitchen. She wondered how many more years she would have to sit here at Christmas, so that Claire could tick her boxes. Five more she reckoned.

Once they were together, Kathy broke the news: 'I'm afraid Sean has said he's not guilty and he'll fight. His solicitor acknowledges that his alibi is blown but they're saying you could have killed the baby after Sean left. He's insisting the child was alive when you saw him leave.'

'The thing is, Ros,' Claire interrupted, 'we were hoping he'd admit it. There's no other evidence. If we go ahead, you could find yourself back in court being questioned about the murder.'

'We can still prosecute him for lying at the original trial but nothing more. My boss is advising that we drop the case. Sean was only thirteen and a jury is likely to be sympathetic about the lie.'

Ros remained still, her face frozen. The fantasy she had held, of staring at her mother across the courtroom as Sean was sentenced, would remain a fantasy. She would have to go on living with an assumed name, always looking over her shoulder. What would she tell Jake when the time came?

She cleared her throat, her voice hoarse. 'Can I talk it over with Nick and Anna?'

'Yes of course,' Kathy replied, 'but let me know on Monday, by Christmas Eve. I'm off for two weeks after that.'

Ros pulled on her coat, her eyes avoiding the sympathy of the older women. She tried to push her way through the glass door, but Claire caught her arm. This time, Ros looked straight into her adviser's eyes and saw that Claire wasn't even pretending not to cry.

'I'm so sorry. Don't give up hope. Something might come up in the future, one day he might confess.'

'Hope is useless,' Ros spat back at her, 'hope is a waste of time.'

Anna looked at her hands resting in the kitchen sink, the veins looking exaggerated and lumpy through some magnifying effect of the water. She tipped a pack of Brussels sprouts into the sink from their crumpled paper bag, bought yesterday from their remaining local greengrocer, and started to slice the tails. Anna wondered how long she could leave Ros to sleep. Jake had been up with the other children since five and it wasn't like her to miss out on his excitement over the Santa presents. Although she would never have said so aloud, Anna thought that being twenty was a bit old for teenage behaviour, but since preparing for her job at Whiteoaks, she'd been reminded that the path to adulthood wasn't always straightforward for children like Ros. She had to be patient, even if she didn't feel like it, particularly since Cara already seemed to be competing for the role of teenage child, with her periods and mood swings at only ten.

Anna needed some help with the lunch. She couldn't risk asking Cara, who was shut in her bedroom with a video game, and she had already turned down Jess, whose enthusiasm tended to be more of a hindrance. She could hear Nick putting in a stellar performance as Christmas Day Dad, but he would soon need a break. Anna regretted her decision to make this an alcohol-free Christmas, since she could really do with a drink herself, even though it was only eleven. She'd dropped the festive abstinence bombshell last January, during their attempt at a dry month, after a Christmas Day when Ros, newly returned from Manchester, had been wary and fragile and Nick had let himself down with an alcohol-induced rage because he couldn't light the brandy on the Christmas pudding. Since she'd made the announcement, Anna felt they had to give it a try. After all, Ros only drank Diet Coke and she and Nick might all too easily sink several bottles of good red between them and start saying things they regretted.

She looked at her watch. Ros had been furious when she'd returned from that meeting, slamming her bedroom door, and refusing to talk about what had happened. Since then, she'd been quiet, helping Anna and playing with the children without energy, her face falling into sadness whenever she thought no one was looking. Anna made coffee and carried Nick's into the playroom.

'Thank God, it's the cavalry!' Nick reached up from the floor to take his mug, Hughie propped between his legs.

'I think I'm going to wake Ros,' Anna said and sat down next to Jessica who was cajoling the two younger boys into a game of snakes and ladders. 'At least for Jake's sake.'

'Yes, do it,' Nick agreed, 'for my sake too.'

Anna watched the children throw a few rounds of the dice. Christopher refused to go down a snake and Jessica began to cry with frustration. Jake stood up and looked around, his eyes searching.

'I'm not playing. Where's my mummy?'

'Good idea, Jake.' Anna pushed herself up from the carpet. 'Let's take mummy a coffee.'

Anna climbed the stairs, the dark-haired little boy holding her hand as he counted each step aloud. They tapped on Ros's door, and hearing a murmur from inside, Anna opened the door for Jake to run into the room and leap onto his mother's bed.

'Santa's been, Santa's been,' Jake shouted, in time with his trampolining.

Ros sat up, pushing her hair out of her eyes, and reaching for Jake, she held the squirming child tight against her chest.

'I'm so sorry. I can't believe I've slept this long.' Ros kissed the top of his head, as he struggled for freedom. 'I can't wait to see what Santa brought for you.'

Anna held out the coffee. 'We'll eat at twelve thirty, the little ones can't hold out any later for their lunch, then I thought we'd let them demolish the pile of presents under the tree. I'll ask Nick to help me in the kitchen, if you could manage to supervise the kids once you're dressed?'

True to the promise she'd made to herself, lunch was a pared-down affair, with minimal decoration and a bottle of cinnamon-flavoured apple juice in the centre of the table, next to Ros's Diet Coke. Looking around the room, Anna missed the riot of colour and sparkle, the garish mismatched tableware and the rows of lit candles, no doubt viewed with nostalgia through warm, alcohol-fuelled memories. But the nightmare of two years ago, when she had accidentally invited Nick's lover for Christmas Day and been accused of trying too hard, was still raw. She nodded in satisfaction and called the family for lunch.

Seating the youngest children in booster seats, with Hughie still in a highchair, took several minutes and Anna noticed that Ros had slipped away.

She quickly returned and dumped a chinking carrier bag onto the table. 'I didn't know what to get you for presents. I hope this will do.'

'If this is what I think it is,' Nick said, reaching for the bag, 'you are my one and only, my everlasting friend.'

'They're chilled because I left them outside the back door last night. It was a bit obvious leaving them in the fridge.' Ros smiled at Anna, as Nick pulled out two bottles of champagne and two bottles of white wine, a film of moisture forming on the icy glass.

Anna had to decide whether to be angry or whether to refuse the alcohol but couldn't remember if she'd actually told Ros about her alcohol-free plan.

'Oh, why not,' she said, holding out her glass. 'Well done, Ros. Merry Christmas.'

By four o' clock the day was over, the sitting room strewn with wrapping paper, half-eaten mince pies and chocolate wrappers. Cara had decided to grace the younger children with her presence and was watching

Paddington 2 with them in the playroom, ensuring their good behaviour and attention as long as she was there. Hughie slept on his mother's knee.

'I've something to tell you both.' Ros spoke softly, so Anna had to strain to hear her above the crackling of the fire, recently replenished with fresh logs. 'The police want to drop the charges against Sean, and I've agreed. The case would have gone to trial, and I risked being questioned all over again by his defence. I can't do it. My mind is made up.'

'But that's so unfair,' Anna argued, 'perhaps we could—'

'That bastard shouldn't be allowed to get away with it,' Nick interrupted.

'Please.' Ros held up her hand. 'The decision is made. I've thought so much about this—my future isn't about my baby brother's murder, it's about what I make of my life now. I've lost the old me, Hannah has gone for ever, along with her family. But I must build a future as Imogen Hope and you two are there to help me. If I do well and become important, like that judge with the spider brooch on her jacket, even if someone finds out that I'm the girl who didn't kill her baby brother, years ago, it will just be a footnote.'

'That's the benefit of a university education right there, to know what a footnote is.'

'Shut up, Nick.' Anna frowned at him. 'Carry on, Ros.'

'I didn't really believe you, Nick, when you said we could be a family, but we are, and no better or worse than any other. We'll let each other down, I'm sure, but hopefully we'll also pick each other up. And Jake will always have you, whatever happens to me.'

Anna watched Nick stare at Ros, open-mouthed. She smelt embers from the fire mingle with resin from the tree and heard children's laughter from the playroom.

'Of course, Ros,' she spoke at last, 'you've made the only possible choice. I'm proud of you.'

'Is it okay if we still call you Ros?' Nick asked.

Anna rolled her eyes and glanced across at Ros, who smiled back.

At least one of us has managed to grow-up, Anna thought.

ACKNOWLEDGEMENTS

I would like to thank my beta readers, Jill Bowler, Alison Timmins, and Charlotte Thompson for taking the time to read 'Broken' at draft stage and for their helpful advice. Any examples of poor practice by the health visitor or social workers in this novel are entirely my responsibility.

My thanks also go to Dr Karen Ette for her thorough copy edit. I am most grateful to Sarah Houldcroft at Goldcrest Books for her professional and efficient publishing of Broken and for designing a terrific cover.

The line from the poem 'When One has Lived a Long Time Alone' is used by permission of The Literary Estate of Galway Kinnell, LLC.

ABOUT THE AUTHOR

Morag Edwards was born and raised in Scotland but has lived in Leicester for most of her adult life. She writes historical and contemporary fiction, short stories, and poetry. Her debut novel, the Jacobite's Wife, was published in 2018.

Morag has an MA from the Manchester University Centre for New Writing and has over thirty years' experience as an educational psychologist.

Connect with Morag:
Twitter: @EdwardsMorag
Facebook: Morag.Edwards39

Also by Morag Edwards and available from Amazon:

THE JACOBITE'S WIFE

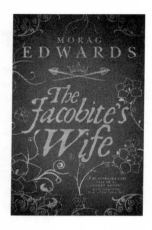

Lady Winifred has had a troubled childhood. Her mother, father and brother were all imprisoned for treason due to their support for the Catholic king. When she falls in love with a handsome young Scottish nobleman, the marriage brings happiness. However, she is forced to rebel when her husband takes up the Jacobite cause and vows to restore the Catholic king to the throne.

While Winifred wants to be loyal to her husband, she also wants to protect him from imprisonment – and worse, the scaffold!

Just how far will she go to save him?

Made in the USA
Middletown, DE
23 January 2023